Laurie Gilmore writes small-town romance. Her Dream Harbor series is filled with quirky townsfolk, cozy settings, and swoon-worthy romance. She loves finding books with the perfect balance of sweetness and spice and strives for that in her own writing. If you ever wished you lived in Stars Hollow (or that Luke and Lorelai would just get together already!) then her books are definitely for you.

instagram.com/lauriegilmore_author

Also by Laurie Gilmore

The Pumpkin Spice Café

The Cinnamon Bun Book Store

The Strawberry Patch Pancake House

THE CHRISTMAS TREE FARM

Dream Harbor Series

Book 3

LAURIE GILMORE

One More Chapter
a division of HarperCollins*Publishers*
1 London Bridge Street
London SE1 9GF
www.harpercollins.co.uk
HarperCollins*Publishers*
Macken House, 39/40 Mayor Street Upper,
Dublin 1, D01 C9W8, Ireland
This paperback edition 2024
24 25 26 27 28 LBC 11 10 9 8 7
First published in ebook by HarperCollins*Publishers* 2024

A catalogue record of this book
is available from the British Library

ISBN: 978-0-00-861074-6

Printed and bound in the United States

For anyone who ever wished Hallmark Christmas movies were steamier, this one might do the trick.

DREAM HARBOR

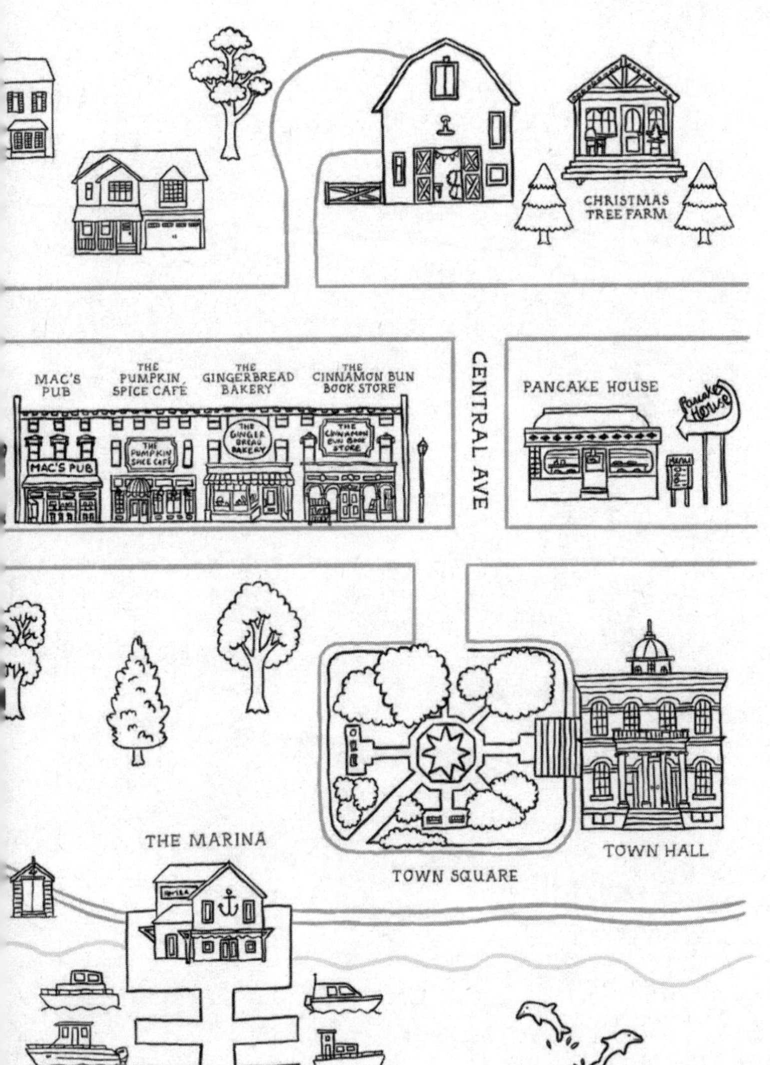
CHRISTMAS TREE FARM
MAC'S PUB
THE PUMPKIN SPICE CAFÉ
THE GINGERBREAD BAKERY
THE CINNAMON BUN BOOK STORE
MAC'S PUB
CENTRAL AVE
PANCAKE HOUSE
THE MARINA
TOWN SQUARE
TOWN HALL
NOAH'S BOAT

Playlist

Christmas Tree Farm - Taylor Swift ♥
Linger - The Cranberries ♥
BIRDS OF A FEATHER - Billie Eilish ♥
Memories - Conan Gray ♥
White Christmas - Taylor Swift ♥
hate to be lame - Lizzy McAlpine, FINNEAS ♥
A Nonsense Christmas - Sabrina Carpenter ♥
21 - Gracie Abrams ♥
the boy is mine - Ariana Grande ♥
Light On - Maggie Rogers ♥
Go - Livingston ♥
Back To December- Taylor Swift ♥
This Town - Niall Horan ♥
Bags - Clairo ♥
From the Dining Table - Harry Styles ♥
I Look in People's Windows - Taylor Swift ♥
Close To You - Gracie Abrams ♥
because i liked a boy - Sabrina Carpenter ♥
Santa Tell Me - Ariana Grande ♥
mirrorball - Taylor Swift ♥
Until I Found You - Stephen Sanchez ♥
All My Love - Noah Kahan ♥
Landslide - Fleetwood Mac ♥

Chapter One

Kira North hated Christmas. Which was unfortunate considering she was currently the proud owner of a Christmas-tree farm in a town that was far too cute for its own good, with residents that couldn't seem to take the hint and leave her the hell alone.

She breathed out a frustrated sigh as she closed the door on her latest visitor. Some guy named George, who'd dropped off a complementary sample of Christmas gingerbread cookies from the bakery in town and a business card, and more than a few hints about a plan to do business together. He was the third one this weekend.

Yesterday, Deputy Mayor Mindy Walsh had dropped by on behalf of the town council to hand her a flyer for the annual Tree Lighting next week, as though Kira hadn't seen half a million of those every time she went into town for food. And just this morning, an entire family showed up, kids in tow with matching Christmas sweaters, asking if they could cut down a tree. She'd pretended not to see the children's tears as she turned them away.

It was all a bit much. She slid down to the floor, her back against the door, and tore open the red and green cellophane protecting the cookies. She picked a Santa-shaped one and bit off his head. Unfortunately, he was absolutely delicious, all nutmeg and cinnamon. Damn him.

The cold seeped through her back as she finished him off one decadent bite at a time. The door was freezing. The floor was freezing. The entire crappy old house she'd moved into three months ago was freezing. She leaned her head back against the door with a soft thud, attempting to pretend that she was fine. It was fine. She would just put on another sweater even though she was already wearing two. She'd put on a warmer pair of socks. People sometimes wore hats inside, right?

The ancient radiator beside the door let out a defeated whine.

Right. Time to get up. Time to get up and get back to work because the 'quaint farmhouse' she'd bought, sight unseen, was actually a decrepit old farmhouse with a heating system on life support, and the 'acres of scenic farmland' was actually a beloved, but totally run-down Christmas-tree farm, and even though she'd sworn not to reopen it, now she had to in order to make some money and fix up this place, seeing as how she'd spent all hers buying it in the first place.

If she wanted to survive the winter and not be found frozen to death by a nosy but well-intentioned neighbor, she needed to get this place up and running. And fast. It was already the Sunday after Thanksgiving, and judging by the family she'd devastated this morning, people were dying to get their trees up.

She grabbed a blanket on her way past the couch and shuffled over to where she'd left her laptop on the ancient wooden dining-room table the previous owners had left behind. They'd left a lot of junk behind, actually. She kept finding old mail tucked away in odd places but hadn't bothered opening any of it. The table was nice though. It fit her farmhouse aesthetic.

She flipped open her computer. Still no Wi-Fi. It hadn't worked right since that power outage last week.

Damn it.

How was she supposed to hire people, set up a website, *and* create a social media presence for this place without Wi-Fi and with an incredibly unreliable cell signal? In, like, two days? She slumped down in the closest chair and practiced not crying. Her tears would probably freeze on her face if she did. She sniffled them back in and tried not to think about how pitiful she must look right now wrapped in a worn comforter, packed into way too many layers of clothing, nose red from cold and crying.

This wasn't at all how things were supposed to go.

First of all, she wasn't supposed to be alone. Her sister should be here with her. Her other half. Her much more competent, reasonable, level-headed half. Her twin and best friend since birth. Chloe never would have bought this place on a whim. Chloe never would have agreed to the sale without a visit and an inspection, at the very least. Chloe would have asked questions like: why do you want to live on a farm in New England despite having no idea how to grow things or cook things or really do anything on your own? Questions that Kira had no desire to answer.

Because this whole plan wasn't so much a whim as it was a last-ditch effort to start over. To get as far away from her old life, her old self as possible. It wasn't a whim so much as a radical reimagining of who she wanted to be.

But Chloe had abandoned her. Ran off and got *married*. And moved to *Denmark*. Denmark! Of all places. And what was one supposed to do when their soulmate, their other half, finds a new other half?

Well, apparently they absorb too much homesteading social-media content, decide they can totally do that, use their trust-fund money to buy a farm, and essentially, ruin their lives. Okay, so maybe this specific plan was a little bit of a whim…

But here she was. Miserable and alone. And really freaking cold.

Kira wiped her cheeks with the back of her hand. This was ridiculous. She had to do something or that image of herself, frozen to death in her bed, was about to become reality. She shoved another cookie in her mouth for strength, grabbed her phone, wrapped her blanket around her more securely, and headed for the back door. She slid on her new boots and stepped outside. It might have been warmer outside than it had been in her house. The sun, however weak this late in November, definitely helped.

If she was going to survive this, she was going to have to get used to these northern winters. It hadn't even snowed yet and she already felt wildly unprepared. The temperature in Georgia rarely dropped below fifty degrees and certainly not in the middle of the afternoon. Today couldn't be warmer than thirty.

She was so screwed.

No tears. Not right now. Not until later when she was huddled under her blankets in bed instead of out here in the backyard where any roaming resident of Dream Harbor could pop up like some kind of jack-in-the-box nightmare of glad tidings.

She held up her phone and started wandering through the rows of trees just past her tiny yard. Surely, if she walked far enough, she'd get some kind of signal. She could probably go into town and work at the library or that café everyone seemed to love, but that would require being out in public, which she did not feel up to in her current state of mental breakdown. So … wandering the fields in her flannel pajama bottoms, ratty old sweaters, and down comforter it had to be.

The trees stretched in tidy rows ahead of her ranging in height from her waist to at least a foot or two above her head. Luckily, the trees had just continued being trees even without an owner for the past few years. They could use some trimming and shaping, but overall, her crop was in good condition. It was the barn that was nearly falling down, and the house that required significant work.

But first, money.

And before money, employees, and a real live business. Something Kira had never done nor aspired to do in her entire life.

But she didn't have time to dwell on that. Not before a giant black blur raced across her path with two smaller blurs at its heels.

Kira shrieked.

The dogs barked.

The man following them skidded to a stop.

'Elizabeth, heel.' His voice was stern and harsh and the biggest dog loped happily to his side. 'Good girl.' He patted her head.

'Odie, Pudgy, heel.' He tried to get the other two dogs' attention with the same stern tone, but it was far too late for that. Kira was already squatting to pet the two little wiggly bodies at her feet.

'Look at you, sweet babies,' she crooned. 'Little angels.' The smallest dog, some sort of Westie mix with wiry white hair, pushed its cold snout into her palm, huffing in excitement. The other one, who must have been at least a hundred years old in dog years, waited patiently for scratches between its floppy ears, its tongue lolling out of its mouth.

'What good doggies you are, so sweet,' Kira went on, petting and scratching and so generally delighted to have such precious babies on her property that she'd nearly forgotten the man until he was towering over her.

'Uh, sorry about that,' he said. 'I didn't realize… I mean,

I thought this place was abandoned. Otherwise, I would have had the dogs on their leashes.'

'It's okay,' Kira said, still crouched low, but now paying proper attention to Elizabeth who was starting to whine at not being part of the lovefest happening with the other dogs. 'Look at you! What a beautiful girl you are,' she told her, and it seemed the larger dog smiled at her. Kira smiled back, for the first time in days. It was nice.

Until she finally stood and looked at the man who had brought the puppies to her farm. The smile dropped from her face. He was staring at her with a mix of confusion and horror.

It was then that Kira remembered her unwashed hair and her red eyes and her blanket-as-outerwear fashion statement. Ugh. This day, this town, these people! They were everywhere!

'Yes, well, actually, I own this farm,' she said, standing to her full height. 'So, you are trespassing.'

Elizabeth whined and Kira scratched between her ears. 'Not you, sweetheart. You didn't know.'

'To be fair, I didn't know either,' the man said, a slight smirk on his face.

'How is that possible? Everyone in this nosy town knows about it.'

He shrugged. 'I don't live in this nosy town.'

Kira frowned. 'Then what are you doing here?'

'Visiting.'

She didn't like his tone. Or his face for that matter. It was too … too … handsome. But in like an obnoxiously conventional way. Too much symmetry. Too much perfect dark hair. It was annoying. And entirely uninteresting.

Too wholesome.

'Well, whoever you're visiting should have told you that I own this land now, so you can't just traipse through here on your little hike or whatever you're doing.'

The man's obnoxiously straight smile grew. '*Little hike or whatever*?'

'I don't know! What's with that vest? You look like you're going on a hike.'

He looked down at his puffy vest and dark jeans and hiking boots and then let his gaze wander over Kira's ensemble.

'You're wearing a blanket,' he observed.

'Yes.'

'And you're making fun of my vest?'

'Yes.' She crossed her arms over her chest, not that he could see that since they were tucked under her blanket, but still. Her stance was defiant. She was pretty sure that came across. She didn't like this guy and his teasing smile. And his light eyes with dark lashes. Really? Ugh, could he be more basic?

Kira only went for men that had 'bad idea' tattooed across their forehead (sometimes literally) and this guy looked like the model for 'the guy your mother wants you to bring home for the holidays to sip cocoa under the tree in your matching pajamas'. Highly undesirable. Downright unattractive in every way, really.

Except for maybe the way his thighs were filling out those jeans.

But that was neither here nor there.

'Sorry again for the misunderstanding. We'll get going.'

Oh, right. He was going to take the dogs with him. Shoot. She *liked* the dogs. She looked down at the three precious faces in front of her and she could swear she could hear their thoughts.

'You might as well finish your walk,' she blurted out, ignoring how his dark eyebrows rose in surprise. 'I mean, you're here now and the dogs need their exercise and I would never deprive them of that.'

'You're a big dog person, I take it.'

'They're better than people in every way.'

His laugh was low and deep and did absolutely nothing for her.

'I agree.'

She gave him a curt nod, expecting him to go on his way, but he was still looking at her like he was working on a puzzle.

'What?' she snapped.

'I just… Are you okay?'

Was she okay?! How dare he?! How dare he presume just because she was wandering around outside wearing bedding and waving her phone in the air like she thought it worked via witchcraft that she wasn't okay?

She smoothed her blanket down with a hand as though it were an evening gown. 'I'm fine, thank you.'

A small crease of worry formed between his obnoxiously

perfect eyebrows and Kira wanted to throw something at him and see if she could hit it.

'It's just … you're walking around with your phone over your head. I thought maybe you were having trouble with it. I work in tech, so I thought…'

A tech bro? Oh, just what she needed! Always trust your first instincts and her first instincts were right. She didn't need some Silicon Valley, let's go for a hike wherever we damn well please because we think we own the whole world, Clark Kent lookalike, to rescue her. Not today, buddy!

'No thanks, Elon. I'm managing just fine.'

'Elon?' Now he looked highly offended. Hmm … *that* did something for her. 'Wow, I was just trying to help.'

'No one asked you to.'

He held up his hands. 'Sorry. You're right. I'll … uh … get out of your hair.'

'Thank you.' She didn't look at him as she said it. The hurt expression on his face had taken some of the fun out of the whole thing. Instead, she crouched one more time to say goodbye to her new friends.

'Bye, sweet babies. Enjoy your walk.' She gave them enough pets to last for a while and by the time she was standing again, the mystery man had already turned and was walking down the row of trees, whistling for his dogs to follow.

And unfortunately, they did.

Chapter Two

'You can stay and sit with me for a few minutes, can't you?' his sister asked, already pulling out a chair at the closest table and gesturing to the one across from it. 'While it's quiet in here? I need a break, anyway.'

Bennett glanced around the temporarily empty Pumpkin Spice Café and then back at his sister, Jeanie. She flashed him her sweetest smile. 'Please.'

'I do actually have to work while I'm here, you know,' he grumbled, but sat down, anyway. He was visiting Dream Harbor for a month, living in his sister's apartment above the shop while she got settled at her new fiancé's house, and he was staying to celebrate the holidays. But he did have to work. He'd set things up to work remotely for the next few weeks, which plenty of his other coworkers already did regularly, but Jeanie seemed to think he was on an extended vacation.

'Just for a few minutes! Jeez, do they not give you coffee breaks at this job of yours?'

'They do, but it's the week after Thanksgiving. I have a lot to catch up on.'

'Right. Computer-y work to do.'

He nearly opened his mouth to explain to his sister for the umpteenth time that he was a software engineer and that he wrote code for multiple online retailers, but he'd given up on that years ago. Probably around the time when she started telling people he was some kind of personal online shopper, for lack of a better explanation. "Computer-y work" was close enough.

'So what did you do yesterday?' Jeanie asked, in between sips of her coffee. Her new engagement ring glinted at him from one hand wrapped around her mug. Logan had proposed to her just before Thanksgiving, and Bennett had had to endure the two of them making heart eyes at each other for the entire seven-hour drive back here from Buffalo, where they'd all spent Thanksgiving with their parents. He'd been very thankful to have his own space when they arrived in Dream Harbor and to have a break from the lovebirds.

Logan was a good guy and Bennett was happy for them, but the ring was another little reminder of how epically bad his dating life had been lately. He couldn't imagine going on a second date with most women he'd met, let alone commit to a lifetime together. Was long-term commitment a thing people even did anymore?

'Slept in, took the dogs for a walk.' He shrugged. 'Nothing much.'

'Where'd you take the dogs?'

'The old Christmas-tree farm up on Spruce.'

Jeanie's eyes widened. 'Oh.'

'Yeah, would have been nice if you'd mentioned the new owner.'

'Sorry! I forgot all about it.'

Bennett leaned back in his chair remembering the woman he'd met in the fields yesterday. The woman who'd simultaneously greeted his dogs with such warmth and affection and frozen him out completely. Who looked like maybe she was in the middle of some kind of crisis but held herself like she was better than him. Who, when he offered her help, had made fun of him instead.

Yeah, he wasn't a big fan of the new Christmas-tree farm owner. Despite how cute she'd looked all wrapped up in that blanket, and how bright her smile had been when she was petting his dogs.

Ben knew plenty of cute women and cute wasn't worth the trouble. In fact, all cute had gotten him in the past few months was roped into helping a woman he just met move out of her ex's apartment while the ex begged for forgiveness from the front porch; a second date with someone he met on a dating app that consisted of a quick drink and then her asking for a ride to the airport, which he gave her because what else was he supposed to do; and three separate women who all disliked dogs, one of whom seemed to have a strong dislike for animals in general. He'd seen her scowl at a bird.

The last thing he needed was another cute woman.

He was done with cute women.

'Did you run into Kira?' Jeanie asked, a guilty grimace on her face.

Bennett shook off the grim thoughts floating through his head and refocused on Jeanie. 'If Kira is the hostile new owner, then yes, I met Kira.'

'She's…' Jeanie paused, tapping her lip as she searched for a kinder word to describe Kira. She didn't find one. 'Yeah, she's sort of hostile, but I think she's probably got a soft spot somewhere. We just have to find it.'

'*I* don't have to find anything. *I* have to get back to work,' he said, rising from his seat. Besides, he already knew what Kira, the hostile Christmas-tree farm owner's soft spot was. He'd heard her croon sweet words to his dogs, her dark eyes lighting up at the sight of them. If the residents of Dream Harbor wanted to get on her good side, he imagined all they'd have to do is head up there with a basket of puppies and Kira would be putty in their hands.

But he had about zero percent interest in getting involved in town drama, of which he already knew too much, thanks to Jeanie. And even less interest in having Kira in his hands.

Jeanie frowned. 'You work too much.'

'Ha,' Bennett scoffed. 'Says the woman who runs her own successful business and is here all the time—which I'm very proud of you for, by the way.'

'Thanks, Ben.' Jeanie waved away his praise as she stood. 'Oh! I have a great idea.' Her eyes lit up in a way Bennett found to be incredibly ominous. 'You should come to the town meeting tonight!'

'I'm going to have to pass on local politics, but thanks, anyway.'

'No, it's fun. It's a whole thing and you can meet my friends and then we all go out for drinks after. Please, Ben.'

'Don't look at me like that Jean Marie.'

'Like what?'

Bennett sighed. He had never been very good at saying no, hence the moving services and airport rides he'd provided lately, but his sister made it particularly hard. 'With those big eyes. You know exactly what you're doing.'

'It'll be fun, I promise. And besides, aren't you here to spend time with me? The loving sister you abandoned to live all the way on the other side of the country.'

'Excuse me, you left Buffalo before I did.' His sister still didn't know the real reason he'd moved out to San Francisco after college, and he had no plans to fill her in.

Jeanie blinked. 'Oh, right. I forgot. Whatever, just come, okay? It starts at seven.'

She brushed a quick kiss to his cheek before hurrying back behind the counter just as a group of retired folks in workout gear ambled in through the door.

'How was your walk today? Chilly out there!' He heard his sister chatting happily to her customers as he slipped away and up the back staircase to the apartment. He was greeted by three wagging tails and a pile of work to do.

And apparently, tonight he was attending the town meeting.

This wasn't even close to a vacation, despite what his sister believed.

Bennett didn't know what to expect from a Dream Harbor town meeting but the raucous laughter and raised voices he encountered when he walked through the doors were certainly not it. He squeezed past a group arguing about the appropriate time to start listening to Christmas music, nearly got knocked out by a woman in a power suit carrying a giant metal menorah, and was about ready to turn around and leave when he was grabbed by the arm and pulled into a row of chairs.

'Bennett! You're here!' A face he had only ever seen from the screen of his phone beamed at him. Jacob, from his sister's book club, pulled him in for a hug.

'Hey, man. Yeah, I'm here.' Here in this bizarre town, feeling more and more like he'd gone down some kind of rabbit hole and landed in another world entirely. And he thought San Francisco was quirky. 'Good to see you.'

Jacob pulled away but was still holding tight to his arms. 'I can't believe Jeanie roped you into coming to one of these. Are you coming out for drinks after?'

'Uh … yeah … apparently.'

'Great!' Jacob gave him one last squeeze before letting go.

Bennett glanced around at the still buzzing crowd although people were starting to find seats now, not that their volume had decreased at all. 'Are these things always so…'

'Crazy? Yeah. But they're usually good for a laugh.'

Ben nodded, distracted by the woman in the suit struggling to run a cord long enough to plug in the giant menorah. Maybe he should go help her?

'That's the deputy mayor,' Jacob said, following Ben's gaze. 'She's probably testing that old thing out for the tree-lighting festival next weekend.'

'There you are!' Jeanie came up behind him before he could untangle himself from Jacob long enough to go help with the menorah.

'Here I am.'

'Sorry we're late,' she said, unwinding a giant scarf from around her neck. Logan stood behind her like he was being marched to his death.

'Hey, Logan.'

'Bennett.' His sister's fiancé gave him a nod and a small pained smile before he shuffled into the row and took a seat.

'And this is Hazel and Noah,' Jeanie was saying, pointing to the two other humans trying to cram into the already crowded row.

'Hey, nice to meet you.' Noah stuck out a hand and Bennett shook it around Jeanie's shoulder. Noah grinned. 'First town meeting, huh? You're gonna love it.'

Bennett was starting to highly doubt that.

The small, curly-haired woman next to Noah must be Hazel, whom his sister talked about all the time. She gave him a little wave as she sat in between Noah and Jeanie. Bennett took the only open seat between Jeanie and Jacob. Logan had managed to scoot his way all the way down the row and was currently reading a book as he leaned against the wall, clearly blocking out the chaos around him.

'If everyone could settle down, we'll get started.' A man with glasses and a hideous Christmas tie was trying to get everyone's attention from behind the podium.

'That's the mayor, who also happens to be Hazel's dad,' Jeanie narrated for him. 'Oh and here's Annie.'

A tall blonde woman swept into the row ahead of them. 'What'd I miss?' she asked, turning to face Jeanie as soon as she was seated.

'Nothing, yet. Oh, but this is my brother, Bennett.'

'Nice to meet you,' he said, sticking out his hand, but Annie ignored it.

'Ben! Hi! I've heard so much about you.' Her gaze flicked from Jeanie to Ben and back again. 'Jeanie, you didn't tell me your brother was like a hot male version of you!'

'I don't normally think of him as hot, actually.'

Annie's eyes were on him again. She was objectively beautiful and definitely trouble, but it didn't matter anyway, because her gaze had already wandered and landed somewhere past his right shoulder.

Bennett turned just in time to see a dark-haired man

wiggle his fingers in a wave at Annie. When Bennett turned back around, she was glaring daggers at the man.

'He's here again. I thought he'd stopped coming to these.'

'That's Mac,' Jeanie whispered for his sake even though Annie could obviously still hear her. 'Annie's arch nemesis. We're all waiting for them to finally sleep together and put us out of our collective misery.'

Annie huffed. 'How dare you?'

Jeanie just laughed and shrugged. Ben knew when it was best to stay quiet and now when he had absolutely no idea what the hell was going on seemed like a good time.

'Attention, everyone,' the mayor tried again but was cut off by a shrill whistle. The crowd flinched. 'Uh … thank you, Mindy,' the mayor said, and the power-suited, menorah-wrangling lady gave him a serious nod before taking her seat in the front row.

'We have a lot to discuss this evening with the Tree Lighting rapidly approaching, the children's pageant in just two weeks, and the toy drive that began yesterday, so let's get started.'

The rest of the meeting went by in a blur of logistics, volunteering, arguing, and a very odd vote about whether or not *Die Hard* was a Christmas movie. Bennett tried to keep up, but following along proved to be impossible. Instead, he found himself scanning the room, trying to match faces with stories Jeanie had told him over the past year. He spotted the book club pretty easily since he'd seen and heard them in the background of his phone calls with

Jeanie. They'd even left a copy of their latest read on his doorstep as a welcome gift and a hint that they wanted him to attend their December meeting.

He'd taken one look at *Daddy December* and was already thinking up ways to be busy that day. The last thing he needed was to read about sex when he hadn't had any in months. He needed something about monks or meditation or suffering or something like that. Not Santa smut.

And why did thoughts of sexy books bring his thoughts back around to that Christmas-tree farm owner? She was so … so rude to him. Not sexy mean. Just plain mean. And … well … sure he'd been trespassing, but he hadn't known he was, and he did offer to help with whatever computer issue she was clearly having and she'd just shut him down completely. It was … well … it had gotten under his skin for sure.

Like a splinter.

A splinter he couldn't seem to stop picking at.

What was her deal? Why had she been out there all alone? Why had she been wearing a blanket instead of a proper coat? Was she cold? Did she want someone to keep her warm…

Nope. Bad. Not going down that road with this strange woman. He knew nothing about her and he was not going to let his overdeveloped need to fix things get in the way of his holiday. He didn't even live here.

Kira North was nothing but a quirky character to add to what he knew about Dream Harbor. Nothing else.

He would absolutely stop thinking about warming her up.

The room had gone quiet around him. He may have let his mind wander a bit too far, because at some point the meeting had taken a turn and now he found himself the center of attention.

'Uh…'

'I was just mentioning that you met Kira yesterday,' Jeanie said with a smile that chilled him to the bone. If he'd been eight and she'd been ten, he'd have flushed her Barbie's head in the toilet all over again.

'Wonderful!' the mayor was saying, oblivious to Bennett's revenge fantasy. 'We could really use a neutral party to go up there and check on her.'

'Neutral party?' he echoed. 'Wait. Check on her?'

'The town has been trying to welcome Miss North,' the mayor went on. 'But she's been … resistant to our efforts. But you, you're just passing through. You're neutral! She wouldn't question your motives.'

Well, that certainly wasn't true. 'And why does she need to be checked on exactly?'

'Uh … well…' the mayor's face flushed red.

'Just in case there's any dead bodies up there,' someone offered from the back of the meeting hall.

'Dead bodies?!' What the actual hell was going on?

Jeanie grimaced beside him. 'It's not as bad as it seems,' she whispered.

'We have no proof that there's a dead body,' the mayor said.

'We also don't have proof that there isn't,' Noah piped up helpfully, earning a smack on the thigh from Hazel. He just laughed and kissed her cheek.

'Alex tells it best. Where are they?' The mayor searched the crowd until a person with lavender hair stood up.

'Hey, everyone.' They gave a little wave before launching into their story. 'So, the Connors owned that farm for generations and when the youngest child Edwin took over, sometime in the eighties, he opened it up for families to come and cut down their trees for Christmas. It grew from there into the business a lot of you were familiar with for years. Edwin and his wife, Ellen, never had kids but they ran the farm for about forty years together. Well, Edwin was rather eccentric and rather ... unpredictable.'

'Scary, you mean.' Someone shouted out from the audience.

'Gave me the creeps for sure.'

'Me too!'

'Anyway,' Alex went on, clearing their throat. 'After his wife died, people saw less and less of Edwin and the tree farm took a downward turn. When he died a few years later, a letter was found in the house.'

'This is the good part,' Noah whispered, loud enough for everyone to hear. Alex smiled at him.

'Right, so the letter claimed that he had buried something important, something *precious* to him on the farm, but it didn't say what or where. Plenty of us have wanted to search up there, but the land was left to some cousin, who was pretty adamant about not letting us snoop around. Highly suspicious, if you ask me.' Alex shrugged. 'So the legend is left unfinished.'

Bennett shook his head. 'And you all think the thing he buried … was a body?'

'His murdered wife, specifically,' Jacob filled in for him.

'What?!'

'She just disappeared one day! I think he buried her for sure.'

'No way, I still think it's something else. Some kind of treasure,' Noah argued.

'Treasure? Keep dreaming, sailor boy,' an old man yelled from a few rows ahead of them, making Noah chuckle.

'It could be money, though. He didn't have any family left. Maybe he hid all his cash instead of putting it in the bank,' Kaori suggested.

'A bit of a crazy theory.'

'Crazier than a murdered wife and a dead body? Please.'

'I think…'

'But what about…'

'Wait a minute!' Bennett raised his voice over the cacophony of theories. Everyone shut up in surprise. 'What the hell does any of this have to do with Kira?'

He heard a snort from the end of the row. 'You don't want to know,' Logan muttered.

'We wouldn't want our newest resident to experience the trauma of accidentally stumbling upon a horrific scene,' the mayor explained like this was all very normal. 'So we just thought…'

'You thought I could stumble over it instead?' Bennett said, an eyebrow raised.

The mayor winced. 'We just thought you could pay her a visit or two and help smooth things over. She's reopening the farm and we're so pleased. We just don't want any surprises.' He wrung his hands in front of him. 'And she won't let any of the rest of us past the front porch.' The mayor's face lit up. 'But you … you were able to get right in there! Jeanie told us you walked your dogs through the fields and chatted with her so … it seems you're the perfect candidate for the job!'

Bennett pinched the bridge of his nose and fantasized about researching flight information for the first plane back to San Francisco.

'I can't. I have to work.'

The mayor and every face that turned toward him looked highly skeptical of this.

'Remote work is still work.'

'But it's flexible, right?' Jeanie asked. 'Like you could just pop up there a few times before the farm reopens? Just to make sure there's no, like, skulls lying around or anything?'

Bennett looked at her and tried to convey just how much he wanted to bury *her* body right now, but she was completely serious about this. And when he looked around the room, so was everyone else.

The entire town was recruiting him to go to their beloved Christmas-tree farm and what? Scan for dead bodies? Find a secret stash of money? Solve the town mystery?

And the hilarious part was they thought Kira was actually going to let him in! Ha! The joke was on them. Judging by the way she'd looked at him yesterday, there was no way she was inviting him for afternoon tea and murder-mystery-solving anytime soon.

But everyone was staring at him like they needed him to do this.

And Bennett hated saying no. Even to crazy villagers he barely knew.

'I can try, but…'

'Wonderful!' the mayor said, already moving on. 'So, Bennett will help with the Christmas-tree farm opening. Okay, what's next?'

I can try but it will never work was what he'd been going to say. Not that it mattered. He'd been steamrolled and now instead of a ride to the airport, he was apparently opening a Christmas-tree farm, or working on a cold case, or treasure hunting…

But most likely just getting kicked out on his ass by the latest scary Christmas-tree farm owner.

Chapter Three

There were dogs outside. Kira could hear them barking as she rinsed her coffee mug and peered out the window over the sink. The one that let in so much cold air, she could feel it on her face as she washed dishes, but she didn't know what to do about that.

Another bark! She wiped the condensation from the window, but she still couldn't see anything.

Maybe she had customers! Customers with dogs! Maybe they'd dressed the dogs in little dog sweaters for a Christmas photo shoot! That would be adorable. And it would look great on the new social media account she'd finally managed to set up when she'd got a weak signal in the far corner of one of the upstairs guest rooms. As long as she stayed perfectly still and faced the wall, the internet worked perfectly.

She should get outside to greet them, even though she'd hired a lovely and very responsible-looking woman to sit in the booth and work the register, but if these were her first customers ever she should go out and see. And get their permission to post pics of their holiday sweater-wearing dogs.

That was why she was scrabbling for her boots and pulling on her new puffy coat so fast. Customers meant money and money meant heat. And new windows.

See, everything was going to be fine. She was going to pull this off all on her own. She didn't need Chloe. If she was being honest, Chloe had probably been holding her back all these years, with her practicality and realistic expectations. It was time for Kira to go big. To live her dream, regardless of how recently this dream had popped up. She was going to make money off this Christmas-tree obsessed town and then she could live off the land just like *@thehomesteadgoddess* and *@selfsustainedliving* and all the other lovely and beautiful accounts she followed. If they could do it, surely she could do it.

Kira hurried out the back door, fantasizing about pickled vegetables lined up in neat rows in her pantry, and cross-stitched aprons, not that she knew how to pickle anything or what the hell cross-stitch involved. She followed the sound of the barking dogs through the lines of trees, up two rows, across three.

There!

Oh.

'You.'

The man from the other day had his head down, as though he was looking for something in the dirt, but it snapped up when he heard her voice. 'Hello, again,' he said, a hand raised in greeting.

'Why are you back?' Kira's dreams of Christmas doggie photoshoots fizzled out. Elizabeth, the biggest of the three dogs, nudged against her hand. Kira gave her head a good scratch. These dogs weren't wearing sweaters, but they were still pretty darn cute.

'The sign said open.'

Kira frowned. 'And you're here to buy a tree?'

The man smiled. 'I'm considering it. If I can find the right one.'

'The right one?' she huffed. 'It's just a tree, not a wife.'

His laugh startled her and the dogs. Odie barked in alarm.

'I have very high standards for my Christmas trees,' he said, his eyes sparking in amusement.

'I bet you do.' He probably had obnoxiously high standards for a lot of things. But if Kira liked that sort of thing she would have stuck around at home for longer.

'You don't?' he asked.

'Not about Christmas trees, no.'

He glanced around at the farm she now owned but luckily for him refrained from commenting about how she should probably care about the quality of her Christmas trees.

Instead, he shrugged and said, 'I like your coat.'

'Thank you. It's so damn cold here, I had to upgrade.'

He chuckled. 'It hasn't even dropped below freezing yet.'

This guy. Ugh. 'Well, it's cold to me. What are you from Alaska or something?'

'Buffalo.'

'Hmph. Well, that's nice for you that the cold doesn't bother you, but it bothers me.'

'Where are you from?'

Kira sighed. She didn't love telling people she was from Georgia, especially people from up North. They made instant assumptions that she didn't appreciate, assumptions that she was dumb or slow or worse. It was why she'd made a concerted effort to ditch her accent when she'd moved. It only slipped out now when she was angry or drunk, or speaking to her sister.

'Georgia.'

The man just nodded. 'No wonder you're cold.'

No rude comments. Interesting.

'I don't know your name,' she said. If this guy was going to keep hanging around, she'd probably need to know what to call him.

He smiled and stuck out his hand. 'Sorry, I'm Bennett.'

Kira took it in hers and shook it. It was big and warm. 'Kira.'

'I know.'

'You know?'

'Sure, you're big news in town. I'm staying above my sister's café and you're all anyone can talk about.'

Odie and Pudgie whined at her feet and she squatted down to pet them. 'You say that, but where is everyone?! I'm open and I haven't had a single customer.'

'Does anyone know you're open?'

Kira huffed. 'The sign says open, doesn't it? And we have a brand new website with all the information and an Instagram profile… Oh, actually could I post a pic of your dogs? So far I just have random tree pictures.'

She peered up at where he still stood above her.

'I don't think anyone is checking for a new website. And I think you did a good enough job telling people to uh … stay out … that no one is driving by to check for an open sign.'

'Oh. Hmm. Good point.'

Now what? How was she going to lure everyone back? Her dreams of perfectly preserved vegetables were quickly fading.

'Why don't you go to that tree-lighting thing? It sounds like a big deal to the town. You could make some kind of announcement about your grand reopening.'

She wanted to tell him she didn't need his suggestions, thank you very much, but that was actually a really good idea. Damn it.

She stood. 'Yeah, maybe.'

He smiled that stupid straight smile. His parents must have paid so much for that smile. Nobody was born with teeth that straight. Well, nobody was born with teeth in general, but that was beside the point! She was getting sidetracked.

'Well, I'll leave you to your perfect tree hunt,' she said. 'If you find one you like, Iris at the booth has saws for cutting it down.'

'You have a person sitting in that old shack out front?' His eyes widened in alarm.

'Of course I do. It's fine.'

'Fine? I don't know about that. Looks pretty run down.'

Kira put her hand on her hip, fully intending to give this know-it-all asshole a piece of her mind, when an image of poor sweet Iris buried under a pile of old wood beams flashed through her mind.

Oh, God, what if this know-it-all asshole was right!

She turned and ran, the dogs hot on her heels. Well, Elizabeth and Odie were. Poor chubby, Pudgie was pulling up the rear.

'Iris! Iris!' she called, racing toward the little cabin on the other side of the farm. 'Iris, you're in danger!' Kira had thought it was rustic. She'd thought it had charm. She'd thought it looked very cute and post-able when she'd strung twinkle lights up along the roof. She had not once thought it might fall down and kill her only employee!

'I don't think it's that imminent!' Bennett yelled to her as he followed behind the dogs. Imminent or not, Kira couldn't risk it. Mostly because she couldn't bear the thought of Iris getting hurt, but also because she didn't have insurance yet and definitely couldn't afford anyone's medical bills.

'Iris, get out of there!' She skidded to a stop in front of the booth. A wide-eyed Iris pulled aside the little window and peered out.

'What's going on?' Iris asked, taking in Kira, red-faced

and panting, the three barking dogs, and Bennett striding in last, but no less harried than the rest of the crew.

'Get out of that death trap!'

'Deathtrap?' Iris's brows furrowed.

'Everyone just calm down,' Bennett said. 'I don't think it's that serious.'

'Not that serious?' Kira spun toward him. 'Not that serious?! Then why did you say it? Why did you waltz in here and just start spouting helpful little tidbits like maybe that booth is a death trap…'

'I never said death trap.'

'Argh!' Kira was out of intelligible words. This guy! Why was he even here?

'How about I just go in and check it out for you?'

'How about you go the hell back to Buffalo!'

His eyes widened at her outburst and the southern accent that was now bursting through her defenses and she was suddenly very thankful she didn't have any other customers right now. That would be … awkward.

She took a deep breath. 'Why would you be qualified to check it out?' she asked through clenched teeth, instead of yelling at him that possessing testicles did not make him a handyman. You had to have actual skills for that sort of thing. You had to know what you were doing.

Not that she did, either … but still.

'My dad's a contractor. I have some experience…'

Kira let out a noise somewhere between a groan and a shriek. 'Of course you do. Fine. Go look.' She gestured toward the little cabin and noticed Iris still staring at them.

Right. She was having an interesting first day of work.

'Iris, why don't you go grab a cup of coffee and take a short break? I just made some in the house.'

Iris's gaze flicked from Kira to Bennett, a bemused smirk on her face. 'Okay, sure.' She came out of the cabin and gave Kira a knowing smile. 'I'll take a break. Try not to kill this guy while I'm gone.'

Did Iris just wink at her? What on earth did she think was going on here? Kira didn't have time to set her straight before Iris hurried away down the drive to the house.

Bennett meanwhile was sniffing around the perimeter of the shack and then peering up at the roof before finally heading through the door. Kira followed him in.

There wasn't much inside, but she'd thoroughly cleaned it all on her own. She'd even relocated the family of possums that had taken up residence inside. And by relocate, she meant she'd screamed when she saw them and they had voluntarily left.

But the wood floors were scrubbed clean, there was a cozy space heater in the corner and a small table and two chairs. She'd lined up the saws on hooks on the wall and had even made a giant carafe of hot chocolate for all the customers she'd imagined having today. Clearly, that wasn't going exactly as planned.

She glanced at Bennett who was examining the small space with a furrow between his brows.

'It's better in here than I thought.'

She wanted to punch him. Unfortunately, manners were still a big deal in the South, so she refrained.

'Thanks.'

He knocked on a few walls and reached up to poke at the ceiling. 'Looks okay.'

Kira ground her back teeth together. 'Wonderful.'

He turned to face her and suddenly the fact that they were crammed into a tiny space together was very evident. He was taller than she'd first realized. For whatever reason that made her angry, too. Like just be average, would you? Ugh.

'I'm sorry for worrying you like that,' he said. 'I was only trying to help.'

'So is that your thing?' she snapped. 'You get off on helping people?'

He blinked. 'I wouldn't say I get off on it.'

'You know what I mean, you like to fix things. You're a fixer.'

'I … well…' his frown deepened. 'Maybe I am.'

Kira scoffed. How predictable. This big Boy Scout liked to fix things. Well, she didn't need that kind of energy in her life right now. This was her big endeavor; she didn't need this guy waltzing in and trying to take over with all his … ideas … and … concerns. However valid they may be.

'And you?' he asked. 'What gets you off?'

'What?' she sputtered, her face immediately heating.

He chuckled, low and deep. 'You know what I mean. What's your deal? You're bad at letting people help you.'

Why was it so crowded in here? Had he stepped closer or had she? For the first time in days, she was warm.

'Actually,' she said, straightening to her full height,

refusing to crane her neck to look up at him. 'My whole life all people did was help me. I rarely did anything for myself ever. I didn't need to. We had people for that.' She sniffed. 'But this is different. This is for me.'

'Accepting help is different than letting other people do everything for you.' He was definitely closer, his light gray eyes locked on hers.

This new coat was too warm.

Kira cleared her throat. 'Yes, well. I think you've done enough helping for one day.'

Chapter Four

He was standing dangerously close to Kira. Dangerous, because she looked like she might strangle him. Dangerous, because he had the sudden urge to pull her closer. Which was insane. You wouldn't try to snuggle with a feral cat, and tugging Kira into his arms right now would amount to the same thing.

Her cheeks had turned pinker the angrier she got with him and at this point were downright rosy. She blew out a breath, fluttering the bangs away from her forehead. He hadn't had a chance to notice just how beautiful she was the other day when she was clearly upset and wrapped in an old blanket, but today … today he was noticing. But he should stop noticing, because noticing would do absolutely no good. Not only was she incredibly not interested in him noticing, but he had very specifically sworn off beautiful women. Not to mention he was only here temporarily.

There were endless reasons why he should step back,

why he should stop holding her fiery gaze, why he should walk right the hell out of here.

But Kira was right. He got off on fixing things. He should have kept his mouth shut about this tree-farm shack, about lots of things he'd said to Kira since he met her.

Except now, looking at her bundled into her new coat with its faux-fur-trimmed hood, like she was ready for an arctic expedition, he found himself opening his mouth again.

'How's the main house?'

She narrowed her eyes at him like he had nefarious motives for asking. 'It's fine.'

'You sure?'

Her internal struggle on how to answer was written clearly across her face. She didn't want to ask him for help, obviously. But that house was at least a hundred years old and had been vacant for the past three, according to Logan. There was no way things were running perfectly in there.

Not that it was any of his business if they were or not. He could just leave. He could tell his sister and her crazy neighbors that he'd found nothing, that he wasn't going back, that he had work to do. He could walk away and leave Kira here with her new farm and her wide eyes and her lack of customers.

But what he wouldn't be able to do was to stop thinking about how she might be unsafe in that house. The town was worried about her encountering some mythical dead body, but what they should be worried about was carbon monoxide poisoning. Or a gas leak. Or faulty wiring.

So, yeah, he wanted to fix a few things for her. If she let him.

Was that so wrong?

Kira blew out a long dramatic sigh. 'I guess if you really wanted to, you could maybe look at the boiler for me. I don't seem to be getting much heat. So, I mean … if it would be fun for you…'

'I'll check it out.'

She might have been rolling her eyes at him, but he had already turned around and walked out of the cabin. His dogs were waiting for him. Pudgie had dozed off under a tree, Odie immediately started yapping at the sight of him and Elizabeth loped loyally to his side.

'Come on,' he said, and Elizabeth and Odie followed, the big dog at his hip and the little one scurrying around his feet. He turned around to see Kira scooping Pudgie up and carrying her in her arms. She whispered something in the old dog's ear. He decided it was best to ignore what seeing her snuggle his favorite dog did to him, turning his insides soft and achy. It was just the sort of thing to have him renovating her entire house by the end of the week.

He shook his head and trudged toward the main house. He was just going to make sure it was livable and then he really would stay away from this farm and this woman who wasn't even remotely interested in him and he didn't need in his life anyway. Regardless of how his dogs felt about her. They also ate trash so they didn't exactly have discerning tastes.

The house was an old Victorian with a big wraparound

porch. It looked like a dilapidated version of a doll's house Jeanie used to have when they were kids. He climbed the front steps, promising himself that he was just being neighborly. He would have insisted on helping even if Kira had been an old man, or a nun, or anyone, really. Although maybe he wouldn't have been quite as eager about it.

'Stay,' he told the dogs, but Kira huffed behind him.

'They can come in.' She cuddled Pudgie closer. 'We can't just leave the poor babies outside,' she crooned.

'Right. Of course.' He opened the door, and Elizabeth and Odie raced inside.

Kira laughed and he added the throaty sound of it to the things he was ignoring.

The temperature in the house wasn't much better than outside. No wonder this woman had taken to wearing comforters.

'Kira, it's freezing in here.'

She put Pudgie gently on the sofa and tucked a fleece blanket around her. He would swear the dog grinned at him.

'I know. That's what I said.'

'You didn't. You said you weren't getting *much* heat. I don't think you're getting any.'

She shrugged. 'Semantics.'

'Kira.'

'What?'

'You can't live here like this.'

Her mouth set in a firm line. He was about to get kicked out on his ass if he didn't scale down the protective vibe.

'I can and I do and I'm fine.' She spun on her heel and marched off toward what he assumed was the kitchen in the back of the house. 'The boiler is in the basement if you want to look at it.' She gestured to a door under the main staircase. 'Otherwise you can feel free to get the hell out.'

She didn't look back, just left him standing in her entryway hall feeling like an asshole for wanting to help her. He should go, clearly. He had things to do other than be abused by irrationally angry Christmas-tree farm owners: things like his actual job. But … but it really was freezing in here and he said he would take a look and, damn it, he couldn't just leave her here like this.

The radiator in the hall clanged like someone was hammering the pipes and then hissed like an angry cat. He took that as a sign. He would just take a quick look. Besides, his dogs were gone; Elizabeth and Odie had totally abandoned him to follow Kira, and Pudgie snored loudly from the couch.

Might as well take a look.

He found Kira an hour later in the kitchen nursing a cup of coffee with all three dogs curled up at her feet. He ignored this cozy picture of domestic bliss and instead launched into his findings.

'You need a new boiler.'

Kira raised a perfectly groomed eyebrow. 'No kidding.'

Bennett sighed and ran a hand down his face in frustration. Why was she making this so difficult?

'Nothing is leaking at the moment, so I think the only real danger is if the pipes freeze. You're getting a little heat coming through, but I don't know if it's enough to keep water flowing.'

Kira's brow furrowed. 'Okay, thank you.'

No snarky comment.

'Okay, so you'll get a new boiler?'

'As soon as I have money for a new boiler, I will get one.'

He swallowed the urge to offer to pay for a new boiler. That would be too much even for him. But still he hated the idea of Kira cold and alone in this house.

'Maybe in the meantime you could have someone come out and get the fireplace operational. You could heat at least some of the house with that until you get the boiler.'

'Why do you care?' She placed her mug down on the table and leaned back in her chair to study him. She was wearing at least two bulky sweaters and fingerless gloves. Inside. She was cold and he *hated* it.

He shifted on his feet. 'You said it, I'm a fixer.'

'Hmm. Well, I'm not a damsel in distress.'

'I never said you were.'

She quirked an eyebrow. 'So, you do this with everyone? This helpful boy-scout thing?'

'I was never a Boy Scout.'

Her lips pulled up in the corner, an almost smile.

'Well, thank you. Thank you for checking the boiler. And for the suggestion about the fireplace.'

'Of course.'

'There's fresh coffee, if you want some.'

He should get back to work, but he'd already missed the whole morning. Passing on coffee at this point seemed silly. Especially if Kira was actually offering it to him instead of biting his head off.

'Sure, thanks."

Kira gestured to the coffee maker. 'Help yourself. The mugs are in that cabinet.'

The house might be old, but Kira's small appliances were top of the line, and her mugs were all matching earthy tones lined up with their handles pointed in the same direction. He had to admit it was all very visually appealing. And it made him wonder about her even more.

'How did you end up here?' he asked, bringing his mug over to the table.

She shifted in her seat, a small frown crossing her face.

'Sorry. We don't have to talk about it.'

'No, it's fine. Just not a terribly flattering story.'

'Oh?' he said, not able to help his teasing smile. 'Now I really want to hear it.'

Kira rolled her eyes, but Bennett had a feeling it was more at herself than at him. 'I was over-influenced by influencers.'

'What does that even mean?'

'I thought I could do this…' She waved her hand around, in a gesture that encompassed everything from the house to the farm outside. 'All this. I thought I could buy an old farmhouse and have a garden and make pickles…'

'Pickles?'

'Yeah, like pickle all kinds of vegetables and line them up in neat little jars and I could just, I don't know, do something for myself for once. By myself for once.'

He nodded slowly, not really sure what the hell to make of any of that, but she was talking to him and he liked it. He didn't want to say something that would make her stop.

'And I don't know. Clearly, I screwed up. And now I'm here in this big, old house with this farm I never intended on having.'

He wanted to ask how that would happen. How do you end up buying a farm without knowing but he knew better than to say that out loud.

'I've never been very … practical. That was Chloe's thing.'

'Chloe?'

'My twin. She's gone.'

'Oh, God. I'm so sorry.'

Kira's eyes widened. 'Oh, no, I'm sorry! She's not dead. She's in Denmark.'

Bennett blew out a long breath. Jesus, he'd thought he'd dredged up memories of her dead twin.

'She's in Denmark with her new husband.' Kira made a face at that as though this new husband was something foul. 'And I'm here alone.'

Alone. And cold.

She shrugged and gave a self-deprecating laugh. 'I

couldn't even survive one day of being open without needing you to rush in and help me.'

'I didn't actually do anything.'

'Well, that's true.'

He laughed and her smile grew, warming him up even in this drafty house. 'How about I call my dad later and see if he has any tips about these old radiators?'

A sharp shake of her head sent her hair cascading over her shoulders. 'You don't have to do that.'

'Consider it a favor to me,' he said, leaning toward her across the table, just a little, just enough to watch her blush spread. 'It gets me off, remember?'

She sputtered. 'I never should have said that.'

'You were right. I like it. I like feeling … useful.'

Her lips twitched somewhere between a smile and a scowl.

'Okay, fine. But that's it.'

'Deal.'

She eyed him over the rim of her coffee mug, and he found he had more questions after this little chat than he'd had before they started.

'I should go,' he said, standing before he could do any more, offer any more. He needed to go before he did something crazy, like suggest he wrap Kira in his arms to warm her up. A pointless daydream.

'Sure. Thanks again.'

There was just one more thing, because Bennett still wasn't smart about women, despite his best efforts. 'Will I see you at the tree lighting?'

Kira scrunched up her face like a child being forced to eat their vegetables. 'I guess so.'

He chuckled. 'It might be fun.'

'Crazier things have happened.'

As he rounded up his dogs and headed out, Bennett refused to think of all the crazier things he'd like to happen with the prickly and intriguing Kira North.

Chapter Five

Did you find anything?

Bennett glanced at the text from his sister. He debated ignoring it. He was already working far later than he wanted to, but he had projects to catch up on after his morning of playing Mr. Fix-It at Kira's. But he hated leaving messages unanswered. It made him feel itchy.

No. Not a single dead body in sight.

Okay. Phew. When are you going back?

He sighed, leaning back against Jeanie's couch cushions. Her small apartment lacked a desk, and he was still trying to figure out the most comfortable place to work.

I don't think I'm going back.

He needed to stay away from Kira. That's what his little visit had proven to him this morning. Seeing her in that drafty old house had stirred up too many things in him and he needed those things to stay buried just like Edwin's dead wife.

You have to! Just a few more times. Just to be sure.

You do know this is insane, right?

Of course I do. But the mayor had a dream and he's rarely wrong.

And what did the wise and powerful mayor see in this dream?

Well … they're always a little fuzzy, but basically something important is buried on that farm.

So, shouldn't we let Kira find it?

Even as he typed it, his stomach dropped at the idea of Kira making a gruesome discovery by herself. And Jeanie knew it, too.

We can't let her just stumble upon something like that!

Fine. One more time.

Thank you, Ben!! You're the best!

He didn't feel like the best. He felt like an absolute sucker who got conned into doing ridiculous errands for his sister because he was too much of a sap to let her down.

But what else was new?

His sister wasn't the first woman to manipulate him into doing things for her and he was sure she wouldn't be the last.

Bennett was back.

She should feel annoyed by that, but she was having trouble summoning the energy today. It was day two of the farm being open and still no customers. A low level of panic had started simmering in her gut. What was left of her trust fund after buying this place was gone after a few months of living here without any additional income.

And now if this Christmas-tree-farm thing didn't take off, she truly had no idea what to do next. This was the first time in her life that she was on her own. She'd spent the first twenty-four years being either coddled or bailed out of every situation. Her parents had the funds and the means to soften the blow of her various bad decisions. Even when she and Chloe moved out of the Georgian mansion they'd grown up in, they hadn't gone further than the recently renovated carriage house.

It was pathetic.

She was pathetic. A barely functioning adult. And when she finally decided to strike out on her own, she somehow thought buying an old farm was the way to go. But she was all in now. She refused to admit defeat.

It *had* to work.

She walked out to the front porch to find Bennett climbing out of his rental car. He had a toolbox this time, but no dogs to buffer their interactions. In her current mood, that didn't bode well for Bennett.

'Back for more fun?' she called and he looked up with that perfect smile.

'I might be able to get those radiators working better.' He strode up her front path like a man on a mission. 'My dad told me some things to try.'

Kira considered not letting him in. It was possible that her first impression of him wasn't exactly right. Maybe he wasn't a misogynist who thought she couldn't do things for herself, but she also didn't know why he was so damn concerned about her house.

What was his angle?

It was an awful lot of work just to get her in bed. And she hadn't really given him any indication she would want him there, anyway. Maybe he liked a challenge?

She didn't have time to fend off well-meaning do-gooders or guys with a masochistic streak when she was too busy failing miserably at her only chance to build something for herself. So whichever one he was, she shouldn't let him in.

On the other hand, she was tired of being cold.

She stepped aside. 'Have at it.'

'Thanks.' Another smile as he passed her and let himself in.

'Maybe later you can find a bunch of old ladies that need help crossing the street.'

He looked over his shoulder with an amused smirk. 'Helping with your heat *and* escorting old ladies? The perfect day.'

Kira huffed and rolled her eyes, but Bennett was undeterred today.

'If it's okay with you, I'll just go around to each radiator and see if I can adjust the vent cans. If not, maybe the service valves.'

'I don't know what any of that means, but go nuts.'

'Great.'

Suddenly, Kira didn't like the idea of just hanging out in her house while Bennett messed around with her radiators. That would be awkward.

'I'm going to go check on Iris.'

'Oh, good, she still works here, then?'

Kira winced. She had not made a great first impression with her only employee yesterday, but the intrepid Iris had shown up again this morning, assuring her that she was not easily scared off. Apparently, she was used to working for crazy people.

From what Kira gathered, Iris had grown up in Dream Harbor and was undeterred by the antics of the townsfolk. She also had plenty of jobs around town and had even invited Kira to join her yoga class. She was probably perfectly fine out there by herself, snug and cozy in the little cabin. But again, Kira had no desire to sit around and watch Bennett work.

So, continuing with her 'fake it till you make it as a Christmas tree farmer plan', she pulled on her boots to head outside.

'Yes, miraculously she still works here after you scared her half to death with your whole "that house is going to collapse and crush her" thing.'

Bennett stopped clanging around in his toolbox for long enough to look at her with a bemused expression. 'I never said that.'

'You definitely did.'

'I wasn't the one who went running and screaming across the farm.'

'It was an emergency!'

'It really wasn't.'

'It could have been. I could have been saving her life.'

His smile grew and Kira was horrified to find her own mouth inching up to mirror his. She shook her head. Time to go. Not time to stand around smiling at this Clark Kent lookalike. Maybe she'd find a biker or a parolee on her way that she could make out with, just to remind herself who she really was.

All this fresh, piney air must be messing with her senses.

It only took an hour for Kira to run out of things to do. She'd checked on Iris and as expected found her totally content, with her nose in a book. She'd swept the little front porch that led to the payment window, straightened the wreath on the door, photographed a few dozen angles of the new sign she'd had commissioned, wandered through the trees, made notes of things to tell the groundskeeper she'd hired who was starting next week, and read through the responses to her ad for a Santa but they were few and far between.

And after all that, she'd really had no choice but to head back to the house, seeing as there still wasn't a customer in sight. Had she really been that terrifying to the locals? Sure, she had told everyone in no uncertain terms that she wasn't reopening, and she hadn't exactly been friendly to the neighbors who'd stopped by, but still. That couldn't possibly have been enough to keep everyone away forever. Where were they getting their trees? Were they all going without one this year?

She could probably ask Bennett to spread the word, seeing as his sister owned the town's favorite café, but she was already uncomfortable with everything else he was doing. She wasn't about to add free marketing into the mix.

She might have to actually go to this tree-lighting thing.

It was that or starve. Or freeze. Or both. A nice freeze-and-starve combo.

She walked inside to find the downstairs empty, but she could hear footsteps above her. She climbed the stairs and found Bennett in the first bedroom (currently being used to house empty cardboard boxes) crouched down next to the radiator. He'd rolled up the sleeves of his flannel shirt and his forearm flexed as he turned some kind of valve on the side of the old metal beast. Squatting there like that, his jeans stretched tight over his thighs and ass…

Time for him to go. 'Almost done?' Kira's voice came out tight and squeaky.

Bennett's head snapped up at the sound. 'I didn't know you were back.'

'I am.' Kira cleared her throat. 'I am back. So, are you leaving soon?'

Bennett stood, that teasing smirk on his face. He wiped his hands on his jeans and Kira could not be faulted for watching the motion. Those thighs were … distracting.

'This is the last one. Hopefully, this helps a bit.'

'Right, I'm sure it will. Any heat is better than no heat.'

'I found this behind one of the radiators.' He handed Kira an old piece of paper he pulled out of his back pocket.

'What is it?' she asked, trying to make out the slanted script across the yellowed notebook paper.

'Not sure.'

She looked again. 'It looks like someone was making a list of their stuff.'

Bennett peered down at the paper, a crease between his brows. 'Two Tiffany lamps, full set of bone china,' he read. 'Hmm, a lot of it is smudged.' He squinted and turned the paper. 'Ellie's baubles.'

'Baubles? Like jewelry?'

Bennett shrugged. 'Could mean ornaments or something like that. Can't make out much more.'

Kira frowned. 'The old owners must have written it.'

'Could be. I've heard the farm was left to a cousin, but maybe they wanted their other possessions to go to different people?'

'So, this is what? Like a rough draft of their will?'

He shrugged again. 'Beats me, but I should go.'

She watched as he gathered up his tools and a spike of panic shot through her. She didn't want him to leave. She didn't want to spend the rest of the day alone in this cold house, on this failing farm.

Kira was a twin. She'd always felt it was against her nature to be alone. She hadn't even been alone in the womb. And now look at her, contemplating chaining this nice, neighborly guy to her radiator just so she wouldn't have to face another dark evening by herself.

She couldn't stop feeling like half a person, like half of her organs had been scooped out and taken to Denmark. This farm, this plan, it was supposed to help, supposed to give her something that was truly hers. And it wasn't working. She'd been the Grinchy character above Dream Harbor for nearly three months now and she had nothing to show for it.

No picture-perfect, organically raised, locally sourced life.

She was an idiot.

When he looked up again, Bennett caught her frowning. At least she wasn't crying, but he had that worried crease between his brows again and she could not have that. Absolutely not.

He had to go. Because unlike the Grinch, Kira had zero

interest in having a heart that grew three sizes. Certainly not if that meant warm and fuzzy feelings toward the man her mother would throw her a parade for marrying.

Marrying?! Dear God. Spending so much time alone had definitely started to rot her brain.

'Okay, well, thanks again. See you around.' She stepped out of the way of the door so Bennett could pass. She ignored the questioning look on his face as he scooted by, his tall, toned body brushing a little too close to hers. She didn't owe him any answers.

She followed him down the stairs, certainly not noticing how broad his back was or that his hair had gotten mussed as he was working. But maybe she did owe him a little something since he had come all the way out here to help her, not that she'd asked him to.

'You can have a free tree,' she said when they were back in the entryway and Bennett was pulling on his coat.

He raised his eyebrows. 'A free tree?'

'Yeah, for your … uh … services.'

He grinned. 'A free tree sounds great.'

Kira sighed. Good. Payment for services rendered and then Bennett could leave and never come back. Perfect. The last thing she needed was to be indebted to this guy.

'I don't have time to stick around today, though,' he said. 'Got a meeting at two. I'll have to take you up on it another time.'

Damn it. Kira kept the fake smile plastered on her face. 'Sure. Another time.'

'And you'll help me pick it out?' His smile was back to teasing which at least meant the worry was gone.

'I don't know if I can live up to your perfect tree-finding standards.'

He held her gaze for a second before answering and Kira wished there was a dog or two between them to break the tension.

'I think you'll live up to them just fine.'

Chapter Six

Bennett had spent the last several days actually working and absolutely not thinking about Kira and her ancient radiators and if they should be making that hissing noise all the time and if the return pipe in the basement should be hot. Though he thought it probably shouldn't be.

If he hadn't been suddenly swamped putting out fires at work, he might have wandered back up to the farm one more time just to check that things were running smoother. But it was probably for the best that he hadn't been able to. Watching YouTube videos of old men explaining steam heat every night before bed was already going too far.

He needed to stop. Kira hadn't even asked for his help. Was it any wonder that his last year of dating had turned into him doing favors for women he barely knew? It was the energy he was putting out in the world. What did Aunt Dot tell him just the other day when he'd had dinner with her and Jeanie? *Your vibe attracts your tribe.* Well, apparently, Bennett's tribe consisted of a lot of people needing favors. Bennett Ellis: free rides, moving services, and now, heating help. Maybe instead of a dating profile, he should just have business cards made up.

He was purposely ignoring the fact that Kira was different than any other woman he'd ever dated and that she hadn't taken advantage of him at all; she'd barely let him in and had only begrudgingly let him help. And she was beautiful and interesting and maybe a little bit sad and a little bit lonely in a way he thought maybe he understood.

But he was going to keep ignoring all of that because he was only here for the month and he had no business chasing after a woman who he would only have to leave behind. Even though he was pretty sure the chase would be great.

He shook that last thought from his head and finished his walk. From the sound of drifting Christmas music and the glow of more twinkle lights than any town should ever own, he was nearly at the Dream Harbor Fifty-Third Annual Christmas Tree Lighting and December Holidays Extravaganza. Or at least that was the name written across the banner hanging over Main Street. According to his sister, this was Dream Harbor's biggest event of the year and that was saying a lot because from what he'd heard, this town loved an event.

He couldn't help the little kick of excitement in his chest. Even at twenty-seven, Bennett loved Christmas. How could you not love it? The cozy lights, the near constant intake of cookies, the secret thrill of finding the perfect gift. And this year, he was back on the East Coast, and it was actually cold. He loved it. His Christmas wish, if he was being honest and wasn't a grown man, was for a snowy Christmas. There was just something magical about snow on Christmas.

His mouth hitched up just thinking about what Kira would have to say about that.

'There you are!' His sister's voice rang out over the music and the general hum of the crowd. Jeanie had one of the first booths on the square. The little wood huts were lined up in a row, strings of white lights running from roof to roof.

'Hey! How's it going so far?' he asked as he joined Jeanie in the Pumpkin Spice booth. There was already a line and Jeanie's cheeks were pink as she handed free cups of cocoa to customer after customer.

'It's crazy! Do you see this crowd?'

He did. This end of Main Street had been closed off to traffic and was filled with people milling around, stopping at the booths along the way. It was already getting dark, even though it was only late afternoon, but the glow of the lights made everything cheerful and warm.

'Do you want some help?' he asked, even as he bumped into Logan who was filling cups. There wasn't exactly a lot of space inside the booth.

'No, no. We're good. My baristas, Joe and Crystal, are coming to relieve us in about an hour. We'll track you down then. They light the tree at six.' Jeanie smiled at him. 'Go enjoy the festival. Maybe buy your favorite sister a gift. I really liked the scarves at Bernadette's handicrafts a few booths down. If you need a starting place.'

Bennett laughed. 'Okay, noted. See you later.'

Logan nodded his goodbye in the middle of explaining to someone for the twelfth time since Bennett had been there that cocoa was free, all other drinks were three dollars, even though that same message was clearly written on the sign out front.

'It's right there, clear as day,' Logan pointed down at the sign and the older woman at the window slapped a hand to her forehead.

'Oh, would you look at that! If it was a snake it would have bitten me!'

Logan grumbled under his breath and Bennett stifled his laugh.

'Good luck!' he called as he ducked out of the booth and back into the chilled air.

He didn't really have a plan of where to go first, so he decided to just let the crowd pull him along. Besides Jeanie's booth, he spotted Annie's bakery, at least five crafters selling handmade scarves, a soap maker, a candle maker, and an artist painting miniatures of the festival. And that was just what he could see in his first scan.

But it was the delicious smells wafting by that made up his mind on where to go next. Just past a crafter selling personalized ornaments and Christmas stockings was a booth with a giant waffle sign posted out front. The air around it smelled like waffle cones and caramel and the line in front was longer than any others. That was enough to convince Bennett that this was the place to be.

He got in line behind a figure in a familiar olive-green parka as he debated if buying personalized stockings for the dogs would be cute or one step too far, even for him.

Kira turned around, her face peeking out from her fur-lined hood. She narrowed her eyes when she saw him, and he couldn't help but smile at her reaction. It made her scowl deepen.

'Of course, you're here,' she said. He knew she was trying to sound like she was annoyed to see him, but he would swear he heard something else, too. Something that said she was glad to not be alone in the crowd anymore, like maybe she was relieved to have someone to talk to.

'I think everyone in a fifty-mile radius is here.'

'Well, I don't need any rescuing at the moment so you can go on your merry way.'

Bennett raised an eyebrow as she tried to dismiss him.

'How cocky of you to assume that I'm here to see you,' he said.

Kira scoffed. 'You've shown up at my house multiple times now. It's not cocky, it's just pattern recognition.'

He laughed and took secret pleasure in the fact that Kira bit down on her bottom lip to suppress her smile.

'Actually,' he said, peering over her shoulder. 'I'm a big fan of'—he read the sign above the booth but there was no way that word was a real word—'of these … waffles?'

'Stroopwafels.'

'What?'

Kira rolled her eyes. 'Stroopwafels. That's what they're called.'

Bennett grinned. 'I'm impressed.'

'You're impressed that I can read the sign? Or that I know that they're thin waffles with caramel sandwiched between them and that they originate in the Netherlands?'

All of it. He was impressed with all of it. With her.

'Impressed that you can say that word with a straight face.'

She did smile then, brief and bright, and Bennett immediately wanted more. But before he could figure out how to make her do it again, he was jostled by the crowd and knocked into her instead.

'Oof.' She let out a small puff of air against his neck as his body collided with hers.

'Sorry.' He grabbed her arms to keep them both upright and the action pulled her even closer to him. His face was practically in her hood with her now, her hair a soft, silky brush against his cheek, her breath warm against his throat.

She was tall, and even when he was standing straight he was only a few inches taller, but now when he pulled back, still a little stooped over, still holding her arms, they were eye to eye. Hers were somewhere between green and brown, like they couldn't quite decide which way to go, with dark lashes. They were wide at the moment, for once not narrowed in annoyance at him.

She was warm and soft in his arms and there it was again, that urge to pull her closer. She smelled like pine and fresh air and that indescribable something that was purely

Kira. Another small breath left her and if he wasn't sure she hated him, he would have called it a sigh. Almost as if she liked being held by him, as if she wanted to stay right here in his arms as much as he wanted to keep her there.

His gaze flicked down to her lips, so close to his in their current stance, so pink and plump, so biteable. Her eyes were dark when he looked up, dark and filled with something he hadn't dared to think about until now. Was it possible that Kira could want him, too?

As if in answer to his unspoken question, Kira cleared her throat and the world around them slid back into place. The crowd, the festival, the weird waffles, the fact that Kira wasn't his to kiss or bite or hold onto like he still was.

He dropped her arms. 'Sorry about that.'

Kira nodded, her gaze still on him, a slight flush to her cheeks that hadn't been there before.

'Right. Well, you're entitled to get waffles, too, if you want them, I guess.' She turned on her heel to face the front of the line and Bennett immediately missed her face. He spent the rest of their time in line wondering how he could go about convincing Kira to spend more time with him.

And if that time led to her lips on his, then that would just be his little Christmas gift to himself.

Bennett smelled like peppermint candy. Kira knew that now that he had nearly knocked her on her ass but instead pulled her close and subjected her to the sturdy heat of his body. And now, as she waited for her Stroopwafel, it was all she could think about. It didn't help that he was still behind her, his body only a few inches from hers, and for a crazy moment she could picture leaning against him as they waited. He would wrap his arms around her and she would rest her head back on his shoulder and it would be like a scene out of one of those romantic Christmas movies she loved to mock with her sister every year.

But, no.

No, no, no.

She was not going to think about Bennett's warm body or her traitorous sister or sappy Christmas nonsense. She was going to get her caramel-y waffle, wait for the mayor to light the damn tree, make her official grand opening announcement, and then she was going to go home.

Back to her dark, cold house.

Alone.

Kira swallowed the lump growing in her throat. It was nearly her turn.

She didn't need Bennett or Chloe or her parents' money or … or … anyone, really. She just needed customers.

'Hello, Merry Christmas!' A tiny white-haired woman who could have won any Mrs. Claus lookalike contest greeted her from the booth window. 'How many?'

'Two, please,' she said without thinking. Two Stroopwafels. Two of everything. She'd always ordered two of everything when she was out with her sister. When had she ever gone out for food by herself? Never. Did people do that?

Well, she couldn't take it back now. The woman had already turned to the young man working with her and he was already pouring batter into what must be an ancient Stroopwafel iron. It was too late. The waffles were in motion and despite her current reputation in this town, she didn't want to insult Mrs. Claus. She was just going to have to eat two of these things. What she hadn't realized until the woman handed her the order, was that each order came with three Stroopwafels wrapped in white bakery paper. So now she was on the hook to eat six and even though they were more like cookies than waffles, she didn't know if she could manage it.

'Here.' She spun to face Bennett, handing him both bundles. 'Hold these.' She pulled out her wallet and paid, bidding Mrs. Claus a Merry Christmas as she pulled Bennett away from the booth by his sleeve.

He was looking at her with an amused smile by the time they found a place to get out of the crowd, tucked behind the food huts. The music was drowned out back here by the sound of multiple generators powering the electricity for the festival, the smell of all the food blending together into a general sweetness that filled the air.

'You could have just asked me to eat with you,' he said. 'I would have said yes.'

Kira frowned. 'That's not what happened.'

'Oh? And what happened, then?'

'I ... well ... I didn't realize that two would actually mean six and then I had too many so ... there you go ... I didn't want them to go to waste.'

Bennett was smiling as he bit into his first waffle.

'I'll just … go now.'

He put a hand on her arm. 'Stay.' He pointed above her head. 'We have a prime spot under a heater,' he added.

Kira huffed. 'Well, I'm not going to say no to a heater.'

Bennett grinned and she bit down on her waffle to avoid doing the same. They were crunchy and chewy at the same time and filled with sticky caramel that oozed out the sides. They were delicious. She might have been able to eat six after all, but she couldn't help feeling relieved that she had someone to stand next to while the crowd meandered by.

It was nice, that was all. It was nice to have someone to eat with after so many nights eating alone as she scrolled through her phone and thought about how she was failing at everything.

'How is the heat at your house, by the way. Any better?'

'It is, actually. The radiators definitely get hotter than they did before. And I got the chimney inspected, so I can have a fire in the fireplace now.'

'Oh, that's good.' The relief on Bennett's face would have been funny if it wasn't so damn sweet. What was she doing talking to such a sweet guy? Had Chloe's departure really screwed her up that badly?

'Yeah, too bad I don't actually know how to start a fire,' she said with a laugh, only meaning to make fun of her ineptitude, but she should have known how it would land with Mr. Fix-It.

He shifted on his feet, took two more bites of waffle, pretended to watch the crowd, did apparently everything in his power not to offer to help her, and it lasted all of about two minutes.

'I could show you how to do it. I mean, maybe. When I come to pick out my tree.'

He looked so earnest, so damn eager. It was too much. Kira didn't do earnest guys. When it came to men Kira required two qualifications: temporary and unacceptable to her mother. Men without steady jobs, men with face tattoos, men who considered themselves 'professional protesters' and smelled like patchouli. One time, she'd brought home a guy who parked his motorcycle on the front lawn and then helped free her mother's prize-winning cockatoos. The birds were probably terrible for the local ecosystem, but it had been the principle of the thing at the time. Her mother had freaked out and her date was on his way to New Mexico for a PETA conference by morning. A win-win in Kira's book.

She preferred the thrill of not knowing if the guy would still be in the country the next morning to the consistency of a guy that texted back. Where was the fun in that? And she was sure Bennett was the type who would text back, like immediately.

But maybe she hadn't needed sweet before. She hadn't needed earnest and consistent because she'd already had all those things in her sister. And now she didn't have Chloe anymore. Her sister had a new soulmate, and a Danish one, at that. Maybe with Chloe gone, Kira needed a different type of man in her life.

Shit.

How annoying.

'Yeah, maybe,' she said, and there it was again, the heat she'd seen in his gaze when they'd bumped into each other in the waffle line. Her gaze snagged on his lips, tipped into that perfect smile. What would it be like to kiss those lips? To lean into this moment and kiss this man and know he would call her back afterwards? And that she might actually want him to?

She swallowed hard, heat creeping across her face. Okay, she'd clearly been alone for too long. When she lifted her eyes to his, he was still looking at her like he had plenty of ideas on how to keep her warm. And they had nothing to do with her fireplace.

Oh, damn.

They were closer to each other than they had been a moment ago, like the force of his handsomeness was pulling her toward him. He reached out and Kira froze as his thumb grazed the corner of her mouth. She felt that brush of his fingertip across her entire body.

'You had a little something there.' He pulled his hand away and Kira wanted to cry at its absence.

'Thanks.' She flicked her tongue out to lick the rest of the caramel-y crumbs from her mouth. Bennett's dark gaze tracked the movement.

Heat flared in Kira's belly.

What the hell was going on here? Was she getting herself worked up over the wholesome guy determined to tidy up her life?

No way.

She took a step back, letting the cold air rush in between them, giving her space to breathe. Bennett's brow hitched up slightly, but he kept his distance.

She avoided his gaze, letting hers rove over the festival instead, willing her body to calm the hell down. She looked over the craft booths, over the strolling families, the excited kids in winter hats and mittens, the bell-ringing Santa. She had to hand it to the Dream Harborians… Harborians? Whoever they were, they sure knew how to throw a festival.

And then she saw it. The perfect thing to distract her from her confusing feelings for this man.

'Reindeer!'

'Reindeer?' Bennett's gaze followed hers to the fenced in enclosure in the middle of the town green.

'Reindeer,' Kira echoed, already moving toward the sweet, furry babies with Bennett trailing behind her. 'Look at them! Where do you think they came from?'

'The North Pole?'

Kira shot him a disbelieving look, but she couldn't keep her grumpy act up when she was in the presence of such adorable animals. She tugged off her mitten, and dutifully ignoring the sign that warned the reindeer might nibble her fingers, she stuck her hand between the wood slates and rubbed the soft snout of one reindeer and then the other.

'So fuzzy,' she whispered.

The reindeer stared at her with big black eyes. The other wandered over to where some squealing children were holding out a carrot, the jingle bells on its harness tinkling as it walked away.

'I want one,' she declared.

'Maybe finish getting the farm set up before you add animals.'

Kira huffed. 'Maybe worry about your own animals and I'll worry about mine.'

'Fair enough.' Bennett took off his own glove and joined her in petting her new furry friend. She kept her hand safely on the other side of the animal's big head. She didn't need their fingers to touch, not when she could still feel the imprint of Bennett's thumb on her lips.

'You want to come home with me, right?' she crooned to the deer. He nudged her hand with his furry head. 'I think you do, you big handsome guy. I'd take good care of you.'

Bennett cleared his throat.

'Yes?' she said, glancing up at him.

'You're making a big mistake here,' he told her.

'Oh, really? And what is it I'm doing wrong now?' This guy. How dare he butt in again? If she wanted reindeer for her Christmas-tree farm, then she was damn well going to get them. As soon as she figured out how.

'You're not nearly as scary as you pretend to be,' he said, his voice dangerously close to her ear.

Kira's eyes fluttered closed for a brief second, but she forced them back open. No. No Christmas magic for her. 'Trust me, I am.'

'I don't think so.' Bennett's warm breath coasted along her cheek. She should have kept her damn hood up. 'And you messed up.'

'I messed up?'

'Yep, every time you talk to an animal, you give yourself away. You show how sweet you actually are.'

Sweet?! No sir, that would not do.

Kira gave the reindeer one more scratch between the ears and straightened to her full height, forcing Bennett to take a step back.

'I have never been described as sweet in my entire life.'

Bennett shrugged. 'Well, you are.'

'No, Chloe is the sweet one. And the sensible one.' The favorite one. She swallowed that last bit.

'I've never met Chloe, but I have three dogs and at least one reindeer that would agree that you are a very sweet person.'

Kira scowled. He only thought that because he didn't know her sister. Her whole life, Kira knew Chloe was her better half. The one who kept her grounded. The one who'd kept her from getting arrested on more than one occasion, with her sweet smile and her southern belle charm. And until very recently, Chloe was the one who kept her from making questionable financial decisions.

'Well, I have an entire town here that would disagree.'

'I don't think so. I think they just want to get to know you, that's all.'

'I didn't come here to make friends.'

'What did you come here for, then?'

'I already told you.'

'Oh, right. Something about pickles … and pouting about your sister's Danish husband.'

'I am not pouting.' At some point Kira's hands had

ended up on her hips. 'I am recreating myself. I am starting a self-sustaining, ecologically friendly homestead. And I am … I am… Okay, maybe I'm pouting a little bit.'

Bennett let out a surprised laugh and she dropped her defensive stance. It was exhausting staying mad at this guy, and maybe she had no reason to. Maybe she should stop lashing out at the one person in town she hadn't managed to scare away.

'It's just… I mean, did she have to move so far away?'

'You miss her a lot?'

'So much.' Oh, no, her voice cracked with emotion. This was why she had to stay mean. There was no in-between for her right now. She could either be angry or sad, and angry seemed like the safer bet. She hastily wiped her eyes with the back of her hand. 'It's ridiculous, really. I'm a grown woman. I should be able to live without my sister, but … I just never had to before.' She sniffled pitifully and she hated herself for it.

'Maybe you should pet the reindeer some more.' Bennett's voice was gentle and teasing. 'It seemed to make you feel better before.'

Kira sighed. He wasn't wrong.

She reached back into the enclosure and stroked the reindeer's soft head. It really did help. Could anyone feel sad when they were petting an animal? She didn't see how they possibly could. It was like the reindeer was sending all its calm energy to her through her fingertips.

'Better?'

She glanced up to where Bennett was leaning against the

wood post of the enclosure. 'Oh, are you still here?' she snapped at him, but he just flashed that perfect smile. It was like he understood that she had to stay mean or she'd crumble completely and, like, maybe he didn't mind.

'So, when are you making your big announcement?' he asked.

'After the mayor lights up the tree.' She sighed. 'I tried to get *him* to just make the announcement for me, but he insisted it would be more effective if I did it.'

'Are you ready for the influx of customers you're going to get after tonight?'

Her stomach flipped at the thought. Customers. Money. Heat. Things she desperately needed. But she was nervous. This was her big moment. The first time she wasn't living off her parents' money, or working for her father's company in that bullshit marketing job he'd made up for her so she could learn some 'responsibility'. Her mother had been banking on her marrying one of their rich friend's sons but that hadn't exactly panned out either.

And now here she was, reliant on this quirky town to want plenty of Christmas trees.

'I'm ready,' she said with more confidence than she felt. 'I hired a few college guys to help load the trees onto people's cars and a groundskeeper to trim the trees.' And that was all she could afford at the moment. If the customers didn't start rolling in, she wouldn't even be able to pay the few employees she had.

'Still looking for a Santa, though.' She let her gaze trail

up and down Bennett's body and couldn't help but laugh at his surprised expression.

'I don't think I'd make a very good Santa.'

'Oh, suddenly you're not so eager to help?'

He chuckled. 'Even I have my limits.'

'That's too bad. I think you'd look cute in red,' she said, as she trailed away from the reindeer, making space for a crowd of kids speculating about the whereabouts of a certain red-nosed reindeer.

She left Bennett sputtering for a response.

Chapter Seven

Cute in red, huh?

No. Absolutely not. He would not let Kira convince him to don a Santa suit. A man had to have his limits. Right?

He tried to follow Kira, but she slipped easily away through the throngs of revelers. Everyone was starting to gather around the big evergreen in the center of the town square, so attempting to go against the flow of the crowd was impossible.

'Ben!'

He turned from his search for Kira and spotted his sister working her way toward him. For a split second, he thought about ignoring her, but that wasn't really in the spirit of the evening.

'Hey, how did it go?' he asked, as Jeanie and Logan caught up to him. Annie was with them, too, her giant fluffy earmuffs and hideous Christmas sweater making her stand out in the crowd.

'It went great. A lot of sales even with giving the cocoa away for free.'

'I told you that was a good idea,' Annie said, nudging her friend. 'Lure them in with free stuff and then start charging.'

Jeanie smiled. 'You were right. You're a very savvy businesswoman.'

'I know. So,' Annie turned to him, eyes lit up mischievously, 'did you find anything interesting up at the tree farm yet?'

'Oh, yeah, several dead bodies, the place is littered with them. I guess I just forgot to mention it.'

Annie laughed. 'I like him.'

'Yeah, he's a riot,' Jeanie said dryly.

'I haven't found anything except an old house and a woman trying to run the place by herself.' He decided not to tell Jeanie and her friends about the list he'd found behind the radiator. If there really was something valuable buried at the farm, that was for Kira to find, not this nosy town.

'Oh, no, Ben.' Jeanie shook her head like she was horribly disappointed in him and he knew he didn't want to hear whatever it was she had to say next.

'What?'

'Not again.'

'Ooh…' Annie chimed in. 'What?'

'Ben has a habit of wanting to fix things for people,

specifically people he's dating,' Jeanie explained. 'And then they just end up taking advantage of him and ditching him.'

Annie winced.

'It's not like that,' Bennett protested. Was this the thanks he got for sharing more of his life with his sister? She just aired out his dating issues on the town square? He never should have told her about those last few dates, and about the favors he'd given out, like he was freaking Santa. Thankfully, he'd kept his sharing to the last few months and hadn't delved back further into this particular dating issue. If Jeanie only knew how screwed up his dating life was, he'd never live it down.

'It's definitely like that,' Jeanie said. 'How many of your last dates involved rides to the airport?'

'Not that many…'

'Oh, Bennett.' Annie shook her head. Even Logan grimaced.

'Why is it so bad to want to be helpful? Isn't that a good thing?'

He blamed Mrs. Brendan, his first-grade teacher. She really got him hooked on those gold stars. And maybe over the years he'd liked the way people appreciated him when he did them a favor, he liked the feeling of being needed, of being useful.

'Not if you let yourself be a doormat for these women. You're too nice, Ben.'

'That's not what's happening here.'

Jeanie raised an eyebrow. 'Then what's happening?'

'Mainly, this insane town forced me to go up there and

then I offered to check the heating in that old house. That's it.' He decided not to mention the computer help, cabin inspection, and potential Santa audition he might have also signed on for. Jeanie and her friends were already looking at him like he was a wounded animal that needed to be put down.

'It's not what you think,' he insisted. 'She doesn't even like me.' Even as he said it, he was remembering the look on Kira's face when they'd collided, the surprise and then the warmth in her eyes.

'Everyone likes you, Ben.'

'Not her. She finds my helpful nature to be very annoying. But I couldn't leave her up there all alone and cold…'

Annie gasped like she had solved some great mystery. 'You *like* her!' she squealed. 'You like the grumpy tree farm lady!'

Bennett cleared his throat. 'What is this, middle school?'

Logan rolled his eyes. 'You get used to it after a while.'

'I don't *like* her.' That definitely wasn't true, but he wasn't about to admit that he did like Kira even though she had tried to give him every reason not to, or that he really wanted to spend more time with her even though that was foolish considering he was leaving after Christmas. Or that he was an idiot for even thinking about any of this, since he'd supposedly sworn off women but had done nothing but think about her since he met her. 'I'm doing what you all asked me to do!' he said instead, putting the blame right back where it should be. On his sister and her crazy friends.

'Oh, right. Back to that,' Jeanie mercifully allowed the topic to change. 'So, nothing weird up there?'

'No. Just trees and an old house. That's it.' Not that he'd been particularly thorough about his search. Unless the old man buried his wife under the boiler, Ben probably wouldn't have noticed, but that was just one more thing he planned to keep his mouth shut about.

The women frowned.

'What? Disappointed I didn't find a dead body?'

'I mean, a little bit,' Jeanie said, at the same time as Annie said, 'Definitely.'

Logan just shook his head.

'Are you going back?' Jeanie asked and Bennett couldn't help but scan the crowd for that familiar coat.

The answer should be a resounding no. How would he ever recover from his 'too niceness' if he spent all his time up at that farm fixing radiators and searching for dead bodies that didn't exist? He should start being more selfish right now. He should tell his sister and this whole town he was done playing detective. But what if being selfish meant he wanted more time at the farm? What if doing what *he* wanted to do meant spending more time with Kira?

'Well, I do still need a tree.'

He ignored his sister's smile and Annie's squeal of delight and stalked off toward the tree-lighting stage to catch a glimpse of the one thing he really wanted for Christmas.

'Ten, nine, eight...'

Kira stood awkwardly on the stage next to the mayor as the crowd counted down to the big moment. She hated being on stage. In fact, she was actively trying to suppress the memories of her disastrous early pageant days, from before her mother quit and told her she never had to do one again. Apparently, peeing your leotard during the talent portion was not exactly Little Georgia Peach behavior. If she was remembering correctly, Chloe won Miss Congeniality that year. Because of course she did.

'Seven, six, five...'

She scanned the faces in the crowd and tried to conjure up some holiday excitement, but it wasn't working. All she saw were strung-out kids, hopped up on candy canes and days of counting down for Santa, and the exhausted parents trying in vain to rein them in. Frankly, it looked like a nightmare. No wonder her parents subcontracted all the holiday nonsense to professional decorators, party planners and various nannies throughout the years. Although, she and Chloe had always managed to make their own fun, sneaking cookies, and in later years booze, to their room to eat under their covers, hiding from their parents' odious friends during the slew of holiday parties leading up to the big day.

How could Kira possibly have a good Christmas without her sister?

'Four, three, two, one! Merry Christmas!' The mayor shouted as he hit the switch and the tree behind her lit up with thousands of colorful lights. The crowd cheered and the high-school band charged right into an enthusiastic, if not technically adept, rendition of 'It's Beginning to Look a Lot Like Christmas'.

Kira attempted to turn her wince into a smile, but probably just looked like she was in pain. Which of course she was. Christmas carols were bad enough but played by a bunch of out-of-tune teenagers, they were a whole other level of terrible.

Her gaze snagged on a familiar, too-perfect face in the audience. Bennett smiled at her, and she really wished she still didn't like him. If only her first impression of him as an arrogant asshole had been correct. Things would be so much simpler. But instead, she found that his smile made her feel better. Just like that. She felt less lonely, less sad.

And if she didn't know he would also leave her in a month, she might have explored that feeling further. But he *was* leaving and Kira couldn't deal with another departure right now. Not when the last one had wrecked her so completely.

She turned away and found the mayor handing her the microphone.

'Um, hi.' The mic squealed and she hastily moved it further from her face. 'Sorry.' She cleared her throat. Oh, good, she hadn't gotten any better at this in the past twenty years. Her mother would be so proud.

'Uh … hi. I'm Kira.'

'Hi Kira!' Someone yelled from the audience, followed by more shouts of 'hello!' and 'hi!' and 'welcome!'

At least the town was still excessively welcoming, even

after she'd acted like a bitchy recluse for the past three months. Maybe things were still salvageable. She took a deep breath. 'Hi. Um … I just wanted to come here and announce the official reopening of the Christmas Tree Farm. This Sunday at ten a.m.'

Cheers rang out around her and Kira couldn't help her smile and the relief that flooded through her. This was going to work. She might not have to sell her organs, after all.

'Right,' she went on, after the noise died down. 'And if you can't make it to opening day, we'll be open every day after that through Christmas Eve from ten to six. The trees are looking beautiful this year so I hope you will come and pick out the perfect one for you and your family.' Her gaze had accidentally found Bennett again and his smile had grown at her mention of the perfect tree. This guy. Ugh, how had he wormed his way into her good graces just by being so damn nice! It was sneaky, is what it was. He was like a sneaky, wholesome ninja who had tricked her into actually liking him.

And now she was smiling like an idiot right back at him.

'Oh, and follow the farm—@mychristmastreedreams—on all your socials!' She quickly handed the microphone back to the mayor before she could do something crazy like burst into a round of 'Jingle Bells', or something equally horrific.

'Thank you, Kira,' Mayor Kelly said, beaming at her like she'd just fixed world hunger. 'I'm sure the whole town will be out in the next few weeks to get their trees. I hope you're ready for us!'

Me, too.

Kira forced her smile to stay put even as her insides clenched in panic.

'Now,' Mayor Kelly clapped his hands. 'Chanukah is still a few days away but we have our menorah ready to go, so look for those lights to go on soon and don't forget to come out for our winter concert on the solstice!'

If the concert was being performed by the school band, Kira wouldn't be going anywhere near that, but she just kept on smiling until finally the local choir from some church or another took over the stage to lead the singalong. At which point Kira hightailed it out of there like her faux fur was on fire.

She may have warmed up to the local nice guy, but there was no way in hell she was participating in a singalong.

She raced down the stairs on the side of the stage and ran headfirst into something solid and warm. Something that said 'Oof!' when she hit it. Something that smelled like peppermint and Stroopwafels.

Kira's body was flush with Bennett's and for a split second she didn't want to pull away. She wanted to burrow further into his warmth. She wanted him to wrap his arms around her and keep her there.

She jerked back and out of his grip. 'Sorry.'

'Hey, where are you running off to?' Bennett asked.

'Uh … I have to get home.'

Bennett's face fell. 'Oh, already?'

This Christmas music had obviously broken her brain because she wanted to stay. All of a sudden, she *wanted* to stay at this absurd display of Christmas cheer. With *Bennett*. That was when Kira realized that this nice guy, this Mr. Fix-It, Clark Kent, was far more dangerous than any of her fresh-out-of-prison boyfriends.

'Yep, I made my announcement, so that's it. No reason to stay.'

'That's too bad. I thought we could go see Santa.'

'Santa?' He couldn't be serious.

'Yeah,' he said with a laugh. 'He's set up over there. I thought you could talk to him about spending some time at the farm.'

'You're just trying to get out of doing the job.' Damn it, she was smiling again. And this was actually another good idea.

Bennett stepped closer, a little smirk on his face. 'Hey, if you have a Santa kink, I'd be happy to…'

'A Santa kink!' She put her hand on his chest to push him away, but her hand forgot to push and instead just stayed there, flat against him, soaking in his heat. 'Is that even a thing?'

He chuckled and it rumbled through her fingertips. 'You'd be surprised. I've been doing some interesting reading lately.'

'I don't even want to know what that means.'

'There's this local book club…'

'Nope, no need to explain your strange habits and sexual perversions.' She grinned and that damn hand was still there, pressed into him and he was so solid and warm in his cream-colored sweater. And now she'd said, 'sexual perversions' out loud and her mind was happily galloping down all sorts of perverse paths. She definitely didn't have a Santa kink but she wouldn't mind if Bennett put her over his knee and…

'So … do you want to go talk to him?'

Kira's face flushed hot. Right. Santa. Regular, not kinky, Santa.

She pulled her hand off the nice man's chest.

'Yeah, uh … yes. That's a good idea, actually.' She started to stride away toward the little gingerbread house on the other side of the square and Bennett fell into step beside her. 'You don't have to come with me.'

'Oh, I have a few things to ask for anyway,' he said, flashing her that smile. Despite her best efforts, she was starting to hate it less.

'And what are you asking for?'

Bennett glanced toward the sky as they walked. 'Snow.'

'Snow?! More cold! Veto.'

He huffed. 'It's Christmas! Don't you want a white Christmas?'

She shrugged. 'I've never had one before. I don't know why I would start now.' Her family was never the sort to head to Aspen for Christmas. Her mother hated the cold as much as she did.

'Well, I've missed snow out on the West Coast. It just doesn't feel like Christmas without it.'

'Australians have Christmas without snow every year.'

'Okay, fine, but it doesn't feel like Christmas for me. I'm not Australian, you might have noticed.'

'So you're asking Santa for snow?'

'Among other things.'

She glanced at him from the corner of her eye. 'Like?'

'Can't tell you or it won't come true.'

'I don't think that's how that works. That's only for birthday wishes.'

'Really? I don't know. Might be different down South.'

She laughed. 'You just don't want to tell me.' They'd reached Santa's house and the line was long and filled with crying children. Two elves were handing out candy canes and trying in vain to keep the line somewhat orderly. The little girl in front of them had laid down in the cold dirt wearing her full Christmas outfit, frilly skirt and all, in some sort of peaceful protest. Her mother just gave them an exhausted smile when they got in line.

'Correct, I don't want to tell you,' Bennett said, picking up their conversation.

'Is it more weird books?'

He shook his head, his smile growing.

'Some kind of Boy Scout badge?'

'Okay, first of all, I told you I was never a Boy Scout. And secondly, you have to earn those. You can't just ask for them.'

'For someone who was never a Boy Scout, you sure know a lot about them,' she muttered and Bennett chuckled. 'Hmm … new tools?'

'I have plenty of tools and why wouldn't I want to tell you that?'

'Because then I would live in fear that you would come back and try to fix more things.'

'I forgot how traumatic that was for you.'

'Truly.' She pushed away the memory of Bennett crouched next to her radiator, sleeves rolled up, forearms flexing. She would not find this man attractive. She *could* not. 'A new puppy?'

'As much as I would love one, I think I'm at my max with three.'

Kira huffed. 'I give up.'

He held her gaze for a second too long and heat rushed to Kira's face. 'I guess you'll have to wait and see if I get it.'

'I guess so.' Why was her voice so breathy? Why was he looking at her like *she* was what he wanted?

The mother in front of them lifted her still prone daughter and moved her a few feet forward and then placed her back in the dirt. The little girl smiled up at her with the face of an angel. Kids were terrifying.

'So what are *you* asking Santa for?' Bennett asked as they shuffled forward, the moment broken.

'Weekend afternoons at the farm from now until Christmas. Hopefully he doesn't have other gigs that pay better. I can't offer him much.' An elf walked past and handed them each a candy cane. 'Thanks,' Kira said, quickly unwrapping hers and sucking it into her mouth. Sweet and sticky. She sighed a little. Maybe Christmas wasn't all bad.

When she glanced back at Bennett, his gaze was fixed on her mouth and the candy cane she was sliding in and out between her lips. Whoops. She slid it out with a distinct pop and Bennett blinked like he was emerging from a trance.

He cleared his throat. 'Uh… What are you asking for yourself?'

'For myself?' Kira's laugh came out harsher than she meant it to. 'I've had plenty my whole life. Too much, really. So I'll just settle for the essentials this year. Heat. Some new windows would be nice. Maybe fix that leaky…' She trailed off, realizing she was just listing all the shit that was wrong with her house. She was probably triggering all the fix-it impulses in Bennett's brain.

But to his credit and Kira's surprise, he just nodded.

'And… I wouldn't be mad if he threw in some cozy socks. Can never have too many of those,' she added, and Bennett smiled.

They were nearly at Santa's candy-covered house now and the little girl ahead of them was standing in front of him listing all her wishes out on her fingers, one by one. The back of her dress was streaked with dirt, but even Kira had to admit that she still looked cute as she stood beside Santa for her picture.

And then it was their turn.

An elf ushered them into the small house and over to Santa's giant chair. He was a pretty convincing Santa. Round belly, rosy cheeks, even his white beard was real. He would do.

'Hello, uh … Santa.'

'Ho, ho, ho! And what would you like for Christmas, young lady?'

Okay, apparently we're staying in character.

'Um, right. Well, I own the Christmas-tree farm and we've just reopened, and I was hoping to hire you, actually.'

The old man chuckled, holding his belly and Kira couldn't really remember how she'd gone from her life of parties and blowing her parents' money to negotiating with a man who thought he was Santa in a house decorated with fake candy. Oh, wait, reckless decisions about real estate.

'Here's my card,' Santa said, pulling a business card with holly around the edges from his pocket. 'Give the office a call and I'm sure we can work something out.'

He smiled. 'Now, what do you two want for Christmas?' he asked, raising his big bushy brows at her and Bennett. 'Perhaps some jewelry?'

Kira just rolled her eyes and pointed to Bennett. 'I'll take a pair of socks, but this guy wants snow.'

'Ho, ho, ho, that's a tall order but I'll do my best.'

'Thanks, Santa,' Bennett said as they left the gingerbread cottage. As much as Kira hated being cold, it was nice to be out of the stuffy house. It smelled like wet wool and children in there.

'Oh, you didn't get to ask Santa for your other gift,' she teased as they walked away.

'That's okay. I decided I don't really need Santa's help with it.'

'Really?'

His arm brushed against hers as they walked. 'Yeah, I should probably do it on my own.'

She glanced at him from the corner of her eye and a secret smile played around his lips. They paused when they got to the edge of the square, back to the craft booths.

'Too kinky, huh?'

He laughed. 'Yeah, that's it. Too kinky for Santa.' He stepped closer. His warm body obviously exerted too much gravitational pull on her because she stepped closer, too.

'Well, I hope you get what you want,' she whispered.

The corner of Bennett's lips tipped up in a smile. 'Me, too,' he said.

Chapter Eight

A distant buzzing pulled Kira from her nest of blankets. It was dark and freezing in the room she was currently using as a bedroom. She'd tried all three at this point and this one won out as just slightly warmer than the others.

The buzzing persisted.

What the hell time was it?

She stuck her hand out into the icy room and patted around on her bedside table until she felt her phone. She grabbed it and pulled it under the blankets.

Six a.m. and Chloe was calling.

'Six hours ahead, Chlo,' she groaned into the phone, not bothering with a greeting. 'How many times do I have to tell you? You are six hours ahead of me.'

Her twin winced, her pretty face filling the screen. 'Oops! Sorry, Kiki. I forgot!'

''S okay,' she said, rolling onto her back.

'Where are you? Some kind of tent?' Chloe wrinkled her nose, like their mother did, but on Chloe it came across as much less judgemental.

'I'm under my blankets.'

'I thought you got the heat fixed!'

'I did. Well, sort of fixed. It's just cold as hell here.'

'Here, too,' her sister said, reminding Kira of how far apart they were, a literal ocean away. 'I hate it, but Erik says I'll get used to it.'

'Right, and how is Erik?' she asked, swallowing every ounce of snarkiness she wanted to put into that question. Kira had met the man exactly once in person and it was at the wedding, but she knew everything she needed to know about him. He'd taken her sister away and so very rationally, she hated him.

'He's good. We looked at the cutest apartment the other day. You would have loved it. It gets beautiful light in the afternoon.'

'Sounds perfect. Send me pics.'

'I will.'

Kira waited for her sister to go on, but Chloe just studied her through the phone, which was unfair really. Of course she looked like a mess. She'd been asleep! Her hair was more nest than hair right now, her bangs sticking up at odd angles. She'd only gotten them in the first place to look different from Chloe. She was tired of people's disappointment when she'd reveal which twin she really was. Like she'd tricked them into thinking she was the better one.

'You're staring at me, Chlo.'

'I just miss you.'

Kira swallowed the hot lump of emotion that insisted on forming in her throat whenever she talked to her sister. It wasn't the same, talking to her this way. It wasn't the same as sitting side by side on their couch, their legs tangled together as they ate ice cream and debriefed on their latest date or a horrible day at work or the last passive-aggressive comment their mother had made.

'I miss you, too. Of course I do, Chlo. But you have that dreamy new husband and that amazing European adventure you've always wanted. Don't waste it missing me.'

Her sister sniffed and wiped her eyes. As much as Kira privately ranted about how her sister had betrayed and abandoned her, she would never, ever, in a million years do anything to dim Chloe's happiness. At least, not anymore. She was determined not to interfere with Chloe's happiness ever again.

'But are you okay there?' Chloe asked, eyes still glossy with unshed tears. 'I'm worried about you.'

'I'm fine. I'm great, actually. The farm is open and I'm sure we'll be mobbed today after my announcement last night. Trust me, these people love Christmas.' She pushed the hair from her face and just kept on lying. 'I'm doing what I always wanted! I've got my own homestead here and this beautiful old house. Once I get everything set up, it's going to be gorgeous. And then you can come visit me.'

Had they been in the same room, had she not been in the

dark, Chloe would have called her on her bullshit. But apparently, the distance really messed with her sister's lie-detecting abilities.

'I just can't believe you spent all your money on it.'

'It's an investment, Chlo. Isn't that what you and Dad were always yammering on about?'

'I meant like a Roth IRA, not a farm.'

Kira shrugged like this run-down farm and the stock market were totally equivalent investments. 'It's what I wanted.' Or at least, what she thought she wanted when she was stress-scrolling through social media in the wee hours of the morning—and that was basically the same thing, right?

'This is a much bigger deal than that time you bought a racehorse,' Chloe went on.

'I rescued that horse, thank you very much.'

'Or the time you booked the country club for that animal-shelter fundraiser and then filled it with stray dogs.'

'How was I supposed to get them adopted if they weren't in attendance, Chlo? That just made sense.'

Her sister rolled her eyes, but a smile played on her lips. She might have always been the sensible one, but Kira knew deep down, Chloe loved her crazy ideas.

'What about the time you brought the guy with the neck tattoos to Mom's Christmas Eve party?'

'Okay, first of all, that was not a reckless plan. That was a very thought-out plan to ensure I would never have to attend the party again. And Jim was a perfect gentleman.'

'He got drunk and peed in one of Mom's houseplants.'

'He was a perfect gentleman until that moment.' She'd also found out the next morning that he was breaking the parameters of his parole by leaving town to attend the party, but her sister didn't need that little bit of added information right now.

Chloe frowned.

'Look, Chlo, this isn't about my questionable choices in men, or about getting under Mom's skin, and it's surprisingly not even about my quest to end horseracing forever. I just needed to get away, start over. That's all.'

'You could have stayed in Georgia. There are farms there, too, you know.'

Kira sighed. 'If I'd stayed in Georgia I would have been too tempted to crawl back home if things didn't work out.'

Chloe's frown deepened. To save her from wrinkles, and because Kira hated seeing her sister upset, she went on sugarcoating the truth. 'But it *is* going to work. It's working out great, actually.' She forced a smile.

'I could lend you some money…'

'No.'

'Kiki, just listen.'

'No. No way. You're not lending me anything. I am *fine*. It was my decision to use my half of the money on this. You save yours for all those little Danish babies you're going to have.'

Chloe's nose crinkled again, but Kira didn't miss the little spark that appeared in her twin's eyes at the mention of babies. God, her sister really was in deep.

'Okay, but you have to tell me if you need help. I cannot

have you so far away from me and know that you are struggling.'

'Ha!' Kira's fake laugh was slightly unhinged. 'Struggling? Chlo, I am thriving over here. I promise.'

Chloe looked skeptical but Kira just kept smiling until her sister moved on. 'Have you made any friends yet?' she asked.

Friends? Hmm. Did dogs and reindeer count?

'Oh, yeah. Plenty of friends.'

'Kiki…'

Shoot, maybe Chloe could still detect some lies.

'I haven't had time for friends yet. I just need to get through the holidays and then I'll have time to hang out with people.'

People, but not Bennett, because he'd be gone by then. And that absolutely should not bother her. It didn't bother her. At all. Why was that guy and his warm sweaters and sweet smile even popping into her head right now?

It probably had something to do with the very detailed dream she'd been having involving her, Bennett, Santa's sleigh, some very provocative candy canes, and a 'naughty and nice' list they seemed to be working their way through.

Dear God, what was wrong with her?

She shook her head. It was way too early in the morning for all this subterfuge. She needed at least another two hours of sleep, preferably dreamless, and a pot of coffee before she had to be greeting customers.

'I should really go. Big day today!' Kira's forced

cheerfulness had Chloe raising her eyebrows, but Kira didn't have the energy to do any more convincing.

'Okay. Love you, Kiki.'

'Love you, too, Chlo'

She hung up before she could get emotional. She had a Christmas-tree farm to open today, hopefully one with actual customers, and she didn't want puffy eyes for her big day.

'Opening day!' Iris chirped beside her, clapping her hands. 'This is exciting.' Her strawberry- blonde hair was done up in a braided wreath around her head today and she looked like she belonged in some sort of Nordic Christmas advertisement. It was the exact vibe Kira wanted, but vibes didn't matter if she didn't have customers.

'Very exciting. As long as people actually show up.'

'Of course they'll show up,' Iris said. 'I know you're new here, but trust me, Dream Harbor shows up for anything resembling a festival, grand opening, carnival, or fundraiser. You should see the turnout for town meetings.'

Kira huffed. 'I have. And it's weird.' She'd attended one back in the fall to convince the mayor and the residents that she had no intention of reopening. And one failing boiler later, here she was.

Iris laughed, leaning back in her rocking chair. They were sitting on the little porch in front of the customer-service cabin, waiting for their first customers to arrive. Or praying they would arrive, in Kira's case. She'd put all her eggs in this one very precarious basket, and she really needed it to work.

The panic of not having money was real, and she'd been so undeservedly lucky to never have felt it before.

'I found these,' Kira said, changing the subject to ease her anxiety about the day. She held out the two old letters and the list of possessions Bennett had found. 'What do you think they're all about?'

Iris took the papers and laid them on her lap. Kira had finally read the letters hoping they'd help make sense of the strange list of items. One had been a letter from what seemed a distant relative of his to Edwin, the last owner of the farm, requesting to come visit the farm so he could 'get the lay of the land'. And the other was a copy of Edwin's revised will from his lawyer.

'Looks like old Edwin was getting his estate in order before he died.' Iris shrugged.

'Don't you think the list of stuff is kind of odd?'

'*He* was kind of odd.'

'The house had a lot of old furniture in it when I moved in, but I certainly didn't find any Tiffany lamps. And what do you think happened to Ellie's baubles?'

'They were probably buried with her,' Iris mumbled.

'What?'

Iris smiled innocently. 'I imagine his wife was buried wearing her best jewelry, right? Or they gave them to a family member.'

'Hmm. Yeah, I guess. I haven't checked the attic yet, though. Too creepy.'

Iris laughed. 'I don't blame you. When we were cleaning out my great-aunt's attic we found an entire family of raccoons living in her luggage collection.' Iris shivered at the memory.

'Aww … cute.'

'Not cute. The little garbage monsters had made a huge mess.'

'Maybe you're right. I'll steer clear of the attic for now.'

They sat in companionable silence rocking in their chairs and sipping their tea while Kira thought about Edwin and his wife and what else he might have left behind in his old house.

'I've never worked on a farm,' Iris said, after a while. 'I like it.'

Kira knew this little fact about her employee, and she'd hired the woman anyway, based almost entirely on the positive energy Iris emanated. She figured it was as good a reason as any to hire someone.

'You've had a lot of jobs?' she asked now, needing a distraction from staring down the empty parking lot.

Iris nodded. 'Bank teller, library clerk, waitress, of course, who hasn't done that to make some extra cash?'

Kira decided not to say she'd never needed extra cash until this very moment.

'Crafts coordinator at the retirement home, dog walker, grocery-store cashier,' Iris went on, counting each job on her fingers. She was quickly running out. 'And now I teach yoga and aquatic aerobics to seniors.'

'Aquatic aerobics to seniors?'

'Yeah,' Iris beamed. 'It's very fun.'

Kira was having a hard time imagining that jumping around in a pool with old folks would be fun, but Iris seemed so enthusiastic about it, she just smiled.

'I'll do pretty much anything. Except kids. I don't do kids.'

'Why not?'

Iris stared at her like the answer was obvious. 'Kids are terrifying.'

'Right, of course.'

'Way too unpredictable.'

'Sure.' Kira bit down on a smile. She had a feeling Iris was pretty unpredictable, too, with her habit of job-hopping, but she didn't mention that, either. Instead she teased her favorite employee. 'There might be some kids here today, Iris. Try not to panic.'

Iris laughed, spraying lukewarm tea from her mouth. And Kira laughed, too.

'I'll try to stay calm,' Iris said, wiping the tea off her boots. 'So have you always wanted to own a Christmas-tree farm?'

'Uh … not really.' She still wasn't convinced she wanted to own one right now.

'Oh. Do you have family in Dream Harbor?'

'Nope.'

'Huh. So you just…' Iris's brow wrinkled in confusion like she couldn't quite figure out how Kira ended up here.

Well, join the club, Iris.

'I decided I couldn't be at home anymore without my twin sister, wasting my life away being simultaneously spoiled and stifled by my parents, so I scoured real-estate listings until I found this place, bought it without really knowing it was a Christmas-tree farm and then had to reopen it to make money to fix up the incredibly old house that came with the property? Yep. That's exactly what I did.'

Iris stared at her wide eyed and then a big grin broke out across her face. 'That's awesome.'

'It is?'

'Of course it is. You just went for it. I think that's fantastic.' Iris gazed at her with a dreamy expression as if leaving behind your whole life to buy a dilapidated farmhouse was the coolest thing ever. Maybe it sorta was.

Warmth spread through Kira's body. Somebody thought this was a fantastic idea. And it felt good. Really good.

Almost as good as looking up and seeing three cars pulling into the parking lot.

'Customers!' She leaped up from her chair and Iris did, too.

'Let's do this,' Iris said, giving Kira a quick salute before heading to her station in the cabin. They'd decided that Kira would make herself available to greet customers and direct them around the farm, and Iris would be in the cabin to take payments and hand out saws. Kira had hired several large college guys to help people heft trees onto their cars. The two men she'd hired for the morning shift were drinking coffee and waiting to be needed. The hot cocoa was made, the Christmas music was playing over the speakers, and the twinkle lights were twinkling; she was ready.

Iris was right. This *was* exciting!

'Hi, ladies, welcome!' She greeted the first group of older women as they approached all bundled up in scarves and hats.

'Hello, dear.' One of the women gave her a friendly smile but the other two were too busy looking around.

'Hi, Carol! Hi, Janet, Marissa!' Iris called from the window of the cabin.

'Oh, there she is! Hello, Iris!' The three women hustled up the steps to the cabin, bypassing Kira entirely. She had to laugh. Of course, Iris was an aerobics-instructor celebrity.

'We had to come see you at your new job.'

'Thanks, Janet. That's sweet of you. I hope you're all here for a tree, too.'

'Of course we are,' the shortest of the three said, with a laugh. 'We left the husbands at home so we can pick the biggest ones!'

'Perfect!' said Iris, passing a saw for the women through the window. 'Have fun, ladies.'

'Will we see you on Sunday?' Carol asked.

'I wouldn't miss it.'

The women all seemed to breathe a sigh of relief. 'We were worried you were leaving us for this new gig.'

'Never! I have plenty of time to do both.' Iris smiled, and Kira wondered where she got all her energy.

'Good, because the woman we had before you was just awful. No sense of humor.'

Iris frowned. 'Did you push her in the pool, Marissa?'

Marissa didn't even bother to look contrite. 'She was asking for it.'

The three women burst out laughing and Kira made a mental note not to cross this crew. They took their saw and waved goodbye to Iris, smiling at Kira as they went.

'Do you need help finding anything?' she asked, now even more pleased with her decision to hire Iris, but also feeling like she should do something for her customers.

'No, dear, we've been coming here for years.' Carol stopped and patted her shoulder. 'We are so glad you reopened the farm. A real piece of history here. We didn't know if anyone would buy it after all those rumors about the former owner.'

'The what? What rumors?'

'Come on, Carol! We have trees to find!' Janet called, already hiking down the closest trail.

'Oh, it's nothing to worry about, dear,' Carol assured her as she followed her friends. 'I'm sure it's not true!'

Rumors about the former owner? What was she talking about? Kira was about to ask Iris why she hadn't mentioned any rumors, when a family with three very excited kids came up asking about where to find a blue spruce, and then a couple who had driven over an hour to get here wanted to fit several trees onto their compact car, and then a family with a new baby who were looking for the perfect first Christmas-picture spot wanted her opinion. By the time

Kira had handled all of that, she'd forgotten the rumor of rumors completely.

Iris was right about another thing, Dream Harbor showed up. By the time she could sneak in a quick lunch break in the cabin, Kira was pretty sure the entire town had stopped by to pick out a tree. It was a Christmas miracle.

Families were wandering between the trees in their matching Christmas sweaters, kids were squealing with delight as the trees fell, old couples were sipping cocoa while their trees were secured to their cars. The whole scene was like something out of a dream.

A new dream.

A dream in which Kira ran a successful farm and didn't freeze to death.

She liked this dream. Maybe everything she'd told Chloe this morning was coming true. Maybe she was thriving here. Or she could, anyway.

This reckless idea might actually work out.

Chapter Nine

Kira's reopening announcement at the tree lighting had clearly paid off. When Bennett pulled up at the farm with Jeanie and Logan, the place was packed. He was riding shotgun in Logan's truck and Jeanie stuck her head up from the back seat to talk to them.

'Wow, it looks great!'

'Crowded,' Logan grumbled.

'It's festive!' Jeanie said. 'I love that she strung up all the lights and look at how cute the little cabin is!'

Bennett had to admit it all looked really nice. Even the cabin looked reasonably safe. Kira had set up a rocking chair on the front porch and a wreath on the door, so it looked more like a house than like a customer-service booth.

'That's where we get the saws,' he told the others.

'No need. Brought my own,' Logan said, pulling the

truck in between two cars that already had trees tied to their roofs.

'Of course you did.' Jeanie rolled her eyes, but her adoring smile made it pretty damn obvious how she felt about her fiancé.

Bennett hopped out of the truck as soon as they were parked. Jeanie's friends, Hazel and Noah, were also meeting them today so they could all pick out trees together. It should be a fun day, but Bennett would be lying if he said he was scanning the crowd for Jeanie's friends.

There was really only one person he was looking for.

'Where should we start?' Logan asked, coming up beside him.

'We have to wait for everyone to get here,' Jeanie said. 'Ooh … but let's get cocoa while we wait!'

'You own a café. Does a hot beverage really excite you that much?' Bennett asked with a laugh as they walked toward the cabin.

'Of course.' She nudged him. 'Isn't this fun? Aren't you glad you came to stay?'

'Yeah, definitely…' Bennett's words trailed off as he got a glimpse of Kira striding across the parking lot. She was heading right toward him.

Definitely glad he came.

The woman walking his way was a far cry from the one he'd met on his first day here. For one, she wasn't wrapped in bedding. She was sporting her new coat with faux-fur-lined boots to match, her long legs in skintight jeans. Her cheeks were pink from the cool air, her dark bangs brushing across her forehead as she moved. And she moved … well … she moved like she owned the place. But the biggest difference was the smile. It transformed her entire face. It transformed the air around her, the very atoms in the air between them. It transformed *him*.

Holy shit. Kira was gorgeous.

'Bennett! Hi!' Her greeting was sweet and friendly and completely unexpected. Who was this woman?

He didn't realize he was just staring at her in silence until Logan clapped him hard on the back. 'Good luck, Ben,' he said with a chuckle as he and Jeanie continued on their quest for hot cocoa. His sister looked back at him over her shoulder, giving him an enthusiastic thumbs-up and knowing smile, but Logan tugged her along.

'Uh … hi,' he managed to finally choke out.

'Hi,' she said again, her smile downshifting into something slightly less spectacular but better because this one was just for him.

'How are things going?'

'Amazing,' she breathed like she almost couldn't believe it. 'We've had customers from all over! One family drove an hour to get here because they wanted a real "New England Christmas experience". Can you believe that?'

Bennett was grinning now, too. 'Sure. This place is quintessential Christmas.' And it really was. All her social-media scrolling had apparently given Kira a real eye for how to sell people an experience: a total 'Christmas vibe'. Folksy Christmas music played over the speakers as families and couples strolled through the rows of trees.

Between the twinkle lights and rustic signs there was no shortage of photo ops, and Kira had even filled the back of a rusted-out pickup truck with holly branches, pine boughs, and ivy. She'd hung a giant red bow on the front, turning trash into something beautiful.

Who *was* this woman?

He wanted to know everything. Bennett crossed snow off his mental Christmas list. There was only one thing on it now and that was more time with Kira.

'So, are you here for your free tree?' she asked.

'Oh, I'll pay for it.'

'No way. I owe you for your heating services.'

Ben laughed. 'I didn't really do anything.'

'You did.' Kira laughed, a real laugh and the sound nearly brought Bennett to his knees. 'Well, you tried anyway.'

'You already bought me some of those funny little waffles.'

'That wasn't enough! You're getting a free tree, now stop arguing.' Kira's mouth was set in a stubborn line and Bennett smiled. 'But just you. Not your whole family or whoever you brought with you.' Kira gestured to where Jeanie and Logan had been joined by Noah and Hazel.

Bennett laughed. 'Okay, got it. Just one free tree.'

Kira nodded, that private smile still playing around her lips and Bennett suddenly didn't want to pick out a tree. He wanted to drag Kira back to the house and personally warm her up with his lips and his hands and his body.

He cleared his throat.

'Uh, come on. I'll introduce you.' He led the way to his sister before his thoughts could take any more distracting turns.

'Kira, this is my sister Jeanie and her fiancé, Logan, and their friends, Noah and Hazel. Everyone, this is Kira, owner of The Christmas Tree Farm.'

'Hi, everyone,' Kira said with a little wave. 'Thanks for coming out.'

'Of course!' Jeanie looked like she was itching to hug the woman, but Bennett sent her a warning look and she stayed put. 'It's so beautiful! You did a great job.'

'It really is,' said Hazel. 'I used to come here with my parents, but it had gotten pretty run down at that time. You really revived it.'

'Thanks.' Kira's cheeks flushed a deeper pink and Bennett had to look away. He'd known she was beautiful before, but today it was blinding, like he'd been wearing sunglasses and without them he was about to drive off the damn road.

'So, where should we start?' Noah asked, rubbing his hands together. 'I'm ready to chop down a tree.'

'You don't chop it, you saw it,' Logan corrected.

'Right. Saw. Either way, I'm ready.' The fisherman grinned and Hazel leaned into him, her head resting on his shoulder. There was no way Bennett could spend too much time with this foursome without feeling like a lonely and pathetic fifth wheel. Who was he kidding that he was swearing off women? During the holidays? That was the worst time to be alone. People wrote songs about it.

'The Douglas firs are down this row,' Kira said, pointing straight ahead. 'Blue spruces are to the left. But if you prefer a Fraser fir, those are a bit of a further walk. You need to head up the hill.'

'A Fraser for sure,' Logan said.

'You just want to make us walk farther,' Hazel argued. 'These close ones look fine.'

'I just want one that smells good,' Jeanie added.

'They all smell the same,' Hazel said.

Noah shook his head and laughed. 'Just let me cut something down!'

Bennett tuned out the rest of the tree argument and turned back to Kira. 'I'm really happy it's working out.'

'Thanks. Me, too.'

'Hey, Kira,' Iris peeked her head out of the cabin window, 'we're out of cocoa again.'

'Okay, be right there.' She looked apologetic when she faced him. 'Sorry that I can't help you pick out your perfect tree.'

'That's all right. You're busy. Which is a good thing.'

She nodded, but maybe she was hesitant to go? Maybe she wanted more time with him, too? 'A very good thing.' She traced an arc in the dirt with the toe of her boot.

He wanted to say more. He wanted to tell her he wanted to see her again, alone. Just the two of them. He wanted to suggest they spend the month together. Naked. He wanted to propose all sorts of crazy and impulsive and objectively bad ideas to her. He wanted to confess that all he wanted for Christmas was her.

But they were in the middle of a crowded parking lot.

And she was working.

And they just met a week ago.

And he was leaving in a month.

And up until five minutes ago, he was fairly sure she hated him.

And this wasn't a Christmas movie or a sappy holiday song.

This was real life, and in real life people didn't lay out all their romantically misguided thoughts in the middle of a Christmas-tree farm even if it was, objectively, the cutest Christmas-tree farm on the planet.

So, he didn't say any of that. But he was sure he'd spend the rest of his time in Dream Harbor thinking about it.

'I should take care of that,' Kira said, pointing to the cabin and the empty cocoa carafe inside it.

'Right, of course.'

'But make sure you say goodbye before you leave. And I'll tell Iris your tree is on the house.' She gave him one last smile before leaving him with his sister and her friends, still arguing about spruces versus firs.

Bennett watched her walk away, knowing that any rational reasons he had for not pursuing Kira were as futile as this Christmas-tree argument. In the end, he wanted her and if there was an inkling of a chance that she wanted him, too, he was damn well going to take it.

Chapter Ten

Things had been going *so* well. Too well. And now it was all about to fall epically apart, and it was only day one.

Damn it, damn it, damn it.

Kira was not going to cry.

She was going to handle this like the capable adult that she was. Or that she was trying to be. Or that she wished she was.

'What are we going to dooooo?' Oops, the question came out in a wail.

Iris looked at her with concerned eyes. 'Um…' Iris frowned. They were in the customer-service cabin together and Kira was starting to sweat. It was too stuffy in here to still be wearing her coat.

'How much weight can you lift?' Kira asked, eyeing her employee. Iris was slight, but maybe she was stronger than she looked.

'I'm pretty strong,' she said with a smile, clearly game for anything. 'But then who will man the booth?'

'Right, good point. Never mind. I'll figure something out.'

'Maybe we should close for the afternoon?'

Kira peered out the window. The place was packed. Think of the money they would lose if she closed now. No, she couldn't do it. Not when things were just taking off.

'No, I can make it work.' Kira tried to give her a reassuring smile as she turned and fled the cabin, but she felt like her face was going to crack in half. Things had been going so well! And now her afternoon help had canceled on her. Her two large college men that were hired to lift trees onto people's cars had bailed—and now what the hell was she supposed to do? She couldn't ask customers to do it themselves, could she?

They already had to cut their own trees, but surely they wanted help getting them on the cars? Oh, damn it, the tears were pushing hot against the backs of her eyes. And, of course, right on cue, Bennett and friends came traipsing out of the rows of trees with their own trees slung over shoulders, and one extra-large tree lay across the bed of one the wagon's Kira had found in the old barn.

She'd really wanted Bennett to see her as capable, and she'd felt so confident this morning, so freaking happy, for once. And now it was crumbling down around her.

Already.

And like a drug-sniffing dog, but for female distress instead of narcotics, Bennett noticed her right away. He was going to come over here and try to fix everything for her and damn it if she didn't want to let him. She *wanted* to lean into him and just let him fix it.

Old habits die hard.

Instead, she sniffed back her tears and rolled her shoulders back, preparing for battle. Bennett lowered the tree from his shoulder and propped it against the side of the cabin as the rest of his group went to the window to pay for their trees. Kira ignored how his arms flexed as he did it.

'Hey,' he said with a frown and a creased brow. He *knew* something was wrong. What, did this guy have some kind of extra sensory perception?

'Hi!' Kira tried to sound perky, but it came out more deranged than cheerful. 'How did it go?'

'It went fine.' He was still studying her. 'What's wrong?'

'Nothing.'

'Nothing?'

'Right. Nothing. Everything is fine. Great, actually. Really, really good.'

His frown deepened. 'Then why is that old couple trying to shove their own tree onto their car?'

Kira's head whipped around to where there was indeed an elderly couple grappling with a giant tree and an SUV that was way too tall for them.

'Shit,' she whispered, already turning and hustling over to them. 'Let me help you with that,' she said, plastering her customer-service smile back on her face. It was very similar to her 'attending her mother's parties' smile. The last thing she needed was to have elderly people crushed by a Christmas tree. Definitely not the vibe she was going for.

'Oh, thank you, dear. We thought we could manage, but we might have picked one that's a bit too big.' The woman smiled at her from under her knit hat.

'I told you it was too big,' the old man grumbled. 'Should have just gotten a small tree from the grocery store again.'

Kira's stomach dropped. Losing customers was almost as bad as killing them.

'No such thing!' said Bennett as he strode up behind her. 'Can never have too big of a Christmas tree! Right, Kira?' He smiled, and before she could stop him, before she could even get her hands on the tree, he was shoving it on top of the car.

Oh, hell, no.

She nudged him aside with a hip check. 'I'll take it from here, thank you, Bennett.'

'Kira, I really don't mind—'

She shut him up with a glare. She must have done a pretty good job communicating with her eyes that she was two seconds away from strapping *him* to the roof of the car instead of the tree because Bennett stepped aside with his hands up in surrender.

Good. Perfect. She could do this.

Right. How exactly was she going to do this?

She stared at the tree. It was enormous. How the hell had these two got it down here in the first place? The man had to be at least eighty years old and the woman was all of four feet tall and maybe ninety pounds soaking wet. The physics didn't make sense, but Kira now had Bennett, the old couple, and several other customers watching her, waiting for her to perform this very unlikely feat of strength.

'Okay, let's get this strapped on, shall we?' she said, still sounding less chipper and more unhinged than she intended. She took the rope from the man's hand and flung it over the top of the tree. It got about halfway and then got tangled in the branches.

Shit.

'I'm just going to open the doors,' she explained with a smile to the man. She refused to look at Bennett, even though she could feel the barely restrained 'I must help you' energy emanating from his direction.

She put a foot up on the floor of the back seat and tried to reach the rope, but between the height of the SUV and the tree branches, she couldn't reach it.

'Just a minute!' she chirped, racing to the other side of the vehicle. Sweat dripped down her back. She climbed up on the other side and stretched across the tree, branches jabbed her in the face like Christmas was personally assaulting her. How festive.

She almost had it…

'Ben! Why are you just standing there?' Jeanie's voice pierced the silence around the car.

'Let me get that.' A large arm reached past her, grabbed the rope and pulled.

'I told you—' She started to snap at the unwanted helper, but reeled it back in when she saw it wasn't Bennett but Logan who had grabbed the rope and was now very expertly and efficiently tying the tree to the car. 'Oh…'

She stepped down from the car and let him work.

Jeanie and Hazel came up beside her. The other guy they'd come with, Noah, had taken it upon himself to help a mom with two little kids get her tree tied to the roof of her minivan. The kids were running around his legs cheering. Bennett was helping Logan make sure the gigantic tree was secure and politely fighting off tips from the old couple.

Kira blew out a long sigh.

Damn it.

She'd failed again.

'I can't believe Ben was just standing there watching you struggle,' Jeanie said, shaking her head. 'That's not like him.'

'I know it's not,' Kira said, faintly. 'I told him not to.'

'Oh. Why?'

'I wanted to prove I didn't need his help. I'm trying to be … independent and all that…'

Jeanie huffed. 'Being independent doesn't mean you don't need help. And besides,' she said, gesturing to the men, 'they love it. Makes them feel all manly and stuff.'

Hazel laughed. 'Wow, Jeanie. How very feminist of you.'

Jeanie scowled at her friend. 'Oh, please. Logan and I are equal partners, but try and tell me it doesn't do something for you to see Noah with his sleeves rolled up and hefting that big tree up over his head. Look at those forearms…'

All three women tipped their heads to the side, pausing a moment to appreciate the sight in front of them. Noah was tying up the tree for the mom, now that the kids were buckled safely in the car, Logan was chatting with the older couple, his muscular frame leaning on their open window, and Bennett had rolled up the sleeves of his flannel shirt and was helping another man carry his tree to his truck. His forearms flexed as he lifted the tree, and Kira was not going to lie, he looked damn good doing manual labor. She didn't hate it.

She shook her head. No. Nope. This was not happening.

She cleared her throat and broke all three of them out of their daze. 'Well, that was very nice of them and all, but I can take it from here.'

'Oh, really? How do you plan to do that? You clearly don't have anyone here to help with the trees and you still have two hours until close. Do you plan on putting all the trees on the cars yourself?' Jeanie asked, her hand on her hip.

'I … well … I will just…'

'We're staying,' Hazel announced. 'Let's get some more rope.' She walked off toward the cabin before Kira could argue.

Jeanie just grinned and followed her friend.

What the hell just happened?

'Cheers to a job well done,' Noah said, and they all lifted their compostable paper cups of cocoa in a toast to their hard work tying trees all afternoon.

'Cheers!' Hazel and Jeanie sang out. They were all gathered on the little porch in front of the cabin, Logan in the rocking chair with Noah perched on the rail of the porch beside him. Hazel and Jeanie were huddled together on the steps, keeping warm now that the sun had set. Kira was freezing but she stood just off the porch in the frozen dirt. Bennett was leaning against the porch on the other side of his sister, and she was still studiously avoiding his gaze. She had been all afternoon. All afternoon while these people she barely knew helped keep her business afloat.

And isn't this exactly what she swore she wasn't going to do? Hadn't she started this whole crazy plan to do something on her own? Something without Chloe's sensible guidance and without her parents' money (other than the money she used to start the whole damn thing, but that was beside the point). Wasn't she here to stop mooching off other people and using them for what they could do for her? She was supposed to be self-sufficient up here on her farm. But she was even further from that goal than she was when she started.

Five people had given up their afternoon for her and she had absolutely nothing to offer them in return, other than watered-down cocoa in cups that would disintegrate if they didn't drink it fast enough.

'I can send over a few of my guys tomorrow,' Logan said, interrupting her thoughts. 'They're always looking for more work in the colder months. They'll help you out and they're reliable.'

'Oh … uh … thank you. That would be great.' Kira chugged the last of her cocoa, wanting to reject his offer but really, really needing a way to keep this stupid farm running. 'And thanks for helping today, all of you. I appreciate it.'

'Of course!' Jeanie smiled at her. Her arm was tucked under Hazel's, the two women leaning in toward each other, and a sharp pang of jealousy hit Kira. Did she miss her sister or just any human contact? At this point, she thought it was probably both.

'It was like being in one of those holiday romcoms Hazel likes to watch,' Noah said.

'*We* like to watch,' she corrected.

'Right, *we* like to watch,' he amended with a grin, and Logan huffed a laugh.

'So, what's the plan for the other eleven months of the year?' Logan asked, steering the question back to business. Kira had learned throughout the afternoon that the man ran a successful produce farm and apple orchard so she should probably ask for some advice. Business advice was different from random help from strangers, she figured. They were associates, fellow farmers. It was different than Bennett trying to swoop in and rescue her. Right?

'Well, I thought I could focus on more of a general garden center. There's an old greenhouse in the south field and we could do shrubs and small trees.' It was the first time she was saying any of it out loud, mostly because she had literally no one to say it out loud to, but also because she was nervous and didn't know if any of it was a good idea, but Logan was nodding so that was probably a good sign…

'Sure, that could work. I'm going to get you in touch with my agricultural engineer. He'll help you get set up.'

'Agricultural engineer?'

'Yeah, name's Gordon. Give me your number, I'll send you his information.'

'Um … okay.' As she rattled off her number, she wondered what the hell an agricultural engineer was and how much they cost, and why the hell running a farm was a lot harder than just planting some seeds.

'What about your pickles?' Bennett asked, speaking for the first time since they'd stopped working, forcing her to finally look at him. *Shit.* He looked good. In the soft glow of the Christmas lights, he looked like a damn holiday card come to life. His dark hair was mussed from an afternoon of working, and his puffy vest was streaked with dirt and pine needles, but his cheeks were ruddy from the cold and his eyes bright and teasing.

Frankly, it was rude to look that good when she knew she was a wreck from the afternoon of running around in a panic, that fake customer-service smile plastered to her face.

'It's possible the internet lied to me.'

His perfect mouth tipped up in the corner.

'What pickles?' Jeanie asked, forcing Kira to tear her gaze away from Bennett's mouth. That stupid, perfect mouth.

'I just thought things would be different when I got here.' She shrugged, like it didn't matter, like she hadn't been completely wrong and delusional about setting up her own little homestead. That she thought she could be self-sufficient and not need things like actual money to fix radiators and windows. That she had lived her entire life in an absurd sheltered reality, where anything broken was fixed for her.

When her gaze flicked back to Bennett he was watching her again. Something was different about the way he was looking at her now. Something decidedly less … wholesome … was lurking in his eyes. Had it been there all along and she just missed it? Or had something shifted between them? Despite the cold evening, heat flared in her cheeks.

'You thought things would be more pickle-y?' Noah asked, pulling her attention from Bennett again.

Kira laughed despite the feeling that her world was falling apart around her. 'Yeah, much more pickle-y. I just … I didn't plan on setting up a business. I kinda thought I was coming here to go off the grid.'

'We can plant cucumbers in the spring,' Hazel told her with a smile, and Kira's heart hurt at how kind they were all being. 'Then you can make all the pickles you want.'

'Right.' Kira cleared her throat. She was not going to cry over pickles. 'Thanks. That would be great.' Her gaze snagged on Bennett's again.

He dipped his head in a nod but didn't take his eyes off her. Kira swallowed hard. Was it possible that Bennett wasn't quite as *nice* as she thought he was? Suddenly this damn coat was too warm.

'We should probably get going,' Logan said, standing from the rocking chair. He reached out a hand and pulled Jeanie to her feet.

'Let's go, Haze. Those Christmas movies aren't going to watch themselves,' Noah said, hopping down from his perch. Hazel stood from the step and Noah hoisted her over his shoulder. She shrieked.

'See,' Jeanie said with a giggle. 'Feeling all manly.'

'Noah! Put me down.'

'Don't worry, I won't strap you to the roof,' he teased. 'Bye, everyone!' He carted Hazel across the parking lot before sliding her down his body and placing her gently on the ground near his car. As Noah's head lowered to Hazel's, Kira turned back to Jeanie and Logan not wanting to intrude on their moment.

'Call me if you need anything else,' Logan said.

'Thanks, I will.'

'See you later, Kira. Make sure you come into the café sometime. Oh, and Annie wanted me to mention that you should call her. She'd love to set something up to sell gingerbread cookies up here.'

Kira winced a little, remembering the business card that was tucked into the free cookies George had dropped off a week ago. She was supposed to call the baker, but time had gotten away from her. 'Oh, that would be great. I will.'

'Great!'

'Bye, Kira.' Logan grabbed Jeanie's hand and the two

wandered back to his truck, leaving Kira alone with Bennett.

'They're my ride,' he said when she dared to look up at him, that new … something … was still in his eyes. 'So, I should probably go.'

'Probably.'

Panic spiked through her. Was this it? Was she never going to see this man again? And why did that matter? Her mind was racing, grappling for reasons to make him come back, for reasons to see him again. Anything! A leaky roof, a creaky floor, a drafty window … technically she had all of those. Would he come if she asked him to?

At some point, he'd stepped closer and she fought the insane urge to lean into him. Get a grip, Kira.

'I'm staying above The Pumpkin Spice Café,' he said. 'If you take Jeanie up on her offer, maybe we'll run into each other.' He was so close now that his words brushed against her cheek.

'Yes,' her voice was a breathy whisper. What the hell was wrong with her? But it had been so long since she had company, since she had … *naked* company, and he was so warm and sweet and…

Jesus, was she describing a man or cinnamon bun?

She cleared her throat and stepped back before he could lure her in further. And there was that smile again. She didn't know if she wanted to smack it off his face or kiss it.

'Yeah, sure, maybe we will run into each other. At the café.'

The smile grew like he knew every single filthy thought going through her mind. 'See you around, Kira.'

'See you.' And despite herself, she was hoping they would.

Bennett Ellis was a complication she didn't need in her life right now. But Kira was not known for doing anything the easy way.

Chapter Eleven

It had been two days since Bennett had seen Kira. Two days of working on his laptop in the middle of The Pumpkin Spice Café, claiming to his sister that he needed a change of scenery. Two days of getting absolutely nothing done. Two days of being questioned by every town resident about what he was working on, how long he was staying, his dating history, and his star sign.

But today he had officially given up. He was taking the dogs on their morning walk and then he was taking his work back up to Jeanie's apartment, where he should have been all along.

Kira wasn't coming.

And he wasn't going up to the farm again. He'd intruded on her life enough already. Whatever spark he thought he'd felt between them, he'd clearly imagined it. Whatever fantasy he'd cooked up about a Christmas fling, was obviously nothing more than a fantasy.

It was for the best. He only had a few more weeks in Dream Harbor, and anyway, he was supposed to be breaking his bad dating habits.

At least that's what he told himself as he walked through the brisk morning. Main Street was decked out for the holidays. Each shop had a wreath or a wintery display in the window. Even the pet store had gold tinsel strung up on each fishtank and gerbil cage.

The sun was barely up and the snowflake lights on each lamppost were still lit. He had plenty of time to admire them since the dogs needed to sniff each and every one.

'Come on, guys. Heel,' he said, tugging on the leashes, though he didn't know why he bothered. They didn't follow commands, anyway, only treats, and he'd forgotten to bring some. He'd be out here sniffing lampposts all day at this rate.

By the time he got to the bakery, his fingers were numb and he was ready to get back to the café and grab a hot coffee from Jeanie before getting to work.

'Let's get some breakfast,' he said, and Elizabeth's ears perked up at one of the few words she knew. *Breakfast.*

But her attention was quickly distracted by Pudgy's whining and Odie yanking on the leash. Once Elizabeth spotted what the other dogs did, there was no hope for Bennett to maintain any kind of control. His loyal companions, man's alleged best friends, dragged him directly in front of the woman he'd just decided to give up on.

'Hello, sweet babies!' Kira's hands were immediately

scratching heads and patting wiggling dog bodies and Bennett couldn't help but feel a little jealous of the affection she so easily poured on his dogs. Were there humans she treated with so much excitement and care? And how exactly did he get to be one of them?

'Morning,' he said, and Kira lifted her gaze from the dogs. When her eyes met his, every lie he'd been telling himself about not wanting her disintegrated completely. And the way she looked at him, he knew he wasn't the only one feeling it.

Even though she was clearly still fighting it.

She glanced away, fidgeting with her mittens. 'Good morning.'

'Are you headed to the café?' he asked.

'Uh … yeah. After I meet with Annie about her Christmas cookie idea.'

'They're amazing. I've already eaten way too many.'

Her lips quirked up just enough that Bennett felt a flare of heat in his gut. 'Me, too,' she said. 'Annie's like some kind of wizard or something.'

He huffed a laugh and a puff of breath floated in the air between them. Kira was bundled up, tucked deep inside her hood, and he resisted every urge in his body to ask about the heat in her house, to ask if it was working, if she'd figured out how to use the fireplace; if she was warm enough. He would not tell her about the videos he'd watched about old, steam heating systems or about the book he'd ordered from Hazel about radiator maintenance. She hadn't asked for any of it.

He cleared his throat. For whatever reason, Kira didn't want his help. Which he was just now realizing left him with no moves, whatsoever. God, maybe he really did have a problem with women. If he couldn't fix anything for her, then what did he have to offer?

That was a grim thought for so early on a Wednesday.

'They'd be a real draw for the farm,' he said.

'Yeah, I hope so. We had a really good turnout last weekend so I'm just trying to keep the momentum going.' She shrugged a little inside her bulky coat. The sun was starting to stretch its rays down Main Street and it gilded the fluff around her hood.

'Well, cookies never hurt.' He was running out of things to say, running out of reasons to keep talking to her. Maybe the women he usually dated ditched him after a few dates not because they were using him, but maybe just because he was *boring*.

'Look, I really am appreciative of all the help your friends gave me on Sunday. I know I haven't been particularly … friendly to you.'

Bennett shrugged. 'You don't owe me friendliness.' But he wanted to earn her friendliness, he wanted it freely given. She'd given him glimpses of it, little tastes, and he wanted more.

She lifted an eyebrow. 'Okay.'

'Okay.' He was definitely smiling like a moron, but she was nearly smiling back so it was worth it.

'So, I was thinking…'

'Oh?'

'Well, I just thought, if you wanted to come up to the farm in the mornings to let the dogs run around before we open…'

'Yeah?'

'I wouldn't chase you off the property.' And there it was, that private smile she'd given him on Sunday like they were sharing a secret joke.

'I might take you up on that. The dogs would love it.'

Kira stooped to give Odie and Pudgy some attention. 'Would you like that? Do you want to come run around and pee on a whole bunch of trees?' She glanced up at Bennett. 'We won't mention to the customers that their family Christmas tree may or may not have pee on it.'

He laughed and Kira smiled bigger, and he was pretty sure church bells rang out in the distance. Elizbeth licked the side of Kira's face.

'Oh, kisses, thank you!' Kira said with a laugh, gently pushing Elizabeth's big face away from hers. She stood up, the smile still lingering around her mouth. Bennett forced himself to drag his gaze away from her lips.

'So, maybe I'll see you tomorrow morning?' she said and beneath the casualness of the question, Bennett heard more. Or he wanted to think he did.

'I think you probably will.'

'Great.' She shook her head, remembering too late to rein in her enthusiasm. 'I mean, good. I will maybe see you then.'

All three dogs immediately started whining as soon as

she turned and strode off toward Annie's bakery. Bennett had to swallow his own whine at seeing her go. But he had an invite to see her tomorrow.

He was sure everyone in The Pumpkin Spice Café would know exactly what the ridiculous smile on his face meant when he walked in, so he took the back alley and went straight up to Jeanie's apartment. If he was going to spend tomorrow morning up at the farm, he'd better get some work done today.

He set himself up on the couch. Laptop, coffee, peacefully snoring dogs: check, check, and check. He had to admit that working from home did have its perks. The Christmas tree he'd gotten from Kira's twinkled cheerfully in the corner of Jeanie's living room and he had his feet propped up on her coffee table in his cozy, Christmas socks. He could get used to this.

Unfortunately, before he could get too deep into his work or his fantasies about Kira, three new texts popped up on his phone and derailed his entire morning. One look at the name on his screen and all the good feelings of the morning dissolved. He should have blocked the number months ago, but he hadn't. Why? Some ill-placed feeling of guilt? Some absurd hope that she'd want him again for more than just a few weeks? That she might need something.

Ignoring everything that was healthy for him, he opened the first one.

Hey Ben. I'm back in town. Want to meet up for drinks?

Bennett sighed and pinched the bridge of his nose, the familiar pull already had his fingers twitching to respond, before he read her next message.

I miss you.

Of course she did, she always did after a while.

I hate to be alone for the holidays and I know you do too... Call me...

And there it was. She just needed someone to warm her bed until spring rolled around or she got bored or she found someone more interesting to spend her time with. Nicole Allen was Bennett's shameful secret. Not even Jeanie knew about her. He'd been way too embarrassed at the time to tell anyone about her, and he certainly wasn't about to tell anyone now.

Nicole was the real reason he'd uprooted his life and moved across the country. They'd dated on and off throughout college, with him always being more invested than she was, not that he would have admitted it at the time. When she'd gotten a job on the West Coast after graduation, he assumed it was officially over between them. It should have been a fresh start for him but instead, she asked him to come with her, tearfully actually, after confessing she was afraid to go alone, to start over on the other side of the country. Of course, it was the exact right thing to say to him. How could he not go? How could he resist the feeling of being her hero?

He'd followed her to California and shared her apartment and her bed for three months, before she realized it had all been a mistake. It turned out that 'freedom' was actually what she wanted. He'd been too embarrassed to come back home and so he'd stayed. And somehow, she was still able to lure him back. Because apparently, the only thing that got him off more than helping people was being *needed* by this woman.

Whenever they were together it was because she needed him or something from him at least. She needed him to chase away her loneliness or she needed him to comfort her while she licked her wounds from whatever the last guy did to her, or she needed him to escort her to holiday parties and ensure she was never under the mistletoe alone.

And damn it, if he didn't feel the pull of her again.

She missed him.

She was lonely.

She wanted him.

He glanced at his tree and the pull lessened. Kira's smile from this morning lit up behind his eyes. Maybe this time, he didn't need Nicole back. He tossed the phone aside and resolved not to answer.

But before he could congratulate himself or manage to write a single line of code, another thought disrupted his workday.

Was he only replacing Nicole with another woman who he hoped needed him? Was Kira's main appeal her need for help? Suddenly, his entire dating history landed in front of him in a heap of disasters and failed connections. Did Bennett seek out people who would ultimately be more than happy to take advantage of him? Was this last year of shitty dates his fault?

Christ, he really did get off on helping people. He had some kind of damsel-in-distress kink. What the hell was wrong with him? Odie let out a soft sigh next to him, like he was equally disappointed in this revelation, and Bennett absentmindedly scratched between the little dog's ears. He needed to fix this. He needed to break this cycle.

He needed to stay away from Kira North.

Elizabeth looked up from her spot on the floor as though she'd heard his thoughts, her dark eyes peering into him. She let out a sad little bark.

Bennett groaned. 'We can't.'

Elizabeth growled.

'I'm trying to be a better person. Don't you want that for me?'

The big dog tipped her head, like she actually understood him, and then gave an indignant bark.

Bennett sighed. He spent way too much time alone with these dogs. 'Fine. Maybe, we can still go for a walk,' he said, and the dog huffed a breath in relief before putting her head back down on her paws. Okay, so he would just keep his helping instincts and his hands to himself.

Easy.

Maybe he wouldn't even see Kira. It was a large farm, after all. He would just stick to the outskirts.

Maybe he'd get lucky and find that dead body. Nothing kills a boner like a murder victim. Right?

Odie sighed again, his disappointment clear.

Bennett was so screwed.

Chapter Twelve

Kira was in way over her head. Buying a farm and opening her own business was one thing. But ice-skating? That was a step too far.

'I think maybe I'll just watch,' she said, wobbling on her rented skates, even though she was still standing on the rubber mats they put around the rink.

'Are you sure?' Iris asked, assessing her from under her knit hat. She looked adorable, in her black leggings and oversized sweater. It was red with white snowflakes on it, and Kira wished she'd worn something more festive than her olive-green coat, but she was freezing as usual.

'I'm sure. I'll just observe until I get the idea.'

Iris laughed. 'I still can't believe you've never ice-skated before.'

'I told you, my family avoided any activities that required freezing temperatures.'

'Right, I forgot. A whole family afraid of being cold,' Iris teased.

'Just be careful out there, Iris. There's a lot of kids.'

Iris nudged her with a laugh and Kira had to hold onto the half-wall around the rink in order not to tip over. 'Ha. Ha,' Iris said. 'I'm glad you came anyway.'

They'd quickly become friends, or trauma-bonded over providing what felt like the entire Christmas-crazed town with their trees in the course of three days, but either way, Kira was happy to have someone to joke with again.

'Yeah. Me, too,' Kira admitted, begrudgingly. Iris had convinced her to come skating at the ice rink after closing up the farm for the night, to celebrate their early success. And while Kira was incredibly pleased with their sales since the grand reopening, she could think of a million other places she'd rather celebrate. But Iris had insisted it was a Christmas-season-in-Dream-Harbor-must-do. So here she was.

Iris glided onto the ice like some kind of winter Olympian, or at least like someone who was unlikely to fall on her ass.

'I'll give you a few minutes to work up the courage, but then I'm coming back for you,' Iris warned as she skated away backwards.

Backwards! Show off.

Kira just waved her off. There was no way she was getting out there on the ice.

Should her feet be hurting already? Even though she hadn't skated a single step?

She shifted a little as she watched the skaters. The outdoor rink was full of people happily skating like it was the easiest damn thing in the world. People of all ages sped past her, but it was the tiny kids with hockey helmets she was particularly afraid of. She had been teasing Iris about her dislike of children, but these kids looked seriously dangerous. They moved fast and apparently had no fear. She could very clearly imagine one taking her out at the knees.

This was a terrible idea.

She caught a glimpse of Iris across the rink; she had stopped to lean against the partial wall that lined the rink and was chatting with a small group of people.

A small group of people that just so happened to included Bennett Ellis.

He hadn't taken her up on her offer to walk the dogs at the farm, but now here he was reappearing in her life where she least expected him to. Damn it. The last thing she wanted was for Bennett to see her sliding across the ice on her face. She needed to get out of here, but she didn't want to bail on Iris, not to mention she could barely walk in these damn skates.

Oh, shit. And now Iris was pointing to her from across the rink and Jeanie was waving and Bennett was skating toward her with complete confidence, like he was born wearing skates and there was nowhere to run.

He was heading straight for the wall she was leaning on like he might crash into it but instead did that hockey stop thing that sprayed ice into the air. It was obnoxious. And hot. And more obnoxious that it was hot.

'Hey,' he said, only slightly out of breath, his cheeks rosy from the cold.

'Hello.' Was she feeling a little prickly with him for not stopping by the farm in the past few days? Absolutely not. She was just cold and her feet hurt. And she was not looking forward to being embarrassed in front of him again.

His mouth tipped up in the corner. 'Are you planning on skating?'

'No. I just came for the ambience.'

'The ambience?' Bennett glanced around at the racing children and the tinny music blaring over the loudspeakers.

'Yep. Just soaking in that Christmas cheer.'

'Sure.' His smile grew. 'Do you want help?'

That question should not have been so loaded. She shouldn't want to yell at him that she didn't need his help with anything. She shouldn't *want* his help so damn much. No, not his help, just *him*. Just his proximity made her feel better. And it shouldn't. She was independent now. Perfectly fine on her own.

'No, thank you.'

'Kira…'

'I don't need your help.'

'Just like you didn't need my help with getting that tree onto the car?'

'Exactly like that.'

'Kira.'

'What?'

'I've been swamped with work. I haven't had time to drive up to the farm for dog walks.'

It irked her that he knew that was why she was acting so grouchy with him. How dare he be so astute.

'Why would I care about that? I've been busy, too.' She sniffed.

'Kira.' He held out his hand to her and she tried her damnedest to ignore it. 'Kira, let me help you.'

'I'm perfectly happy watching.'

'You'd rather stand there, wobbling on those skates and freezing your butt off than let me help you?'

He had a point. She *was* freezing, and flailing around for her life as she made her way around the rink would probably work up a sweat. Iris and Jeanie waved to her from across the rink, beckoning her to join them.

Iris thought she was cool for leaving her life behind and starting the farm. She couldn't let her new friend, her *only* friend, down.

Ugh.

She took Bennett's hand. It was comforting and warm and her fingers immediately started to defrost.

'Okay, we're just going to take it slow,' he said, soothingly, like he was talking to a spooked horse, which may have been how Kira looked as she stepped through the opening in the wall and onto the ice.

One skate, two skates. There. She was on. She kept her death grip on Bennett's hand and he smiled at her.

'Now we have to move.'

Kira frowned. 'Are you sure? I kinda feel like this is good enough for my first time.'

'Kira…' he coaxed. 'Come on. One foot in front of the other.'

She glared at him, but slowly slid one skate forward. Unfortunately, the other one did not follow and she nearly did a full split before Bennett hauled her back upright.

She clung to the front of his sweater.

'I got you.'

'No. Nope. I almost fell.'

'But you didn't.'

'But I almost did.'

He had an arm wrapped around her back now, holding her steady as a rush of child skaters moved past them, his strong body protecting her from tiny people with hockey helmets and no concept of personal space.

'I got you,' he said again but this time his lips brushed the sensitive shell of her ear. A shiver ran the entire length of her body. She pulled away just enough to see his eyes darken and his perfect lips tip up in the corner. Uh-oh. Skating was even more dangerous than she thought.

'Let's try again,' he said, taking her hand in his. 'Push with one foot and then glide. Push and glide.'

'Push and glide. Right. Piece of cake.' Staring at her skates was a good excuse not to look at Bennett's lips, so that was what she did. Push and glide. Push and glide. There. She was doing it. Well, sort of. Her pushes were very small and her glides were pretty choppy and they were making incredibly slow progress around the rink, but she was upright.

She forgot to keep her eyes on her feet and glanced at Bennett. Damn it, this man was just made for outdoor excursions. He looked rosy and healthy and the stars twinkling behind his head just added to the whole dizzying effect of him.

'Ta-da,' she whispered and his smile grew.

'Very good.' He dipped his head closer to hers so she could hear him over the music. 'You continue to impress me, Kira.'

Her sarcastic response died on her tongue as he ran his thumb over the soft skin of her wrist beneath her coat. Suddenly she was very aware of her hand in his, of his long fingers woven through hers. If she had any confidence in her ability not to get grievously injured, she would have let go. But instead, she had no choice but to let Bennett's body and words warm her.

'Look at you!' Iris cheered as she skated by, spun on her skates and turned to face Kira. 'You're a natural.'

Kira cleared her throat, emerging from the trance of Bennett's proximity. 'That is definitely not true. But if I stay off my ass, I'll consider it a success.'

Iris smiled at Bennett as she leisurely skated backwards, somehow avoiding other skaters and the wall. 'I'm sure Bennett will keep track of your ass.'

Bennett choked on nothing, a startled cough escaping his lips.

Iris laughed. 'To keep it off the ground, I mean.'

'Keep what off the ground?' Jeanie asked, skating up beside them.

'Me,' Kira said, out of the corner of her eye catching the blush that had worked its way up Bennett's cheeks.

Jeanie smiled. 'I'm sure he will.' She skated off with Iris, the two of them giggling and Kira started to wonder if there was something in the water in this town.

'Those two are weird,' she said.

'Very.'

'I will obviously keep track of my own ass.'

'Obviously.'

She snuck another glance, and saw he was looking at her like he had other ideas in mind. Again, his thumb was tracing circles over her wrist, and she wondered if he knew he was doing it. If he was driving her crazy on purpose.

How had she ever thought he was wholesome when he was looking at her like *that*? Like he was thinking about her ass. Like he wanted her. Which was insane considering she was currently wearing the world's bulkiest parka and was creeping around the rink like an elderly turtle.

But he was. That heat was back in Bennett's eyes and Kira was getting dangerously close to stoking the flames. Would it be so bad to give in to that look? To see what this good guy had to offer?

He was still looking at her when the pee-wee hockey player nailed them from behind and they both went crashing to the ice.

'Shit, shit, shit.' Bennett hit the ice hard, his legs tangled up with Kira's. She let out a scared little squeal as they went down that would probably haunt his dreams forever.

'You okay?' he asked, quickly sitting up. He looked down at where Kira was sprawled on the ice. 'Can you get up?'

Kira winced. 'If you mean, am I too injured to get up, the answer is no. If you're asking if I am physically capable of getting up, the answer is also no.'

He huffed a laugh, relieved that she was okay enough to crack jokes.

'Here.' He took her by the arm and eased her up to a seat. The kid that crashed into them had already skated off, unscathed by the collision.

'A hit and run,' Kira said with a scowl. 'I don't even know which one it was. They all look the same with those helmets.'

'What would you do if you knew who did it? Seek retribution?'

'Something like that. Get their mom to yell at them at the very least.'

Bennett shook his head with a laugh. 'All right, let's get up before we get run over.' He managed to get himself back on his feet but Kira was slipping and sliding all over the place, her flailing threatening to knock them both over again.

'Maybe I should just crawl,' she said with a groan as she fell back on her butt.

'You're not crawling.' He leaned down, put his hands on

her waist and hoisted her up to a stand. Her eyes went wide when he then scooped her into his arms.

'What the hell are you doing?'

'I'm carrying you.'

'No way.'

'You going to skate back?' He raised an eyebrow in challenge and Kira glanced across the rink. They'd made it halfway and it had taken a hell of a long time to get here.

Kira frowned but relented. 'I will allow it.'

He laughed and started to head toward the exit. And it was fine, totally just a friend helping a friend, until Kira leaned her head against his chest and *sighed*. Sighed like she liked being there. His fingers tightened on her thighs. First her hand in his, then all this talk about her ass, and now this? Kira in his arms, her silky hair tickling along his throat, her scent washing over him? And all he could think about was the soft skin of her wrist and how he'd wanted to replace his thumb with his tongue, how he'd wanted to explore a lot more than her wrist.

What the hell was he doing? He'd resolved to stay away from her, to tamp down his 'rescuer' instincts, and he'd ended up with Kira in a bridal hold as he escorted her off the ice. He was obviously failing epically.

'Uh, the ice-skating lifeguard is blowing his whistle at us,' Kira said, distracting him from his thoughts.

'Ice-skating lifeguard?' Bennett looked in the direction Kira was pointing. 'Oh, the high-schooler with a whistle and a safety vest? I'm not worried about him.'

'He's yelling that you have to put me down,' she said with a smile in her voice.

'I'll put you down when we get there.'

'Uh-oh, Bennett, I thought you were a rule follower,' she teased as they approached the exit. 'A good boy.'

He slowed down, ignoring the way she'd purred those last words, and stepped carefully off the ice. He lowered Kira to the ground and tried desperately to ignore the way her body pressed against the entire length of his as he did. She didn't pull away, just looked up at him with a mischievous grin.

There were so many rules he wanted to break when it came to Kira, mostly the ones he had made for himself. He wanted to take her home, he wanted to take her to bed, he wanted to dive headfirst into this thing with her that made no sense and would land him exactly where he always landed, alone and confused about what he'd done wrong this time.

But the answer was clear: he kept doing the same thing over and over again. Falling for women that he had no future with. His home wasn't here. His life wasn't here. He'd already been down this road before, and he couldn't do it again.

Kira was not the one for him.

And he needed to remember that, even as she leaned forward and pressed a kiss to his cheek.

'Thanks for rescuing me,' she said, her voice light and teasing in his ear. 'I hope it was good for you.'

He bit down on a groan. This woman was going to kill

him. She was so close; her delicious lips were *right there*. A slight turn of his head and his mouth would be on hers. It took all his strength to pull away.

Kira raised an eyebrow, a playful smirk on her face and damn, did he want to play with her. But it just wasn't meant to be.

'Real good,' he said, and Kira's smile grew. 'But I have to get going.'

Her face fell. 'Oh.'

'See you around, Kira.'

'Right. See you around, Bennett.'

Chapter Thirteen

The sky was white this morning. According to her weather app, they were under a winter storm warning which to Kira sounded quite ominous. What did one do to prepare for a winter storm warning? Did she need to stock up on toilet paper and canned soup? She already had plenty of those.

She probably just needed working heat.

But that was still a pipe dream, so instead of preparing she just stared forlornly out the window at the eerily white sky. She didn't love the idea of being trapped here alone for whatever this storm might bring, but she didn't have much of a choice now, did she? What was she going to do? Trap Bennett here when he, hopefully, came for a walk? Bat her eyelashes until he agreed to stay and keep her company?

Ha, ha. Nope, of course she wouldn't. That would be crazy.

And Kira was done manipulating people like that. Or

she was trying to be. She'd replayed the whole scene from last Sunday over and over in her mind, searching for evidence that she'd somehow conned Bennett and his friends into helping her when her employees didn't show up. But she hadn't found any. She was pretty sure they'd all just stayed out of the kindness of their hearts. Which was … odd. And made an uncomfortable, but decidedly warm feeling settle in her chest. Uh-oh, maybe her Grinchy heart was growing.

She shook her head and reread her sister's text message from this morning.

Morning, Kiki!

Love you! Hope you have a great day and sell so many trees!

Xoxo

The whole thing was followed by several tree emojis and far too many hearts. Chloe was overcompensating. She only used emojis when she was feeling bad about something. Somehow her twin knew that she was struggling here, despite all her protests.

And if she didn't get her shit together soon, Chloe might do something crazy like come back, and as much as the thought made Kira's heart surge in her chest, she absolutely could not allow that. Just as much as this was her chance to do something on her own, it was Chloe's, too.

It had taken some distance for her to see it, but Kira realized how much she had pulled Chloe down over the years. How many times had she nearly gotten them both into trouble? If that cop that showed up to pull a half-naked and very drunk Kira out of the neighbor's pool hadn't had a huge crush on Chloe all through high school, they'd probably both have been arrested.

And Chloe could have been a functioning member of society so much sooner if Kira hadn't kept them both behaving like spoiled brats for so long. Chloe had a real job, like with numbers and money, and she'd gotten it all on her own.

God, Chloe had been so damn proud of herself when she'd come home after that interview. An interview that had nothing to do with their father's company, the one he hadn't had to make up for her. And Kira had panicked. Her twin was moving on. Her twin was growing up. And when Chloe had casually mentioned getting an apartment of her own in the city, Kira had freaked out. Well, freaked out in a way that no one but her twin would notice, but Chloe knew. Chloe knew she didn't want her to go. She'd quietly dropped the whole thing, putting her life on hold for Kira.

It wasn't until Chloe had met Erik on that dating app that she finally had the courage to leave. And Kira had tried so damn hard since then to make sure she didn't get in her sister's way again.

She took a deep breath and pressed her forehead to the cold window. She didn't like to think about it, her past behavior. How entitled she'd acted for so long. How often she'd put herself above others, even her sister.

Sure, she'd donated more of her trust fund than she'd

spent, but karmically, it didn't seem to be helping. As it turned out, being a good person was kinda hard.

Sighing dramatically for no one's benefit but her own, she put her coffee cup in the sink and decided to head outside just to … check on things. Not to maybe accidentally bump into a certain perfectly symmetrically-faced man. Definitely not that.

Actually, screw it. She absolutely was going to look for Bennett because he was pretty to look at and he was nice to her and she was lonely, damn it. And if she wanted a little Christmas flirtation, a little holiday hookup, she was perfectly within her rights as a grown woman.

She tugged on her boots and took her coat off the hook. She strode out the back door with a new determination in her step. Bennett had been looking at her with all that steam in his eyes for days. He'd practically been drooling over her at the skating rink until he had to leave. And who was she to deter him when she could really use a friendly roll in the hay?

Besides, this was the perfect solution. Bennett was leaving after Christmas. It was the perfect out. She'd let him fill her stocking and then he'd be out of her life. No need to worry about seeing her mother's smug face when she met him, because she never would.

Bennett could just be a Christmas fling.

She smiled as she pulled on her coat. Why hadn't she thought of this sooner? She'd been too bogged down with this whole running-a-business thing, and fighting off Bennett's attempt to fix her life. She didn't need him to fix anything but she sure as hell would let him give her a hand with a few things in the bedroom.

She nearly laughed to herself, but she already felt a little bit like she was hunting the nice man, so she probably shouldn't add villainous laughter into the mix. Not that she was about to force him into anything. He'd been making those sexy eyes at her for days and she'd been stubbornly and rather stupidly ignoring it. Well, she was done with that.

It wasn't manipulation if he wanted it, too, right?

It was just finally giving in to what they both wanted.

Now she just had to find him.

Kira's confidence faded a bit when she found Bennett on the edge of the farm, out by the old barn. It was possible that she had been grossly underestimating his attractiveness. He looked good this morning. Like, really good. Like Henry Cavill good. And suddenly she felt less sure of her seduction plan. Maybe she had hallucinated the tension between them? Maybe it wasn't sexual at all, maybe it was just regular old hostile tension. And he did kinda run away after carrying her off the skating rink. Maybe he wasn't into her, after all.

And besides, how was it that a man this good looking and this kind and handy, and who filled out his jeans like that, was single? Maybe he wasn't? Oh, God, what was she even doing out here? It was that text from Chloe that had her all mixed up. And this storm warning. Something in the atmosphere had made her briefly think that this man might want her. Never in her entire life had Kira been attracted to a well-adjusted man—or attracted one, for that matter. Instead, she picked up delinquents, deviants, and general trouble wherever she went. Men that looked and acted like Bennett Ellis had never factored into the equation. Despite her mother's best efforts to set her up with plenty of upstanding citizens (or at least men that appeared that way from the outside; plenty of them had pinched her ass and called her sweetheart when her mother wasn't looking), Kira had resisted at all costs.

But all that was beside the point, she had a lot on her plate. She didn't really feel like adding rejection by a hot man into the mix today. She should just go.

A cacophony of barking stopped her in her tracks.

'Kira?'

Shit. Caught.

'Oh, Bennett, hey,' she said, as casually as possible for someone lurking in the trees and spying on him like a creeper. She was thankful the dogs were here so she could look at them instead of Bennett's face. Her feelings had swung back to annoyed at its perfection, now that she realized he would definitely reject her if given the chance. Asshole.

'Hey.' He was closer now, that damn peppermint scent filling her senses. Why did he smell like that? Did he eat candy canes for breakfast?

'What are you doing out here?' she snapped.

His brows rose in surprise. 'I thought… You said we could come for a walk.'

'Right. I know.' She shook her head. *He didn't actually reject you, you lunatic. You made that up. Be nice.* 'Sorry, I just meant, you're really far out here.'

'Oh, yeah.' He glanced away from her, his gaze scanning the decrepit old barn. 'You're not using this building, are you?'

Apparently, he was here on a safety-inspection mission and not to see her, which is what she'd been stupidly hoping.

'No, officer, I'm not using this building. Don't worry.'

His hands flexed at his sides, his jaw clenched and released, like he was holding back.

Kira couldn't help her smile. 'It's killing you, isn't it?'

His gaze flicked back to hers. 'You want to lecture me about this barn,' she went on, 'or offer to rebuild it or something equally insane. It makes you crazy that it's just sitting here all dangerous and broken. I might walk in there one day and the whole thing could collapse on me.'

He visibly winced at that image, which Kira had to admit she found quite satisfying. A crease formed between his brows. She wouldn't be surprised if he was sweating beneath that vest.

'I'm not going to rebuild your barn.'

Kira laughed. 'Are you telling me or yourself?'

He frowned at her. Good. It was respite from that perfect smile.

'I didn't come up here because of the barn. I just needed a longer walk today.'

'Oh.' Well that was a little bit … disappointing.

Bennett ran a hand over the back of his neck and Kira noticed that he looked tired today. Stubble was visible on his square jaw and his eyes had dark smudges beneath them. Teasing him was significantly less fun if he was upset about something.

He glanced up at the sky and then back at her. He opened his mouth to speak but then closed it as though he'd thought better of it.

'I should probably go,' he said.

'Right, the storm.'

He shrugged. The unimpressed gesture of a man who'd lived through many a snowstorm and lived to tell the tale. 'Shouldn't be too bad.'

'Maybe not for you northerners,' she said with a small smile, hoping he would return it, but that frown hadn't left. He studied her a moment longer before letting out a defeated sigh.

'Did you get the fireplace working?' he asked, and why did that question make her warmer than the actual fire.

'I did. I'm a real pro at lighting it now, too.'

'Who showed you?' There was an edge to the question like he was angry that it hadn't been him.

'You'd be amazed what you can find on the internet, Bennett.'

He gave another tense nod. His energy was weird today. What was going on with him? Wasn't it just last night that he'd been all smiles with her at the skating rink? This whole conversation felt like a rejection, and she hadn't even attempted her seduction. Is this what nice guys were like? Hot and cold and generally confusing?

'I just…' He shook his head. 'Make sure you stay warm, okay? And that the flue is open,' he added like he couldn't help himself.

'Got it,' she said, stifling the urge to add that he could stay and keep her warm. This half- rejection was bad enough. She didn't need an explicit one.

'Good. And if you need anything…'

'Yeah?' Her dumb, recently enlarged heart paused, waiting to hear what he would offer.

'… Call Logan. He has a plow.'

Logan? What the hell? Her heart shriveled to its previous Grinchy size. Maybe even smaller.

'Sure. Okay. Thanks, I guess.'

'See you around, Kira.' He called to his dogs that were currently scattered through the trees, sniffing and probably peeing on her merchandise.

'Bye, Bennett,' she said, but it didn't really matter. He was already walking away.

Chapter Fourteen

He'd nearly made it back to his rental car, ready to make his escape, away from this farm and Kira and an impending snowstorm and barns that were most definitely death traps, when a familiar voice called his name.

'Ben! Hey!' Jacob from Jeanie's book club was waving to him from the dirt patch that served as a parking lot.

Bennett glanced at his watch. He'd stayed longer than he planned. It was after ten and the farm was officially open. Not that anyone else appeared to be here.

'Jacob, hey. What are you doing here?'

The younger man smiled at him like he was an idiot. 'This is a tree farm, Ben. We're here for a tree.'

Bennett was about to ask who the 'we' was, when he spotted Nancy, Linda, and Kaori climbing out of Nancy's hatchback.

'It's a book-club field trip. Or at least some of the book club,' Jacob explained. 'What are you doing here?'

'Uh…' *Using all my strength not to fall back into bad habits.* 'Just out for a walk with the dogs.' The dogs in question were happily sniffing around Jacob's feet.

'Right,' Jacob said with a wink. 'A walk … got it.' He winked again and Bennett had no idea what he was hinting at until the women came over and Linda immediately asked if he'd found anything suspicious yet.

Kaori shushed her. 'Quiet, Linda! Remember we're trying *not* to traumatize the new owner.' Kaori turned her gaze on Bennett. 'How is Miss North, by the way? We hear you've gotten to know her.' Her smile made him wonder if he could make a run for his car before they could catch him.

'She's…' *Funny, sharp, a little lonely, so beautiful it hurts…* 'She's done a lot to get the farm up and running. I think she'll be good for the uh … town.'

'Hmm, yes, good for the town.' Kaori's smile grew but there was no time for a more thorough interrogation. Another young man was striding toward them.

'Looks like they're closed,' he said, linking his hand with Jacob's.

'Ben, this is Darius, my boyfriend,' Jacob said with a huge grin, ignoring Darius's proclamation that the farm was closed.

'Nice to meet you.' Bennett shook the man's hand and Darius gave him a big smile in return before turning back to Jacob. 'There's no one in the cabin. Maybe because of the snow?'

Jacob frowned. 'But it's barely started!'

The snow had been falling in large, fat flakes since Bennett had run away from Kira, and now it was coming down faster. Already the trees had a light coating, making the farm look like it had been dusted with confectioners' sugar. It was pretty at the moment, but Bennett figured they only had another few hours before the roads were a mess.

'We'll just go by the honor system,' Nancy declared, waving her saw around.

'The honor system?' Darius asked, clearly skeptical and maybe a bit nervous about the jagged blade the older woman was brandishing.

'Sure. We'll cut down our trees and leave the money. Like we used to do. No need for all this fuss.' Nancy waved her hand at all of Kira's hard work. Her decorated cabin and strings of lights, her cute hand-painted signs and photo-op spots. It made Bennett irrationally angry to have it brushed aside like it was nothing.

'Maybe you should just come back another time,' he suggested.

'Do you know how hard it was to find a day we could all come?' Kaori asked. 'And we're still missing members.' She gave her head a determined shake. 'I'm with Nancy. It has to be today.'

'Yay!' Jacob clapped his hands. 'Let's go!'

The little group marched off toward the trees, snow already piling up on their hats and shoulders.

'Come on, Bennett!' Jacob called over his shoulder. 'We'll help you look for bodies while we're here!'

Bennett glanced toward Kira's house, down the dirt road from the parking lot. He thought about her in there, alone and cold. He thought about her rummaging around in that old barn, or stumbling over some grisly discovery, or most likely looking out her window and seeing the Dream Harbor Book Club stealing her Christmas trees, and he wanted to protect her from all of it.

He blew out a long sigh.

This test was too much and he'd definitely failed it.

'Wait up,' he called after the group and followed them back into the trees.

'I'm starting to think maybe there isn't a dead body, after all,' Jacob said, like he was horribly disappointed they hadn't found a murder victim.

'Of course there isn't,' Bennett grumbled. They'd ended up by the old barn again, mostly because Jacob thought it looked like a good place to hide things and partly because the biggest trees were up at this end of the farm, and apparently Kaori required a twelve-footer for her cathedral ceilings. Bennett was cold and tired and now carrying Pudgy who was snoring loudly in his arms.

The women had already headed back down the hill, their trees on the back of a sled. But Jacob insisted they check out the barn. So here they were, inside the building that just this morning Bennett had warned Kira to stay away from.

Trespassing.

Snooping.

'Maybe it's not a body. Maybe Noah was right. Maybe he buried some kind of treasure. Or money,' Jacob said, as he peered around an old tractor.

'And if he did, it's not ours to find. So, let's go.'

'He's right,' Darius chimed in from his spot huddled inside his coat near the door. 'We should go, babe.'

'Okay, fine,' Jacob agreed with a huff. 'I guess the old guy was just screwing with us with that letter.' He shrugged. 'Well, you're off the hook, Ben. You don't have to keep coming up here for walks,' he said, with another wink, before following Darius out of the barn.

Bennett didn't have to keep coming here. He shouldn't keep coming here. He didn't need another Nicole in his life. Not that Kira was anything like her, but the situation was too tempting for him. It was like a sugar addict getting a part-time job at a candy factory.

He glanced at the ceiling, where the beams had separated and the roof had caved in. Snowflakes swirled in through the opening. There was nothing else in here except for some old farm equipment and damp hay. Nothing of much use.

Except for maybe that…

Bennett spotted the old shovel and the bag of rock salt shoved into the corner of the barn. He doubted Kira had thought about how she would clear her path tomorrow. She wasn't used to the snow.

He could just bring these down and leave them on her porch for her.

And then he would go.

He wouldn't think about her digging herself out of her house, alone, tomorrow. Nope. He would drop these off and then go home.

It was a good plan. A compromise with himself.

He looked down at the sleeping dog in his arms and the two circling his feet.

'Hey, Jacob, wait up.' He followed the other men and found them loading their tiny tree onto the back of a sled. Perfect.

He put the salt and the shovel next to their tree, but kept Pudgy with him. She was too old to go bumping around on the back of a sled. They all slipped and slid their way back down the hill, with Jacob and Darius spontaneously breaking out into a very spirited version of 'Let it Snow' on their way down.

It reminded Bennett that this was what he'd wanted. A white Christmas. A quintessential New England December. Noah was right, the farm looked like the set of a holiday movie. But it wasn't enough. Bennett's thoughts kept returning to his other Christmas wish.

And his resolve to leave the snow supplies and run was weakening with every step.

'Can you guys drop the dogs off at Logan's for me?' he said when they got back to the cars. Logan's farm was on the way back to town or he wouldn't have asked, but he didn't know how much longer he'd be here, and he wanted the dogs taken care of.

Because, who the hell was he kidding? There was no way he was leaving until he was sure Kira was equipped for this storm.

'Sure, Ben.' Jacob smiled at him, shaking snow from his coat. 'Sticking around a little longer, huh?'

Bennett didn't reply. He was getting tired of this book club and their knowing smiles and remarks.

'Have fun, anyway!' Jacob sang.

Bennett bundled the dogs into the car and watched as they drove away. The dirt parking lot was completely covered in several inches of snow now, but the car made it out and onto the road safely.

Bennett stood there, the snow seeping through his jeans, thinking about how he should leave, about how bad of an idea it was to go check on Kira, about how he was repeating patterns that had only made him miserable in the past.

But the thing about bad habits was that they were very hard to break.

Chapter Fifteen

Kira was less than pleased that she had to untangle herself from her blanket pile to go answer the door. She was all hunkered down in front of the fire, ready to sit out the storm. She'd already called Iris and the few farm hands from Logan's and told them not to bother coming today. So who could possibly be at her door?

She pulled it open to find a scowling Bennett on her porch.

'Uh… Hi.'

'Here.' He pushed a rusty old snow shovel into her hands, like he was either mad at her or the shovel. She couldn't tell.

'Thanks? Bennett … what are you still doing here?'

His frown deepened. His cheeks were red from the cold and his pants were soaked up to the knee. What the hell had he been doing since she left him over an hour ago?

He blew out a long sigh. 'I ... well ... the book club showed up.'

'The book club?'

'Yeah.' He shook his head, sending clumps of snow tumbling off his hat. 'I just wanted to make sure you had a shovel for the morning.' He winced like this whole conversation was killing him.

'Oh.'

'And I brought some salt, too.' He glanced down at the bag by his feet and then clearly noticed the shovel and bucket of rock salt that was already next to the door. The one she'd bought yesterday on her trip to the hardware store. 'Christ. You already have one...' He huffed a brittle laugh.

'Yep. My first one. Bought it yesterday.' She gave him a smile, but he still looked like a man in pain. 'I even called Logan. He's going to clear the parking lot for me tomorrow once he digs himself out.' She probably didn't need to tell him all this and she definitely shouldn't feel as proud of herself as she was, but she *was*. She was figuring shit out and ... apparently, she wanted Bennett to know about it.

He nodded, still frowning, still not celebrating her ability to buy her own snow shovel. *Rude.* 'That's good. Uh ... I'm glad you have it under control.' He cleared his throat. 'I should go.'

Kira's heart sank. 'You can't go.'

'I really should.' He gave her a grim smile. 'You don't need me here.'

'So?'

He raised his eyebrows. 'What do you mean, "so"?'

'So, what if I don't need you. What if I just want you to stay?'

'You *want* me to stay?' Why did he sound so damn incredulous about that? Like she couldn't possibly want him to stay if she didn't have odd jobs for him to do? Did he really think she was that shitty of a person?

She was a reformed shitty person! Or trying to be, anyway.

'For safety,' she said, still wanting him to stay. Wanting to show him that she wasn't a shitty person anymore.

She gestured around them, the snow swirling past the porch. 'The storm.'

'It's not that bad.'

'Look, Buffalo Man, just because you're not scared of snow doesn't mean it's not dangerous. I can't in good conscience let you drive off in this.'

His gaze met hers and she didn't know why he was so torn about this decision, but he clearly was. This man, who had pushed his way into her house to check her heat just a handful of days ago, now couldn't seem to convince himself to cross the threshold.

Kira huffed. 'You're getting snow in my house. At least come in and have this decision-making crisis inside.'

Bennett blinked. Kira ignored the snowflakes glistening on his long eyelashes. Details like that were absolutely not helpful at the moment.

'Sorry.' He left his shovel next to hers and stepped

inside. Not that it was much warmer in the drafty entryway, but Kira had solved that problem.

'Leave your boots and coat there and follow me,' she said, leading the way to the cozy nook she'd made in her living room. She pushed back the blanket she'd hung in the doorway separating the living room and the front hall. She had another one tacked up in the door between the living room and the kitchen. They helped keep the heat from the fire in the room. It was actually quite toasty.

Bennett stepped in after her. He looked around, taking in the roaring fire and the blankets— the clear lack of smoke or freezing temps, obviously throwing him for a loop. His mouth opened and closed in an attempt to speak but nothing came out.

Kira couldn't help her smug smile.

See. She could do it. She could take care of herself.

'Okay, take your pants off,' she said, turning to him.

Bennett coughed. 'Take my … what?'

'Take. Your. Pants. Off,' she said slowly, like he just hadn't understood her and not that he was horrified at the suggestion. 'They're all wet. I'll throw them in the drier. Probably your socks, too.' She glanced down at his holly-printed socks.

When she looked up, a blush had crossed Bennett's cheeks. He blushed?! Ugh, just when she'd decided not to seduce him, he had to go and blush like that? Unfair. Absolutely underhanded move.

'I can't just … sit here without pants on.' He crossed his arms over his chest. 'I'm fine like this.'

'You're not fine. You're wet, you stubborn ass.'

A flare of excitement went off in her gut at his surprised expression. Why was it so fun to tease him?

'I'll get you something to put on,' she said, hustling out of her grown-up blanket fort and up the stairs. It was a good twenty degrees colder up here, so she didn't waste time grabbing something for Bennett to wear and heading back down again.

He still had his pants on when she reappeared. Disappointing.

'Here. To preserve your modesty.' She stuck the old bathrobe out between them, but Bennett just stared at it.

'You want me to wear that?' he said at last, taking in the very fuzzy pinkness of the whole thing.

'It's all I have that will fit you. It's this or…' she raised her eyebrows suggestively, '… or nothing.'

Bennett snatched it from her hand, his cheeks turning an even brighter red.

She laughed, tempted to stay and torment him a bit further, but she didn't want to scare him off quite yet.

'I'll go make us some coffee while you change.'

The freezing temperature of her kitchen sobered her slightly while she waited for the coffee to brew. What exactly was she doing with this man? If she was trying to be a better person, it seemed important to examine her motives. But, like, quickly, because she was freezing her ass off out here.

She reached for two mugs and poured them both fresh coffee.

'How do you take it?' she called.

'Milk and too much sugar for a grown man,' he replied and she bit down on a smile.

Damn it. At some point, she started *liking* him.

What would her old self have done in this situation? If she could figure that out, she could just do the opposite and that would probably be what a decent human being would do.

Hmm. She didn't actually know what her old self would have done in this situation, because her old self probably wouldn't have invited the nice man in in the first place.

'Do you need help out there?' His voice came through the blanket again.

'Nope, all good. Be out in a sec.'

Right. Okay. What were the facts here? She went over them as she poured milk into Bennett's mug and heaped in two teaspoons of sugar.

Facts: It was snowing out. Probably dangerously so. There were actual safety concerns here.

On the other hand, she had very inconveniently started admitting to herself that she found Bennett attractive, and she'd managed to get him out of his pants. That sounded kinda manipulative. Kinda like something her old self would have done, decided she wanted something and then just taken it.

On the other hand, she hadn't lured him in here under false pretenses or to *do* things for her.

She just liked him and didn't want him to get hurt.

Holy crap! She was doing it! She was being a good person.

Kudos to me, she thought as she carried the mugs back through the blanket door. *I'm being a better person and I get a buddy to sit out the storm with.* Karma was finally back in her corner.

She looked up, half expecting Bennett to still be stubbornly wearing his wet pants. He wasn't.

Any thoughts about being a good person, or being 'buddies' with him immediately left her brain at the sight of him sitting on her couch wearing her robe.

He looked … well, he looked absurd wrapped in pink fleece, but he also looked … ugh, he looked damn good. His hair was damp from the snow and curling slightly around his ears and his furious blush had lessened to a rosy glow. His eyes when they met hers were a stormy gray, but he was smiling again.

He'd taken off his pants and sweater and was left in a white T-shirt under her robe and whatever other undergarments he might be sporting that Kira definitely wasn't thinking about.

She thunked the mugs onto the coffee table, sloshing hot liquid over the rim.

'What'd you do with your clothes?' she asked, ready to take another little break to put them into the drier.

'I remembered where the drier was downstairs, so I just threw them in.'

'Oh. Right. Good.'

'Are you going to sit down?' he asked, that little smirk

returning. Apparently, whatever internal crisis he'd been having earlier had been resolved. But she was still hovering over the coffee table trying not to look at his legs or think about his underwear.

'Uh … yep.'

She shoved some of the blankets away from the end of the couch and curled up in the corner. She'd taken to sleeping down here in her warm nest and the blanket and pillow situation had gotten a little out of control.

'Where are the dogs?' she asked once she was settled as far away from Bennett's naked legs as she could get. It would help to have a few furry bodies between them right now.

'I sent them home with Jacob.'

'Jacob? Oh … yeah. Why exactly was the book club here?'

Bennett rolled his eyes like he was just as befuddled by the Dream Harbor Book Club as she was. She'd run into them once at the bookstore and had avoided them ever since.

'They came for Christmas trees, but you were closed so they went by the honor system.'

'Honor system?! Did they *steal* my trees?'

Bennett laughed at her outraged tone. 'No. Here you go,' he pulled a wad of cash from the pocket of the robe. 'They left money.'

'Oh, well in that case…' She smiled. 'I hope they had a lovely experience.'

'They seemed to enjoy themselves.'

'And you stayed to…?'

He smiled ruefully, shaking his head like he was disappointed in himself. 'I thought I should. Just to make sure…'

'To make sure the book-club party didn't trash the place?' she asked with a teasing smile.

He laughed. 'They seem like they can get wild.'

'I believe it.'

He held her gaze. 'And I wanted to make sure you were okay. With the storm and everything.'

'I am.'

'Clearly.'

'But I'm glad you're here anyway.'

His lips curled up, that beautiful, perfect smile directed right at her, and the room got warmer. 'Me, too.'

'So you'll stay?'

His gaze slipped and landed on her mouth for just a breath before tracking up to her eyes again. She had been right, after all. He *did* feel it too.

'Yeah, I'll stay.'

And now that they were stuck here together for as long as this storm lasted. Kira found herself hoping the weather wouldn't clear up anytime soon.

Chapter Sixteen

Kira had been inching closer to him all morning, and by afternoon she had her legs draped over his and her face pressed against his shoulder as they started their second holiday movie of the day. Apparently, Kira had not only fixed her heat problem, she'd also bought a new router and now had working Wi-Fi in her living room. She was right. She didn't need his help.

Kira wasn't using him. She wasn't Nicole.

And unlike all of the women he'd dated this year, he actually liked spending time with her. If anything, him staying here wasn't some selfless act of imagined heroism, it was *selfish*. He wanted more of Kira, and with her currently pressed against him he thought maybe he could have her. Just for a little while, he could have her.

Luckily, he was back in his own clothes. That robe hadn't provided much protection between him and Kira's warm body in his lap. Jeans were slightly safer.

Although not by much.

He was trying very hard to focus on the convoluted premise of the movie, but Kira's body was incredibly distracting. And now that he'd stopped worrying about replacing one bad habit with another, all he could think about was other ways they could be spending their time together.

Other less *nice* ways.

He shifted a little and Kira rearranged her legs. They were long and lovely, and he wanted to peel off her leggings and kiss them from ankle to…

She giggled next to him and he marveled at the soft sound, like she was showing him a completely different side of herself. 'This part is so absurd,' she said, gesturing to the laptop that was balanced precariously on a throw pillow on the coffee table. 'I mean, her best friend can't even tell that's not her! As a twin, I can tell you, it's not actually that easy to switch places with someone even if you share one hundred per cent of their DNA. And she just swapped places with a princess. There's no way.'

'I think she's a duchess.'

'Whatever.'

'So, she's just acting with herself right now?'

'Yep. By the third movie, she's playing three characters.'

'There's a third one?'

Kira laughed. 'Yep.'

Bennett groaned and she elbowed him in the side. 'Hush, or I'll throw you out in the snow.'

He chuckled and moved so that his arm was draped

around her shoulder. 'I thought you didn't even like Christmas,' he said.

She peered up at him. 'What makes you say that?'

'Well, you have zero decorations in here. You don't even have a Christmas tree and you own a Christmas-tree farm. And you cringe every time you hear a Christmas song.'

'Christmas music is objectively terrible.' She crinkled her nose at the thought, and God, she was *cute* when she wasn't trying to scare him away.

'And yet you love these objectively terrible movies.'

'Hey! This movie is a cinematic masterpiece.'

His laugh rumbled through them and Kira nuzzled in closer. Her body was so warm and *right*. He hadn't felt like this in so long, like he clicked with someone, like he could actually imagine wanting to be with them.

'Why do you love them so much?'

She sighed. 'Watching crappy Christmas movies was one of the few holiday traditions I liked. Me and Chloe, every year we watch the worst ones and eat our weight in Christmas cookies and do our best to avoid my mother's over-planned events.'

'Sounds fun.'

'It was. Except the year we tried to make it a drinking game.'

'Less fun?'

'Well, less fun because they said the word "mistletoe" so many times I almost got alcohol poisoning, and Chloe nearly ran bare-ass naked through my mother's famous Christmas Eve party, but luckily she passed out in the hallway before she made it downstairs.'

'Wow.'

'Yeah. Poor Elaine, our housekeeper, had quite a shock in the morning.'

'I bet.'

'Don't worry I gave her an extra good Christmas gift that year.'

'What did you get her?'

Kira huffed a disbelieving laugh. 'Cash.'

'Oh, right.'

'I'm guessing your Christmases were a bit different.'

'Uh … yeah. I mean there was no household staff and no big parties, and definitely no naked drinking games, but we had fun.'

'Did you wear matching pajamas and sing around the Christmas tree?'

Bennett laughed, his breath rustling Kira's hair. Her head was tucked right beneath his chin. 'Nothing quite that cute. We used to see all my cousins on Christmas Eve, and we'd do a Secret Santa gift exchange.'

'That's pretty cute.'

'Not that cute. We liked to mess with each other and tried to one-up each other on giving the worst gift.'

'Who won?'

'Probably my cousin Andrew, the year he got me a bottle of lube when I was sixteen.'

Kira burst out laughing and he couldn't help but join

her. In hindsight, it was kinda hilarious. At the time, he'd wanted to crawl under the tree and die.

'Lube?!'

'Yeah. I opened it in front of my grandma. It was mortifying.'

'Oh, God, no!'

'It got worse when she saw what it was and said "Oh good, a practical gift, you'll get a lot of use out of that."'

Kira was nearly rolling off the couch with laughter now, gasping for breath as she sat up. 'That is amazing.'

'At the time it was the worst. I didn't masturbate for like months after that. Every time I saw the lube, I thought of my grandma.'

Kira snorted. 'Why did you keep it, then?' She was laughing so hard, tears were streaming down her face and the trauma of his grandmother commenting on his lube usage was totally worth it for this moment of seeing Kira completely undone.

'I don't know! It seemed rude to throw a gift away.' He laughed, too, more than he had in a while. The kind of laughter that makes your stomach hurt and you forget why you're laughing but you can't seem to stop. It felt good. It felt like maybe he'd been missing something for a while and hadn't noticed, hadn't even realized it until right now.

Kira sighed, wiping her eyes with the back of her hand.

'Thanks,' she said, still smiling at him. 'I needed that.'

'Yeah, I think I did, too.'

She held his gaze, her hazel eyes warm in the glow of the fire. He wanted to kiss her. He wanted to pull her close to him again. He wanted her naked and panting beneath him.

He suddenly wanted a lot from Kira North.

'How about lunch?' she said.

'Uh … sure.'

'Okay, follow me. I'm sure we can find something…'

He grabbed her hand and pulled her back down to the couch. Her eyes went wide.

'Wait.' His voice was gruffer than he'd meant it to be, but he'd spent the morning with Kira curled around him, her breasts against his arm and her legs nudging his cock and he just needed to know which way this day was headed. Was there a chance this could go further?

'Okay…'

'Can I do something first?'

Kira arched an eyebrow, a small smile tugging at her lips like she knew exactly what he wanted to do. And she wanted it, too.

'What is it you want to do, Bennett?'

He brought a hand to her face, cupping her jaw, his fingers in the hair at the nape of her neck. Her eyes fluttered closed.

'There's a lot of things I want to do, but how about we start with this?' He dipped his head and kissed her, a soft touch, a gentle nudge of his mouth against hers, so light that he could feel the delicate curve of her smile.

'That's a good start,' she whispered, pressing her forehead to his for a breath. 'Let's try a few more things.' She kissed him back and he knew then that she'd been thinking about this just as much as he had. There were things she wanted to do to him, too, ways she wanted to kiss him and touch him, and it was so nice to not be in this feeling alone.

She ran her fingers through his hair as she deepened the kiss, her tongue sweet and warm against his. A soft groan rumbled in her throat and Bennett was undone. His hands were on her waist and he was pulling her on top of him before he could think better of it. He kissed her, deep and strong and urgent, now that this experiment had started, he didn't want to stop. She straddled him, those beautiful legs bracketing his, and he traced her thighs with his fingers. Kira wriggled in his lap and he thought he might die.

'Kira,' he ground out, stilling her hips with his hands.

She looked at him with a wicked grin on her beautiful mouth. 'I think I was wrong about you,' she said, rocking just slightly forward.

He groaned and dropped his head to the back of the couch. 'Oh, yeah?'

'Yeah, I thought you were too … wholesome.' She whispered the words against his exposed neck, following them with her tongue.

Bennett squeezed her ass and she yelped.

'Too wholesome because I didn't grab your ass in public?'

She laughed, breathy and low. 'No. You just seemed too nice. You're not like the guys I'm usually attracted to.'

'Because you're usually attracted to assholes?'

'Basically, yes.' She rocked again, and the friction was

too good. It had been too long. Things were about to get decidedly less wholesome if Kira kept doing that.

'But you're attracted to me?' he rasped.

'Mmm,' she purred against his neck where she was back to kissing him, her teeth scraping gently across his skin. 'Yes, definitely.'

'And … you're attracted to me?' she asked, her eyes meeting his again and it was an absurd question considering how his erection was pressed against her core, but if she needed him to say it, he sure as hell would.

'Have been since the moment I met you.'

'Liar,' she said with a breathy laugh.

'It's true. Scout's honor,' he said, with a teasing smile, dipping his head to kiss her neck, wrapping his arms around her.

'You weren't a Scout!' she said between giggles and sighs, as he sucked the delicate skin between her shoulder and her neck. Bennett didn't typically believe in things like pheromones, but he couldn't think what Kira smelled like, other than like something he *wanted*. He breathed her in.

'Okay, so maybe not since that very first moment, but every moment since.' He brought his face back to hers and found her with a charming blush on her cheeks. 'You are gorgeous. You must know that.'

She rolled her eyes like she was tired of hearing it, but a shy smile played around her lips. 'Still nice to hear every once in a while.' And the way she said it made him think she hadn't heard it nearly enough.

'Those assholes you dated must not have said it

enough.' He kissed her again, unable to stay away now that they'd started. 'You are fucking beautiful.'

'Language, Bennett! I'm shocked.'

He grinned. 'Bet I can think of plenty of other ways to shock you.'

She kissed his smile. 'I'd like that.' But even as she said it, she was pulling away, standing in between his splayed thighs. 'We have all day and night.' She tugged him up by the hand. 'Let's not rush it, okay?'

He might have been disappointed if it wasn't for the wicked look Kira gave him over her shoulder as she led the way to the kitchen. It wasn't just a look. It was a promise of all the fun to come.

Bennett had always liked snow. But this was already his favorite snowstorm ever.

Holy crap. Okay, so nice guys could kiss.

Kira welcomed the cool air of the kitchen on her overheated skin. What the hell had just happened? One minute they were watching her favorite crappy Christmas movie, and the next she was straddling Bennett and his mouth was on her neck. And it was *good*. Like really good. Like toe-curling good, and they still had all their clothes on.

And in a totally uncharacteristic move, she'd stopped him.

It had all happened so fast, she found herself wanting to make it last.

'Christ, it's freezing out here.' Bennett's voice rumbled behind her as he followed her into the kitchen.

She turned and her breath caught at the sight of him. Hair tousled from her fingers, cheeks pink, his stormy gray eyes on her. He smirked a little, like maybe he knew just how freaking hot he was, like he wasn't nearly as wholesome as Kira had imagined.

'The blanket fort isn't the perfect solution,' she said with a shrug, turning back to the cabinets, unable to face him for too long, especially not with the visible erection in his jeans. Holy shit. Her storm preparations had not prepared her for this.

'It was pretty clever, though,' he said, and she heard the scrape of a kitchen chair against the old floorboards as he sat.

She let out a self-deprecating laugh. 'Every once in a while, I have a good idea.'

'I'm sure you have a lot of good ideas.'

Kira snorted. 'You don't know me very well.'

'I think I know you well enough.' His voice coasted over her as she kept her eyes trained on the cabinet in front of her as though it was taking a long time to choose between chicken noodle or vegetable soup. 'I know you set this farm up all on your own,' he went on. 'I've seen plenty of your good ideas out there. It takes a lot of courage to start over—'

'Stop.' She spun to face him.

His eyebrows rose just a fraction.

'You don't need to make up bullshit compliments to get in my pants.' She tried to laugh but it came out strained, his kind words doing weird things to her insides. 'That's a done deal. You're in. Okay? Just don't … do that.'

'They're not bullshit compliments, Kira.'

She crossed her arms over her chest. 'I made some really dumb decisions to get here. Let's not romanticize it.'

Bennett shifted in his chair, his gaze not leaving hers. 'Let me ask you this: why haven't you asked your family for a loan? From your stories, you clearly come from money. I'm sure your parents would pay for a new boiler.'

'No way.'

'Why not?'

Kira huffed. 'You really want to know who I am, Bennett?'

He nodded.

'I am the reckless, spoiled daughter of an investment banker and his debutant wife. They were already rich because their parents were rich. I've spent most of my life assuming I could waltz through life doing whatever the hell I wanted, because I could. My father's money meant I never had to think or care about anything. I treated people like crap for years because I could.'

She stalked closer, resting her hands on the kitchen table in front of him but he didn't flinch. 'While you were out helping old ladies cross the street, I was caring exclusively about myself. Elaine, that housekeeper I told you about, was working herself to the bone just to put her daughter through college.'

'Kira—'

'No.' She shook her head. No, he wasn't going to

convince her that she hadn't been a shitty human. Elaine had been making Kira's bed in between doing her two other jobs to make sure her daughter got an education. Something that Kira had completely taken for granted. Her college years had been nothing but parties and bad decisions. She never would have graduated if her family's name wasn't on the library. It was unacceptable.

And the worst part was, Kira hadn't known any of this until Elaine had to call in sick for the first time since Kira knew her, and she only noticed then because she didn't like the way the new woman made her coffee in the morning. Crappy coffee was what made her pay attention to the fact that the woman who'd taken care of her home for most of her life was missing, was home sick. Sick because she'd worked herself too hard.

Kira still hadn't forgiven herself for that. Even after making sure that tuition and room and board were covered for Elaine's daughter, it wasn't enough. Elaine had washed her clothes, fed her, and bailed her out of plenty of sticky situations over the years.

And Kira had treated her like she was invisible.

'But you're not like that anymore.'

Kira threw up her arms. 'You've known me for two weeks!'

'And I know that you're not that person that you're describing. Not anymore. You left.'

She sighed, feeling the fight go out of her. It was one thing for Bennett to be a nice guy, but now he was just being delusional.

'I had to leave. Chloe left. I couldn't be there without her.'

Chloe had left and Kira'd become a broken half-person. A broken half-person with so little awareness of the people around her, she didn't even notice when they were working themselves to death. Moving here was a desperate attempt to find herself without her sister, to see if there was anything worth finding. And so far, she really wasn't sure there was.

'What happened to the rest of your trust fund, Kira?'

'What do you mean?'

He shrugged. 'If you're as rich as you say, there's no way you'd be this broke now. There's no way this farm cost that much.'

She tried to turn back to the soup cabinet but Bennett grabbed her wrist, holding her in place, his eyes on her. 'What'd you do with it?'

'I don't want to tell you.'

'Why not?'

She sighed. 'You're going to get the wrong idea.'

'What'd you do with it, Kira?'

She blew out a long sigh. 'I gave it away.'

He smirked. 'Gave it away to whom?'

She rolled her eyes. He was getting this all wrong. She wasn't some kind of saint. Giving her money away had just been a new way to piss off her mother. 'I gave it away to some women's and children's charities. And a few animal shelters.' She tried to wave it away like the donations hadn't enraged her mother. *How will this look to our friends?!* her mother had asked, and by *friends* she'd meant the conservative folks from the country club who would not approve of funds going to single mothers and women's healthcare. They didn't care much about stray animals, either. Kira couldn't help but smile grimly at the memory.

'See,' Bennett said, smug as hell. 'You have plenty of good ideas.'

His fingers were still curled around her wrist, his thumb tracing distracting circles over her pulse.

'Maybe. Sometimes,' she conceded. 'But it was the least I could do…'

'Other people would have done less.'

Kira frowned. It still didn't feel like enough, but Bennett's warm gaze was making her feel like maybe she was on the right track. Like maybe she didn't have to punish herself forever.

'Okay. But let's not pretend buying a farm, sight-unseen, and thinking I could somehow figure out homesteading overnight was a good idea,' she said, tired of unearthing her past.

He laughed. 'Okay, so maybe that wasn't your *best* one. But you're here now. Making it work.'

She swallowed the lump of emotion in her throat. Why was she getting choked up about this?

'Yes, well. Can't go back now.'

'Brave.'

She gave a slight shake of her head and Bennett's fingers tightened on her wrist. He stood and pulled her closer.

'Brave, clever girl,' he said, brushing a kiss on her forehead.

Never in her life had she been called either of those words. Wild, stubborn, reckless, yes. But never brave. Never clever.

Bennett's fingers left her wrist. 'So, soup?' he asked, moving past her, leaving her reeling from his assessment of her.

Apparently, kissing wasn't the only thing nice guys were good at.

Chapter Seventeen

The wind rattled the old windows, and from her spot on the couch the view of the outside world was a blur of white and gray. This wasn't pretty Christmas card snow anymore. The storm lashed icy shards at the windows and the wind shook the trees behind the old farmhouse. This was shut-the-roads-down-stay-indoors-and-pray-the-power-stayed-on snow.

Inside, the fire crackled cheerfully in the fireplace and Kira was thankful for the delivery of firewood she'd ordered back in the fall. And that she wasn't alone.

Bennett's phone buzzed on the coffee table, rattling their empty soup bowls.

He'd gone to the bathroom and his phone had buzzed at least five times in the two minutes he'd been gone. Maybe she should check it. Maybe it was an emergency. Maybe her foot might accidentally nudge it off the coffee table and she might have to pick it up…

Just as her toe brushed the edge of his phone, Bennett came in through the blankets. She pulled her foot back and tucked it underneath her. *Bad foot.*

'I really hope you sell a lot of trees. It is not pleasant using the bathroom right now.'

Kira laughed. 'Yeah, I know, right?'

Bennett sat down next to her, but he didn't reach for his phone.

Curiosity was killing her. 'Uh … your phone was buzzing a lot while you were gone.'

'Really? I let Jeanie know where I was and I canceled all my meetings for the day…' his voice trailed off as he looked at his phone. Clearly, the messages were not from his sister or his job. He frowned at the screen and then put the phone back on the table facedown without answering whoever it was.

'You can answer if you need to,' she said, dying to ask more. 'I mean, I don't mind if you need to be on your phone.'

'I don't need to answer.' His tone left no room for questions.

'Oh.'

'Wind's getting bad,' he said, gazing out the window.

'That wasn't your wife or anything, right?' Kira said with a laugh, thinking maybe teasing him would get him to let her in on who was texting him. 'I mean, nice guys don't make out with people when they have wives back in California, right?'

Right?

Her laughter petered off when she saw the stricken look on his face.

'Bennett, please tell me you're not married.' As much as she'd looked for trouble in the past, she'd never fooled around with a married man. It was a line she refused to cross. Pretty much the only line.

And now here she was, making out with a man she thought was a nice guy who was very clearly hiding something, and she was right back where she started. But this was worse. At least the guys she'd been with in the past never kept it a secret that they were assholes. They never pretended to be sweet or helpful. They never plied her with kind words and lulled her into a false sense of security.

Oh, no, the guys she'd slept with in the past had never hidden the fact that they had no intention of staying, no intention of being reliable or trustworthy or really anything other than a quick fling, designed primarily to piss her mother off. And they'd been good at it. And that had been their entire appeal.

But here was Bennett acting all … all … sweet. And good. And *nice* to her. And she'd let him in, she'd started liking him. For once in her life, she'd chosen a man's company because she actually liked him as a person and not as a means to an end. Only to have it end like this? With Bennett hiding something huge from her?

She should have known. There was no such thing as a good guy. But she'd actually thought Bennett was different.

'I'm not married.'

'Oh.' She blew out a sigh, the rage seeping from her

body, before another thought crossed her mind. 'Engaged? Got a girlfriend back home? I may have been a shitty person in the past, but that is not something I would ever…'

He grabbed her wrists, his fingers on her racing pulse again. She shouldn't care this much about him but she did.

'Not engaged. No girlfriend.'

'Oh. Okay. So…' Her gaze drifted back to the discarded phone and Bennett dropped her wrists with a sigh.

'You're not the only one that makes bad decisions sometimes.'

'So, it's a bad decision calling you?' she asked.

Bennett's mouth tipped up in the corner. 'Yeah, exactly.'

'And does this bad decision have a name?'

'Nicole.'

'Hmm. Nicole.'

He nodded, looking more pained than she'd seen him since the 'oh, you already have a shovel' incident.

'And Nicole isn't a girlfriend or a fiancée or a wife?'

He shook his head. 'Not anymore. Not for a long time, actually.'

Kira leaned back in the pillows, waiting for him to go on. She'd told him all the ugly bits about herself, she deserved a story or two about Bennett's messy love life. She raised an expectant eyebrow. A part of her recognized her gesture as something her mother used to do when she was waiting for an explanation about Kira's latest exploits, but she wasn't going to think about that right now. Besides, the eyebrow always worked.

He sighed again. 'It's kind of embarrassing, actually.'

'Embarrassing?' She asked, even more intrigued than before. She'd love to hear something embarrassing about this almost-too-perfect man. And she'd love to hear an explanation for why this woman was blowing up his phone. 'So, you didn't break poor Nicole's heart? She broke yours?'

Bennett glanced back at the windows. 'Maybe the storm's not that bad. I could probably make it home.'

Kira smacked his arm. 'You're not going anywhere. Now spill it.'

He huffed an embarrassed laugh. 'Tale as old as time really. I was into her way more than she was into me. I followed her across the country. And then she ditched me.'

'When?'

Bennett winced. 'Five years ago.'

'Five years ago?! Why didn't you go back home?'

'No one knew I went to California for a girl. They thought I went for a job. I couldn't just come back.'

Kira frowned. 'I've met your sister. She loves having you here. I'm pretty sure you could have gone home. Or come here.'

'Probably.' Bennett let his head lean back on the couch cushions and Kira watched his throat muscles as he swallowed. 'But at the time, it felt like I couldn't.'

'That doesn't explain why Nicole-of-five-years-ago is texting you now.'

He closed his eyes. 'Well, it gets worse.'

'Uh-oh.'

'Every year or so, we kind of end up back together

again. But not really together.' He pinched the bridge of his nose. 'She usually just needs something from me.'

'Oh, Bennett.'

No wonder he was acting so weird this morning. His ex was trying to slide back into his life, and he was trying to fight every Mr. Fix-It instinct in his body. He had a history of being taken advantage of. Did he worry she would do the same thing? The last thing she wanted to do was hurt him, but she didn't have a lot of practice being *nice*.

'I know. I'm a complete sucker. Nicole calls and I come running. Every damn time.'

'If you were in California right now…'

He swallowed, his Adam's apple bobbing in his throat. 'She doesn't like to be alone for the holidays.'

'And what do you get out of all this?' Kira huffed, irrationally angry at a woman she never met. How dare she drag this sweet man along all these years? Even someone with a damaged moral compass like herself could see that Bennett didn't deserve that.

He lifted a shoulder in a defeated, half-shrug. 'I usually get a few weeks of sex, a date to my office holiday party, and a New Year's resolution not to let it happen again once she runs off. I told you, it's embarrassing.'

'Do you love her?' The question slipped out. She shouldn't care if he loved her. As long as he and this Nicole person weren't together at the moment, she could sleep with him guilt-free. Why should she care what he did when he got back to California?

Despite all that, she waited with her breath stuck in her throat.

His eyes stayed shut, his head tipped back, and she thought he wouldn't answer. Or worse, maybe he would confess to being in love with Nicole, and then what? They play Parcheesi the rest of the afternoon and sleep on separate ends of the couch? Not nearly as fun as the day she'd envisioned.

But then he sat up and faced her, his gray eyes clear and honest.

'No, I don't love her.'

Breath rushed back into her lungs. Relief. 'Oh.'

'I don't think I have for a long time.'

'Well, then maybe it's good you're here. To … you know … break the pattern.'

His gaze held hers. 'It's definitely good that I'm here.' He reached for his phone and turned it off, the cocky little smile returning to his lips. 'There's nowhere else I'd rather be.'

Kira's smile was involuntary, immediate, and wide.

Bennett returned it and that was the last thing she saw clearly before the power went out.

'Shit.' Kira's voice was breathy, a hint of fear in it.

'I'm guessing you don't have a backup generator.'

He could see her scowling at him even in the dim lighting. It was late afternoon and between the storm and the early sunset, the room was nearly completely dark now that the lights had gone out.

'Of course not, I don't have a backup anything. I barely have an upfront anything.'

He huffed a laugh. 'It'll be fine. We have the fire. And all these blankets.' He fluffed the pile of blankets between them. Kira looked at him, a highly skeptical look on her face.

'We'll starve.'

'Kira, you have a gas stove.'

'So…'

'So, it will still work. And I don't think you can starve in a twenty-four-hour period.'

'Maybe *you* can't.'

He laughed again. 'How about a flashlight? Or candles.'

She perked up at that, her eyes big in the semi-darkness. 'I have candles! Upstairs.' She grabbed his hand and pulled him up from the couch. 'Come with me, it's scary up there in the dark.'

He followed her out of the cozy warmth of the living room and up the stairs to the second floor. The stairs groaned with every step. Kira still held tight to his hand as she led the way. He hated to think that if he hadn't come back, she'd have been here by herself, scared. She'd obviously have been fine, but he hated it, anyway.

She led him down the hall to the last bedroom.

'They should be in here somewhere.'

It was the only bedroom with furniture. A bed in the

center, a dresser, two bedside tables. But the room didn't feel lived-in.

'You don't have sheets on the bed,' he observed as Kira rummaged through a dresser drawer for candles.

'I don't sleep in here. Too cold.'

'Where do you sleep then?'

'Living room. On the couch.'

'The couch?' He was trying very hard to swallow his thoughts on Kira sleeping on the couch, but it had been a long day. A day filled with unplanned confessions and rapidly shifting barometric pressure. And Bennett was tired of suppressing his natural instincts.

He liked Kira. A lot. Too much probably. But he did.

And he showed people he cared about them by taking care of them. It was just who he was, damn it. And just because Nicole had abused that side of him, didn't mean he needed to get rid of it completely.

And just…

Sleeping on the couch?

Because she was cold?

In this fucking drafty old house by herself?

He couldn't *stand* it.

'I'm bringing this mattress downstairs.'

Kira turned from the dresser, her arms filled with candles in varying sizes and shapes. Her brows rose until they vanished beneath her bangs.

'Excuse me, you're doing what?'

'Don't argue with me about this, Kira. I'm bringing the mattress downstairs. You can set it up on the floor in the living room. It will be more comfortable.' He was already tugging the mattress off the box spring.

'Bennett…'

'I said don't argue.'

'Ha! Okay, you said it so obviously, I will just agree with you.'

He sighed, lowering the corner of the mattress. 'Please.' His voice was rough and raw, and this mattress meant way more than it should right now, but it did. He'd just realized that he didn't *want* Nicole anymore. He didn't *love* her anymore. And all he wanted was the woman in front of him and he didn't know what to do about that.

All he knew was he needed this mattress downstairs.

He needed Kira warm.

He probably needed therapy, but that was an issue for another day.

'Please?'

'Please, let me do this for you.'

Kira stood in front of him, her mouth slightly open, like for once she didn't know what to say. So he lifted the mattress again, tipping it to its side so he could shove it through the bedroom door. He pushed it out, angling it to get it down the hall.

Kira followed behind him, still in silent shock.

The stairs were a bit trickier, but he was a man on a mission now and he managed it, not entirely gracefully, but he managed it. Kira didn't speak again until the coffee table was pushed aside and the mattress was laid out on the living room floor, right in front of the fireplace. The warmest spot in the whole damn house.

'Show-off,' Kira muttered as she arranged the candles on the mantle and the side table next to the couch.

And he couldn't help his smile.

He grabbed the pack of matches by the fireplace and started lighting the candles.

'This candle smells like *Meet Cute*? What does that even mean?' Lilac, champagne, and citrus, apparently.

'Chloe got me that set.'

'Morally Grey, Enemies to Lovers, Grumpy-slash-Sunshine,' he read off the other candle labels. 'Slow Burn, at least that one makes sense for a candle.' He set the last candle down and found Kira laughing at him.

'Here this one suits you best,' she said, handing him a candle with Cinnamon Roll written on the side.

He sniffed it. 'Smells good. Still don't get what any of that means, though.'

'Doesn't matter.' Kira shook her head, her laughter petering out. 'But you should probably pay more attention when your sister talks about books.'

'Books?! I thought we were talking about baked goods.'

She patted his arm as she made her way around the mattress that was now taking up most of the room. 'Nope. Romance tropes.'

'Romance, huh? So is a cinnamon roll … like a sex thing? Is there frosting involved?' He waggled his eyebrows and Kira laughed harder.

'Sounds sticky,' she said, wrinkling her nose as though

she didn't like the idea, but Bennett's mind was already happily imagining a naked Kira with vanilla icing drizzled over her body and his tongue tracing the pattern…

'Help me with this.' Her distressed plea broke through his inappropriate but delicious daydream.

At that moment, a fully dressed Kira was struggling to put a fitted sheet on the mattress. Every time she pulled one corner down the other popped up.

'Would it kill the fitted sheet makers of the world to make them a tiny bit bigger?' Kira groaned in frustration. 'It's times like this that I miss Elaine. That woman was a treasure.'

Bennett laughed and grabbed one corner while she took the other, and together they managed to tug it over the mattress. Once the sheet was on, Kira collapsed, arms and legs out like a starfish in the middle of the bed. The firelight gilded the side of her face, dancing gold over her dark hair.

She grinned up at him. 'Well, I don't know where you're sleeping tonight. I take up a lot of space.'

'I'll take the couch.' His response was so fast that Kira's eyebrows rose in surprise. A frown crossed her beautiful face.

'I was kidding.'

'Kira, I don't want you to think—'

Kira cut him off before he could cock-block himself any further. The last thing he wanted to do was sleep on the damn couch.

'Let's agree that overthinking anything that happens during this storm is a bad idea, okay? Let's just…' She bit her bottom lip, her gaze meeting his again. 'Let's just live in the moment.'

'Live in the moment, huh?'

'Yeah. Let's pretend there's nothing outside these walls. Nothing after tonight. We don't have to worry about the consequences. This storm, this day … it's a free pass.'

A free pass? God, what a tempting thought.

A purely selfish moment. He'd wanted Kira North since he first saw her on the farm wrapped in her duvet, and now he could have her. For today, for this storm, for this moment. And he didn't have to wonder what would happen after, or who would have to uproot their life for whom, or when she would get bored of him and leave. There would be none of that.

Only today.

Kira stared up at him from the mattress. He was still kneeling beside it after helping her with the sheet. He could tumble into bed with her and stay there for the rest of the night. He could have his perfect Christmas gift.

He didn't know what it was about this girl that had him so into her after knowing her for a short time. But no, that wasn't true, was it?

He knew exactly what it was. It was the way she sparred with him, teased him, and didn't back down. It was the way she'd decided to change her life and then actually *did* it. It was the way she smiled at him like that, like he'd earned it.

'So … what do you say?' she asked, hesitation seeping into her question.

He leaned forward, bracketing her body with his arms, his legs straddling hers. 'I say, I told you so.'

'About what?'

He let his mouth tip into a smile. 'About you being full of good ideas.'

Kira's smile grew then, the uncertainty leaving her face. 'Yeah?'

He dipped his head, letting his chest brush against hers and he felt her breath catch. He kissed the corner of her mouth.

'Definitely.'

Kira blew out a dramatic sigh. 'Oh, good. I was worried you were going to go all nice-guy on me and refuse to take advantage of me or something.'

Bennett huffed a laugh, as he nuzzled behind Kira's ear, placing another kiss on the soft skin he found there.

'Do you *want* me to act like a nice guy?' he asked, lowering his hips and pressing lightly into hers. She squirmed a little beneath him.

'No.'

'No?' he asked, teasing, brushing against her center again.

'No, I don't want you to be a nice guy right now, Bennett.'

He smiled against her throat. 'Good.'

Chapter Eighteen

Bennett's chuckle rumbled through her body, the vibration echoing in her toes. Her legs were wrapped around his middle and his mouth was on her neck and all she could think was, *thank God* because she really needed this.

She needed out of her head and out of this new life just for a freaking second. She needed a break, a day off from everything. She needed to just … *be*. And at the moment, the best place to *just be* was underneath Bennett's body. How had she not noticed how broad he was? How solid?

She was still reeling from him single-handedly wrestling her pillow top mattress down the stairs like it was his life's mission and now the feel of him between her thighs, strong and sure, it seemed insane that she had ever underestimated Bennett Ellis.

'Does anyone ever call you Ben?' she asked, raking her fingers through his hair.

He raised his head, a half-smile on his lips. 'Some people.'

'Can I call you Ben?'

His smile grew. 'Only if I get to call you a nickname.' His answer was suspiciously fast, as though he'd already given this some thought. Had Bennett been thinking about her that much? As much as she'd been thinking about him? She liked that idea probably more than she should.

'I don't have any nicknames.' She let her fingers trail across his shoulders and he shivered a little against her.

'No nicknames, huh?'

'Well, Chloe calls me Kiki, but that's off-limits.'

He dipped his head again, kissing along her throat. She arched into him and he groaned, the sound rumbling through her.

'Peaches,' he murmured against her skin.

'No way.'

He was grinning when he lifted his head again. 'My little Georgia peach.'

'Absolutely not.' She hadn't even told him about her traumatic pageant past and still he'd landed on that nickname. *Wonderful.*

'It's perfect.' He ran his nose along her skin. 'You're sweet and soft just like a peach.'

'And fuzzy and I bruise easily?'

He laughed and she was starting to like that sound a little too much, like she might want to hear it past today. Like she might want it in her life permanently.

'Okay, point taken. I'll work on it,' he said, his smile

softening. The glow of the fire and the candlelight flickering across the ceiling cast him in yellows and golds. His hair was disheveled, undone. His body was still wrapped around hers, warm and safe. She didn't say it out loud but at this moment she felt like she would let Bennett call her pretty much anything.

She might even let him call her *his*. For today. For tonight. For as long as the storm lasted. Because that was what they agreed on. That was the only way this made sense. He lived in California and now, for better or worse, she lived here.

'Kiss me,' she said, the safest thing she could say. Bennett's lips met hers without hesitation, without a second thought. She asked and he answered. She opened and he met her tongue with his. And then she was drowning in it, in this kiss, in Bennett. His breath was hers, his heartbeat matched her own, his body heat was seeping into her chilled bones. Had she ever been warm enough before this moment?

It was a kiss unlike any other. A kiss that left her melted into the mattress, a vaguely Kira-shaped puddle. She gasped, coming up for air and Bennett sucked and nipped at her neck as she breathed in and breathed out and clawed at his back and pulled him closer and arched against him and wanted more and more and more.

'I want you naked,' he rasped between kisses. 'I can't stop thinking about it. About you.' He was just as frantic as she was, his mouth hot and insistent on hers, his hips moving against her like he couldn't help himself.

'Okay, yes,' Kira panted, pushing against his chest. 'I want that, too.'

He lifted off of her but then dipped again, kissing and nipping at her lips like he couldn't stop. Kira felt the same way. She was dizzy with it, with this fire between them.

Finally tearing himself away, Bennett sat back on his heels. His breath was coming nearly as fast as hers, his cheeks flushed red. His hair stood up where Kira had been tugging on it. He looked wild. Nothing like the mild-mannered Clark Kent she'd met in her fields a couple of weeks ago. He looked debauched. And like he had a list of ways to do the same to her running through his mind.

'You can't stop thinking about me naked?' she asked, sitting up to face him. She still couldn't resist an opportunity to tease him. Just a little.

That new cocky smirk tipped the corner of his mouth. It was so different from the perfect toothed smile he'd given her at first. This one was secret. *Bedroom Bennett.* She liked it.

'It's becoming a problem, actually.'

'Oh, yeah?'

'Distracting.'

'Poor Bennett.'

'Take your clothes off, Peaches,' he practically growled the command. Maybe she didn't hate that name as much as she first thought. 'Unless you want me to do it. You know how I love to help.' The smile was downright wicked now. And Kira was starting to think that Nicole must have some sort of head injury because why on earth would you let go of a man who was so damn sweet out of bed and so damn hot in bed? Why would you walk away from that?

Well, it was her loss.

Kira smiled. 'And you know I have to insist on doing things myself.' She tugged the sweater over her head and tossed it aside. Unfortunately, she'd been freezing when she got dressed today so she had to pull off two more layers before she was finally in just her bra. The slight delay did nothing to put out the fire in Bennett's gaze though.

'Goddamn, Kira,' he cursed and she liked that too. 'Keep going.' His voice was a husky rasp, and the sound of it licked across her bare skin.

'I can't reach the clasp.'

His gaze darkened.

'Will you do it?' she asked.

His hand was on her hip, tugging her closer before the question was even out of her mouth. 'At your service,' he whispered, his breath skating across her cheek as he leaned in, his hands reaching behind her back. Her eyes fluttered closed as each hook came free. Slowly, too slowly, his fingers trailed up to one strap, siding it down her shoulder. He took the other strap down too, letting the bra fall between them. And then he stopped.

Kira whimpered but he still didn't touch her. They stayed locked like that, kneeling in front of each other, his lips brushing across her cheek. Kira thought she would combust. She breathed deep and her nipples brushed against the front of his shirt.

'Bennett,' she groaned.

'Yes?'

'Touch me.'

And like her words were magic, his hands were on her, tracing the lines of her curves. He cupped her breast, letting his thumb run lightly back and forth over her nipple. Kira ignited.

His forehead dropped to hers and her eyes closed. His touch was firm, confident like he knew exactly what he wanted to do to her, like he'd imagined it before. Heat pooled between Kira's thighs. God, they'd barely done anything yet, but Bennett's hand on her breast, his other clamped tight to her hip, holding her in place was already making her crazy for him. For more.

'Take off the rest,' he rumbled. 'I want to see all of you.'

He pulled away, his gaze dark and hungry on her body. There didn't seem to be a point to playing coy now; she wanted him just as badly as he wanted her. She slipped off her fleece-lined leggings and panties in one move. By the time she had her cozy socks off and was back to kneeling naked in front of Bennett, he was looking at her like a man destroyed, like she'd just ruined his entire life by taking her clothes off.

'Kira,' he said, squeezing his eyes shut and giving a quick shake of his head. When he reopened his eyes, they held her gaze. 'I've never seen anything so beautiful in my life as you right now. You're … you're unreal.'

Kira swallowed the emotion rising hot and fast in her throat. She'd had men tell her she was sexy before or hot or even beautiful, but never like that. Never like Bennett. She tried a smile but her lips felt wobbly, her whole body felt wobbly, off kilter because of this sweet man's words.

'I'm real.'

She grabbed his big hand and put it back on her hip. His fingers flexed, digging into her flesh.

'See,' she whispered.

'Yeah, I see.' He tugged her close, his hand moving to grab her ass, the other buried in her hair. 'You're real and so gorgeous.' He tipped her head and she could see the storm building in his eyes. A whimper escaped her lips and he smirked.

'I'm going to spend the rest of the day taking care of you.'

And for once, Kira didn't argue.

How was the real Kira even better than the one he'd made up in his head? Bennett wasn't sure, but, holy shit, she was. All long limbs and glowing skin, he wanted to lick every damn inch of her. Maybe it was because he'd only ever seen her in layers of sweaters or bulky parkas or queen-size comforters, but the sight of her completely bare in front of him felt like a gift, a miracle. Like something he didn't deserve and had no right to ask for but was so damn happy to receive.

'Now you.' Kira tugged at the bottom of his Henley. 'I want to ogle you, too.'

He chuckled as he pulled the shirt over his head, loving

that she hadn't suddenly changed her personality just because they were about to have sex. He had a feeling that Kira would be Kira no matter where she landed or who she was with.

And that was refreshing as hell.

Kira ran her hands over his chest, a little purr of appreciation humming through her.

'No wonder you're never cold,' she said, her fingers trailing across his chest hair. 'You have fur,' she said, with a teasing smile, and it didn't feel anything like the summer Nicole convinced him to wax his chest and he'd nearly lost a nipple in the process. He wasn't that hairy of a guy but he'd been self-conscious about it ever since. Not enough to let any woman come at him with hot wax again, but still.

It helped that she had leaned in again and ran her tongue along the edge of his ear after she said it.

'You're really hot,' she whispered. 'For a tech guy with a fixer complex.'

He ran his hand down her back, letting his palm coast over the perfect curve of her ass. He thought about giving it a little smack, but he squeezed it instead and pulled her closer. 'And you're really hot for a spoiled little rich girl with a heart of gold.'

Her laugh vibrated through him and he nearly joined in, but Kira's fingers at his waistband stopped the laughter in his throat.

'Now these,' she murmured, her fingers following the trail of dark hair below his belt. His entire body shivered and she grinned. 'Take your pants off for real this time.'

He didn't hesitate. His hands replaced hers at his waistband and he quickly ditched the jeans he'd thrown in her drier just that morning. This morning already seemed like forever ago, this morning when he thought it would be best to stay away from Kira.

Ha! Now he was on his way to being as close to Kira as humanly possible and it felt exactly *right*. Maybe it was because there was no future here, no worries about what would happen next, or maybe it was because Kira was the most genuine person he'd met in a long time, but this moment felt like exactly where he was supposed to be.

And he was pretty sure that wasn't just his cock talking.

Although it was currently straining against the front of his boxers like it couldn't wait another damn minute.

Kira felt him through his boxers, her hand wrapping around him and he trembled again.

'You are just one pleasant surprise after another,' she said, that flirty smile on her face again. She stroked him, the fabric bunching beneath her fist, and pleasure shot through him, hot and urgent and aching. Bennett's legs shook with the effort not to pounce and pin her to the mattress.

She grinned, like she knew exactly what he was thinking.

'Don't be nice,' she whispered and Bennett's restraint snapped.

She was under him, her hands pinned above her head before his brain could register what he was doing. She let out a breathy gasp, her cheeks pink and eyes wide.

'You like that?' he asked, his grip tightening on her

wrists just slightly, just to see how into this she was. She whimpered, her breath short and fast. She was into it, but he needed to hear it. He needed her to tell him.

They barely knew each other.

He needed her permission to let loose. To be free with her.

'Yes.' She raised her head, capturing his mouth with hers. She bit his bottom lip and he growled, pinning her hips with his. 'Yes, I like that. Don't be gentle with me, Bennett. Don't treat me like I'll break.'

He held her gaze, feeling the fluttery pulse in her wrist against his palm. 'Say stop and I will'

'Okay.'

'I mean it. At any time.'

'I know you will.'

Her trust in him nearly did him in. He hadn't felt that in a long time. Sex had been purely transactional lately, both parties were just there to get off. But this felt different. Even if it was just for today, it felt like they fit. His hands on Kira's body just made sense in a way nothing had in a long time.

And now that he had her here, he wanted every inch of her.

He released her wrists, noticing the slight flicker of surprise in her eyes when he did, like she thought he would just pound into her without taking the time to experience every last thing about her. Like the way her back arched when he flicked his tongue over her nipple, one sweet peak and then the other. Or the way she moaned when he sucked it into his mouth. Like he would have missed out on the feel of her thighs beneath his fingers, or the hitch in her breath when he demanded she open her legs for him.

Like Bennett would have ever skipped tasting Kira, licking her until she was his new favorite flavor? *Never.*

There was no way in hell he was going to miss Kira moaning his name, her fingers clawing at his shoulders as he kissed her center, his tongue swirling around that sweet bundle of nerves that made her ankles dig into his back.

'Ben … damn it … you're good at that, too.'

He paused, looking up at her from his position between her thighs. 'Does that bother you?' he asked with a grin. Kira looked back at him over the long, golden expanse of her naked body.

She huffed. 'A little,' she pushed his head back down, 'but keep going.'

He chuckled against her, the vibration causing another gasp from Kira. He licked and sucked, letting Kira's words guide him.

'Like that,' she breathed. 'Like … oh … like that but a little to the left … holy … shit … yes, right there.' Her fingers dug into his scalp. 'Don't move,' she breathed out the words, demanded he stay, begged him to stay right there. And he did. He stayed and licked and sucked and his fingers dug into the soft flesh of her ass, and he thrust his hips mindlessly into the mattress because he couldn't help himself, because the higher Kira climbed the more turned on he got, and when she broke, trembling and babbling about how good he was, how sweet and hot and *good*, he nearly came all over the newly made bed.

'Who are you?' Kira was asking when he pulled away, resting his head on her still-shaking thigh. 'I mean, really, where the hell did you come from?'

He couldn't help his satisfied grin as he ran his hand idly up and down Kira's side. Goosebumps pebbled her smooth skin.

'Are you cold?' he asked, already sitting, already grabbing a blanket from the couch.

'Maybe, a little.' Kira shrugged but he tugged the blanket harder from the bottom of the pile. It came loose and brought with it a small pink oval-shaped thing that landed on the mattress between them.

'What's this?' he asked, but Kira was swatting his hand away and grabbing the little pink object.

'Nothing.'

'Nothing?' he asked, raising an eyebrow like she had earlier to get him to spill his guts.

'I'm not sure how you'll feel about it, and I don't want to ruin the moment,' she said, holding her hands behind her back. The fact that she was still naked, and the position did very fantastic things to her breasts, only convinced him further that nothing she said next could possibly ruin the moment.

'Try me.'

She held out her palm, the vaguely tear-shaped pink thing sitting on her hand. She pressed the side and it started to buzz.

'It's my vibrator.'

Bennett's eyebrows rose. 'You keep your vibrator in the living room?'

'The living room is currently my bedroom so … yeah. And I didn't realize it was lost somewhere in the couch. But I can just put it away…'

He grabbed her wrist before she could run off with the vibrator.

'Don't.'

'Don't?'

'Don't.' He let the cocky grin return to his face. 'I want to see you use it.'

The color rose in Kira's cheeks as she processed his request. 'You want to see me … use it?'

He nodded, the idea alone making him harder than he'd been in months. 'I want to see you use this cute little pink device to get off.'

Kira swallowed, her gaze wide and dark on his face.

She didn't bother answering, just laid back into the blankets he'd pulled onto the mattress and spread her legs. Holy shit.

Best. Snowstorm. Ever.

She brought the vibrator to her center and the image of a naked Kira in front of the fireplace pleasuring herself was sure to haunt him for the rest of his life.

Bennett was watching her like she was the sexiest thing he'd ever seen. Which was nice since he was currently the sexiest thing she had ever seen. He was kneeling on the mattress again, towering above her, his dark gaze never leaving her, but flicking from her face to her body to the device buzzing happily between her legs. The feel of it, of his appreciative stare, sent shivers down her body.

He'd shucked the boxers at some point and gave himself a few rough strokes as he watched her. His thick thighs trembled each time he did it and Kira licked her lips at the sight.

'You are killing me,' Ben groaned.

Kira smiled, moving the vibrator back and forth. She gasped, arching her back a little, suddenly wanting Bennett's hands on her again. 'You asked for it.'

He chuckled, low and deep, scratching a hand through the dark hair on his chest. 'True. I did.' He thrust into his hand again and Kira whimpered. She was close, but she wanted more.

'You didn't happen to bring a condom, did you?'

The cocky smirk returned. 'I did.'

Kira couldn't help her laugh, dropping her hand and her little buzzy friend to the side. 'You came to my Christmas-tree farm with a condom in your pocket?'

'Two. In my wallet.'

'You cocky bastard.'

He let go of his erection to lean over her again, caging her in. 'I tried to pretend I was going to stay away from you.' His lips brushed over hers. 'But I can't.' His nose ran along hers. 'Don't want to. I *like* you, Peaches.'

Kira swallowed.

'Get the condom,' she said, her voice somewhere between breathy and bossy. Bennett's grin grew.

She only had about thirty seconds to think while he was up and fishing through the wallet he'd left on the coffee table while his jeans were in the drier. Only a mere thirty seconds to consider that she liked this man more than any other, maybe ever, and that he liked her and that this sex so far was off the charts and that inevitably it would suck when he left. Which he was going to do. And then she would be alone again, but somehow even more alone because she'd have the memory of this day to look back on and miss.

But then he was back, and he was big and warm and safe and it was hard to remember that he would leave and she would be sad. It was hard to remember that this whole thing was just for today.

It was hard to remember anything but Bennett.

'Spread your legs for me,' he rasped, and she did it, loving that he was taking charge again, that his big hands were digging into her hips, and that he had listened to her. He wasn't treating her like she would break. He made her feel strong.

Instead, he pushed into her, both of them groaning when he did.

'Goddamn, Kira,' he growled. 'You feel so damn good.' He thrust into her again and again, and the heat from the fire and Bennett's body coursed through her.

'So do you,' she purred. 'So good.'

He paused, kissing her neck, his body pinning her to the mattress. 'Where is it?' he asked.

'Where is what?' What was he looking for? She already knew he didn't need directions to the exact spot she needed him—

His hand fumbled around in the blankets next to them. 'Here!' He held up the forgotten vibrator in triumph. He put it in her hand. 'Use it.'

He pushed away from her, angling her hips up with him. Shallow thrusts that she felt down to her toes.

'Holy shit.'

He grinned. 'I know. Now use it.'

She pressed the vibrator until it turned on and then held it to her clit while Ben kept thrusting and … she wasn't a religious woman but was anyone else hearing a choir of angels singing?

'Oh, God,' she gasped, gripping tight to Ben's forearm. 'Oh. My. God.'

'Yeah?'

'Holy shit, yeah. Don't stop.'

'I wouldn't dream of it.'

He kept going, his hips thrusting into hers, his fingers digging into her and the fact that he wasn't at all intimated by the buzzy little robot in her hand just made the whole thing hotter. As it turned out, she had found some kind of magical sex unicorn in her fields.

Pleasure shot through her, a hot flash, so intense it almost felt like pain.

'That's right, just like that. Let it all go.' Bennett's words rained down on her overheated skin and she broke.

Sobbing and babbling, her orgasm tore through her like Bennett had performed some sort of sex exorcism, wringing every last bit of worry and stress from her body and replacing it with pleasure. She dropped the vibrator when she couldn't take any more.

Bennett lowered her legs, leaning over her again, dropping kisses along her sweaty brow.

'You okay, Peaches?'

She could barely nod, barely whimper, 'Yes.' Because that damn nickname was too sweet and she liked it far too much. This all was too much. She couldn't. She shouldn't. But he was there. Still there, kissing her and shushing her and telling her she was beautiful and perfect and it was all *too* good.

She didn't deserve it. Any of it. But she *wanted* it.

Bennett was still moving inside her, gently, slowly as he kissed her.

Kira ran her hands down his back and he shivered. 'I need you,' he whispered, his voice rough. 'Just a little more. I need you, Kira.'

She wrapped her legs around him, kissing him deep, nipping his bottom lip, giving him permission to go harder, to thrust into her until he came, too, with a fierce curse, his body trembling with the force of it.

He pressed his forehead to hers when it was over, her legs dropping to the bed.

'Did I hurt you?' he asked.

Kira shook her head, amazed that the first words out of his mouth were concern for her, but of course, they were. 'No, I always cry during sex,' she said, afraid of the emotions sweeping through her. Teasing was safer.

His low chuckle ghosted across her cheeks. 'Okay.' He dropped another kiss to her nose.

'But that was better than sex with an asshole, I'll give you that.'

He let that slow grin cross his face, and it was even sexier now that she knew it was warranted. 'Glad to hear it, Peaches.'

'We have not agreed on that nickname.'

'Oh, right. I forgot' One more kiss and he got up, braving the cold to deal with the condom. He came back cursing. 'Goddamn, Kira. You need to raise the prices of those trees. You need that boiler now.'

She laughed, standing up to wrap a blanket around him. 'Come on, let's go take a nice, hot shower. The storm isn't over yet.'

She threw a flirty wink over her shoulder on her way out of the living room, hoping she was covering the panic currently flooding her veins at the thought of all this ending as soon as the snow plows came rolling through.

She should have known this was another one of her bad ideas. Another example of her taking what she wanted and giving no thought to the consequences.

But at least this time, she'd be the only one to get hurt.

Chapter Nineteen

'So how long do you think the storm will last?' Kira asked as she studied her letter tiles. They had found an ancient Scrabble board in the back of the closet Kira had been using for her towels and it was now laid out between them on the mattress.

After their shower, he'd built the fire back up and it crackled and popped, filling the room with warmth and calm. They'd just finished what Kira called a snowstorm-empty-the-refrigerator-charcuterie-board for their dinner. It consisted of cheese and crackers, several types of pickles, leftover rotisserie chicken from the little grocery store in town, grapes, and chocolate-covered almonds that Kira bought in bulk. It was delicious.

'Seems like it's already winding down.' He'd been avoiding looking out the window for a while now, not wanting to confirm that the snow had significantly slowed down, although the wind continued to rattle Kira's old windows.

Kira looked up at him, a trace of worry between her brows. 'Roads are probably still bad though,' she said.

Bennett bit down on his smile. She didn't want him to go. Which was good since he was in no hurry to leave, either. A fact he was trying very hard to ignore.

'Probably. I doubt they'll get the roads cleared until morning.'

Kira blew out a little sigh and arranged her letters on the board. '*Touch*. Double word score.'

'Nice one,' he said, smirking at the board. Kira had already played, *lick, taste, nibble, clench,* and *hard*. She was winning. In more ways than one. He was half hard again thinking about how and where he wanted to lick, taste, and touch her.

She grinned at him in that wide-open way that he'd just discovered about her. It was unexpected. She was unexpected. This whole day had gone so differently than he'd planned this morning when he left the house. It felt like a lifetime ago that he decided staying away from Kira was the best course of action.

He didn't know who that Bennett was anymore. The one who'd never seen this goofy Kira grin. The one who'd never seen her naked, kissed her skin, felt her come. He didn't envy that guy. That guy was severely missing out.

The fact that he would be that guy again soon, the guy without Kira in his life, weighed heavy in his gut.

'How do you think the dogs are doing?' she asked, distracting him from his thoughts.

'Probably being spoiled by my sister,' he said. He grabbed his phone to check for messages from Jeanie. Nicole's name flashed on the screen as soon as he turned it back on, but he swiped away her texts without reading them. He was finally ready to put his toxic relationship with her behind him.

'Jeanie sent pics,' he said, holding up his phone for Kira to see. The dogs were snuggled in front of Logan's fireplace sound asleep.

Kira giggled. 'I guess they're settled in.'

'They don't even miss me.'

She was studying him as he put the phone down.

'What?'

She gave a little shrug. 'Between the condoms in your wallet and sending the dogs off to a babysitter … seems like you planned this whole thing.'

He huffed a self-deprecating laugh. 'And I thought I was swearing you off for good.'

She smirked. 'Guess it didn't work.'

'Guess not. My subconscious knew what I was up to.'

Kira fidgeted with her letter tiles, rearranging them on her rack. She blew out a little sigh before she spoke. 'I'm not like her.'

His eyebrows rose in surprise.

'I mean, I just want you to know, I'm not trying to like, use you and leave you … but that's kinda the situation we're in … and I don't want you to … I don't know … hate me?'

'I won't hate you. We both know what this is. It's entirely different than me uprooting my life for Nicole. This is just two people who mutually agreed to have a fun snow day.'

Is that what this was?

'Right.' She nodded but still wasn't meeting his eye.

'I don't leave until after New Year's,' he said, forgetting about the game, forgetting about why he should stay away from Kira.

'Okay…' Her gaze met his again, suspicion in her dark eyes.

'Let's extend this thing.'

She raised a brow. 'You want to keep playing old board games and eating the scraps from my pantry?'

'Yes.'

Kira laughed. 'Okay, Bennett.'

'I do. I want to do all of that. I want to do … whatever. I just want some more time with you.' If all Kira wanted to do was hang out for the rest of his time here, he'd be into it. He just wanted to see her again and he was out of dumb excuses to come up here. He wanted to come see her, just to come see her.

She stopped laughing, the look on her face somewhere between incredulous and afraid. 'I don't know if that's a good idea.'

Ben nodded, taking his gaze back to the board, not

wanting to pressure her. He played the word *please* and caught Kira's small smile when she read it.

'Won't it make things harder when you have to go?' she asked, her voice small, as though she didn't want to ask the question, like it revealed more than she meant to.

'Maybe. But I like you. I want to spend time with you.'

'You keep saying that.'

'Saying what?'

'That you like me.'

'Because I do. Why does that surprise you?'

She shrugged like she didn't care, but her face told him otherwise. 'I guess I've never been particularly likable before. I mean people liked me for my money or the places I could get them into, or they liked me long enough to sleep with me, but'—she laughed a little, a bitter sound— 'yeah, I guess people don't typically just *like* me.'

'Then they obviously don't know you.'

'Ben.' She sighed, but he couldn't help his smile because he liked it when she called him that.

'Yeah?'

'You don't have to be so damn sweet all the time.' She was scowling at him like she was angry, but the next word she played was *good boy* which was technically two words but he decided to allow it.

'So … is that a yes, then?'

Kira blew out a long sigh, like he was trying her patience, but her lips had tipped up in the corner. 'Under one condition.'

'Okay, name it.'

'At the end of this … thing … you need to go home.'

'Kira. Of course, I'm going home.'

'No, I mean it. I am a mess, Ben. I will continue to be a mess for the foreseeable future. This whole farm will be a mess. You absolutely cannot get it in your head that you are going to somehow stay here and fix it, fix me.'

'I don't want to *fix* you. You don't need fixing.'

She scoffed, but that was bullshit, so he grabbed her wrists, making her pay attention. 'I think it's awesome that you are starting over, that you are trying to do better, but don't ever for one second let anyone make you think you need fixing. Do you understand me?' His voice was rougher than he intended, but he needed her to know this. He'd wanted to help her, to keep her warm and safe, but he had never once thought that she *needed* him to fix things for her.

Her eyes widened in surprise, the color high in her cheeks. Her pulse raced beneath his fingers. He relaxed his grip.

'Sorry.'

She pulled her hands from his and swiped the Scrabble board off the bed in an instant. The tiles scattered across the wood floor.

'Kira, what—'

She tackled him before he could ask what the hell was going on. She kissed him hard on the mouth, before pulling back. 'You stupid, sweet, infuriating man.' She kissed him, a little softer this time. 'I like you, too.'

He smiled. 'Sorry.'

'Yeah, me, too. I really tried not to.'

'I know.'

'But you have to promise me, you'll go,' she whispered. 'After New Year's, you'll go back home to your real life. I might get selfish … fall back into old habits. I might try to keep you.'

He nodded, feeling his cheeks flush, liking the idea of her wanting him to stay a little too much. But no, he wasn't going down that road again. 'I'll go.' Of course he would go. He had a life to get back to. This was a vacation, a Christmas fling. Just because he wanted to extend it a little longer didn't mean he'd forgotten the dangers of giving up everything to fit into someone else's life. He was determined not to do that again.

No matter how tempting Kira might be.

'Okay.' Kira nodded. 'Deal.'

'There's something else I have to tell you.'

'Okay…'

'The whole town thinks there's a dead body buried somewhere on your farm, and they sent me here to find it.'

'The whole town thinks what?!' Obviously, Bennett's solid body beneath her had impaired her hearing somehow, because what he'd just said made absolutely no sense.

He winced. 'The town thinks the old owner buried a body here. They didn't want you to find it and be … traumatized … I guess. Honestly, their reasoning is all a little fuzzy at this point.'

Kira pushed up on his chest, but she wasn't in a hurry to move off of him completely. Bennett was very comfortable. 'And why do they think this?'

'Something about a cryptic letter left behind after he died. The town seems split between a possible dead body and some kind of treasure, or maybe money…'

'Treasure?! Money?! Bennett!'

His eyes widened as her voice rose.

'If there is a treasure on this farm, I need it!'

He let out a chuckle and she felt it rumble through her chest. 'I don't think there's anything here, Peaches.'

She didn't bother to correct the nickname. It was growing on her. The fact that he'd wanted to give her one was growing on her, too.

'That's probably what that cryptic list was all about, the treasure!'

'Kira…'

'And I found his will. Edwin didn't have many relatives. He left a lot of stuff here in the house. Maybe there *is* something valuable here.'

'It seems unlikely.'

'Oh, and why is that, detective? You did such a thorough search while you were walking your dogs and banging around in my basement?'

'What was I supposed to do? Start digging holes between your trees?'

'You were supposed to tell me!'

'Right. Sorry about that. But in my defense…'

She rolled her eyes but was having trouble keeping the

smile off her face. Especially since Bennett had started rubbing up and down her back with his big warm hands.

'You didn't seem open to input when I first met you.'

She huffed and he laughed.

'And after that, I just wanted an excuse to keep coming up here.'

'Because of your love of Christmas trees and bad hot chocolate?' she teased.

'Yep, that was exactly it.' He planted a kiss on her chin, and she tipped toward him, letting him capture her lips. 'Oh, and I love to be verbally abused by local business owners.'

She giggled and he kissed the sound from her lips.

Kira had been undervaluing kissing her entire life. Kissing Bennett, being kissed by him, was an event in and of itself. And right now, it was lazy and delicious and warm. She felt like she could do this forever, kiss him in front of a crackling fire.

She didn't want it to end.

Stretched out on top of him, his hands on her body, Kira had never felt more content.

It was scary.

And dangerous.

She pulled away and sat up, straddling a rosy-cheeked, swollen-lipped Bennett and he looked so damn good it scared her even more.

It was going to hurt like hell when he left.

And if she was already a half-person without Chloe, how much of herself would even be left?

How had she let this happen?

Why was she incapable of making a single good decision?

'What happened?' he asked, brow suddenly furrowed in concern.

Kira bristled. 'What do you mean? Nothing happened. I just needed some … oxygen.'

Bennett watched her, one hand running idly up and down her thigh. 'Okay.'

'So are there any other details about this treasure? Like a map or something?'

'Sorry to disappoint you, but I'm pretty sure this is just a crazy town rumor.'

She frowned. 'Right. Probably.'

'Hey, come here.' He tugged her back down and her body went without her permission. He was so warm and comfortable, she couldn't help it. Bennett was a bad decision wrapped in a good decision package, but it was too late to fight it now.

He rolled them a bit and tucked her into his side.

I could live here.

She sighed and he misinterpreted her change in mood.

'I am sorry I didn't tell you sooner. And I'm sorry I got your hopes up, but the farm is doing great and I'm sure you'll have a shiny new boiler in no time.'

'Sure, yeah, probably.' Maybe if she started selling her organs along with Christmas trees she could fix up the whole house.

He rested his chin on the top of her head and she

nuzzled her face in the crook of his neck. *This.* This spot right here was where she would set up her new home if she could. She was such an idiot.

'You're doing great, Kira.'

And she didn't know if it was his words or his hands stroking her hair or the warm fire or this crazy day, but her feelings threatened to overwhelm her again. It was a rare thing for someone to tell her she was doing a good job and actually mean it.

She sniffled a little and Bennett tried to pull back to see her face, but she clung tight to him like a desperate little barnacle. She wasn't ready to leave this warm cove of his body yet. Not until she was forced to.

'I'm fine. Just … just keep doing that to my hair.'

She felt his soft laugh ruffle her hair.

'At your service, Peaches.'

Chapter Twenty

The next morning dawned bright, blinding, and white outside her windows. She needed to get darker shades for this room if she was going to keep sleeping here. She was about to burrow deeper under the covers, when she realized the body that had kept her warm and cozy all night was missing.

God, last night had been so … perfect. So life-alteringly perfect. She didn't want to think about it in the light of day, but it was too late. She was already thinking about it. Thinking about how Bennett had held her until she was done with her little emotional breakdown and then how he'd rolled her over and made her come like five more times, and how each time her defenses came down a little more until she was completely exposed, and there was nothing she could do about it.

And the only consolation was that he seemed to be feeling the same way. That he seemed just as undone as she was. That each time he slid into her, he seemed just as awestruck as she was, just as destroyed. And she didn't know what to do now, except to keep going with this bad idea. Because she was stupid to go down this road, but she wasn't stupid enough to stop now.

She had Bennett until New Year's, and she was going to hold onto him with both greedy hands until then.

'Bennett?' she called, peeking out into the chilly room. The fire had died down in the night and now it was cold even in the confines of the living room blanket fort.

'Ben?'

No answer. But when she sat up, she found a travel mug next to her side of the bed. Weird. She took a sip. Piping hot coffee from her own kitchen. He'd put it in a travel mug to keep it hot in this damn house.

Why was he so thoughtful?! Her resolve not to chain him to the radiator and keep him here forever was weakening. *Keep it together, Kira.*

She took another sip, fortifying herself, and then emerged from the blankets. Where did he go? She padded over to the front window in her fuzzy socks, a necessity for walking across these freezing floors. The world outside was white.

The sun had come out and the snow on the trees sparkled like fairy dust.

It was objectively beautiful, even Kira had to admit it.

And she found an unexpected excitement building up in her belly. She wanted to go play in the snow! A feeling nearly as foreign as wanting to keep the man she'd slept with last night. Quickly donning several more layers, her boots, coat, hat, and gloves—ugh playing in the snow was hard already—Kira stepped out into the brilliant morning before her enthusiasm could wane too much.

Bennett, apparently giving up on fighting his helper instincts, had already shoveled the walk from her door to the driveway. After that, footprints had plowed through the snow and into the tree fields.

Even after all the storm warnings and the high winds of yesterday, the snow wasn't actually that deep, less than a foot, she would guess. So Kira followed the footprints into the trees. The snow was light and fluffy, a cold, sparkly powder.

She didn't have to walk far before she found him.

Bennett had cleared the snow away from one of her trees and was kneeling beside it, sawing it down. He had on that vest of his and had rolled up the sleeves of his Henley. Kira watched his arms flex and bunch as he sawed.

'Aren't you cold?' she asked, and he looked up at her in surprise. The smile he gave her warmed her to her toes.

'Nah, worked up a sweat shoveling.'

'Thanks for doing that.'

He shrugged. 'You weren't supposed to find me.' He gestured to the tree. 'It was supposed to be a surprise.'

'A surprise that you were trying to run off with another free tree?'

He laughed. 'You caught me.'

'I knew it, you seduced me so you could continue your quest for the perfect Christmas tree.'

'That's definitely not why I seduced you,' he said, holding her gaze, his breath a visible cloud in front of him.

Phew. Somehow, she had worked up a sweat, too.

He grinned and went back to sawing, and Kira went back to objectifying him while he did it. A few more pushes of the saw back and forth through the trunk and Bennett reached up and pushed it over. Just like that.

Lumberjack fantasies that Kira didn't know she had rushed into her head.

'It's for you, actually,' he said, standing up next to the tree.

'For me?'

'Yeah, you didn't have a tree yet, so I figured…'

'You cut down a Christmas tree for me?'

'Yes, I just thought…'

She launched herself at him and he caught her with a surprised laugh. He looked down at her and planted a kiss on her lips.

'Morning,' he said with a grin.

'Good morning.' She couldn't stop smiling at him like the big dummy that she was, but he cut her a tree! He did manual labor for her and, God help her, but it was hot. 'Thank you for my tree.' And the best part was that he did it just because he wanted to, because this beautiful man did things for the people he cared about and she was one of those people. He didn't do this to get something from her in return.

Or worse, just because her parents had paid him to do it.

'You're welcome.' He held her a minute longer, just

staring at her in the bright morning light, like he didn't want to look away, like he was memorizing her. She could tell because she was doing it too, memorizing him, soaking him in. 'We should probably get it inside,' he said, finally.

'Okay,' she said as he put her back down in the snow, but there was one more thing she wanted to do to complete this Christmas-card-perfect morning. She stooped down and grabbed a handful of snow. Bennett was eyeing her skeptically when she straightened.

'Whatcha doing, Peaches?'

She squeezed the snow attempting to make a ball but the whole thing just kind of exploded in her face.

Ben laughed. 'Are you trying to make a snowball?' He stooped down to grab his own handful of snow and Kira thought she may have miscalculated this little plan. He grinned at her before he nailed her in the side.

'Hey!' She shrieked and ducked behind a tree. 'No fair!'

'No fair? It was self-defense.' Ben chuckled.

Kira picked up more snow and squeezed it a bit more gently this time until she had a decently packed snowball. Then she popped out from her hiding place and launched her attack. Bennett ducked and the snowball hit the nearest tree. Oh, she had definitely miscalculated. She ran behind the next tree, scooping up snow as she went. Bennett threw three more rapid-fire snowballs into her hiding place. Snow rained down from the branches.

'You're supposed to go easy on me!' she yelled.

'That's not how this works,' he said, laughter clear in his voice. That bastard. She'd show him.

She grabbed more snow and packed it tight. She jumped out from her hiding place and whipped the snowball at Bennett. The ball exploded against the side of his head, snow spraying everywhere. He froze.

'Oh, shit.' Kira clamped her mittened hands over her mouth. 'Oops.'

Bennett stared at her, his eyes narrowed as the snow dripped down his neck.

Uh-oh.

He ran straight for her, and Kira tried to turn and run but she was too slow. He grabbed her around her waist and took them both down into a snowbank.

Kira shrieked, her world suddenly tipped sideways. Bennett loomed over her, panting, his face red from where she'd hit him.

'No face shots, Peaches,' he growled, but his eyes were lit up with mischief.

'I was not informed of the official snowball-fight rules,' she said, tamping down a giggle, her own breath coming out in short gasps.

'Well, now you have to face the consequences of your actions.'

Kira's eyes widened. 'What are you going to do to me?'

Bennett's smile grew wicked as he reached up to the tree branch above them.

'Ben … what—'

He shook the branch and snow rained down on her face. She shrieked and pushed him over, rolling on top of him in the snow. He laughed, the sound shaking her body.

'Sorry,' he said between laughs. 'I couldn't help it.'

Kira wiped her face with her mitten. 'And here I was, thinking you were such a nice guy.'

'I am a nice guy.' He pushed the snow-crusted hair out of her face, his smile softening around the edges. 'I just take snowball fights very seriously.'

She huffed, trying to pretend to be mad but the way he was looking at her was quickly melting her resolve. He looked too damn cute and too damn happy, like a kid home from school on a snow day. He raised his head and planted a kiss on her nose.

'How can I make it up to you?' he asked, and Kira got a mischievous look of her own.

'Well, I don't have anything to decorate my tree with, but I thought we could check the attic. I've been too scared to go up there alone.' She fluttered her lashes at him, damsel-in- distress style and he laughed.

'I'm sure I could find time for a trip to the attic this morning.'

'Yay! Now let's get out of this snow. I'm freezing.' She wiggled her way off his body in an entirely unnecessary way that had him red-faced by the time they were both standing again and not because of the cold.

'Let me help you carry it back,' she said, gesturing to her tree, attempting to ignore the heat in his gaze.

Bennett raised an eyebrow.

'I can do it,' she insisted, not willing to be outdone in her snowball-fighting and tree-carrying skills in one morning.

Ben shrugged. 'You get the top and I'll get the bottom.'

'Okay.' She grabbed the spindly top of the tree and Bennett hefted the back and she was sure she wasn't doing anything but leading the way and getting her gloves all sappy, but it was nice to feel helpful.

'I might be starting to understand why people like this,' she said, glancing back at Bennett, who was definitely carrying the bulk of the weight. She got distracted by his arms again and almost led them into a snowbank.

'Oh, yeah?'

'Yeah,' she said, steering the tree and getting them back on a straight path. 'It's very … festive.'

Bennett chuckled again. 'Glad you're coming around to it.'

They trudged back up her front path. 'And you look hot as a lumberjack.'

Another low chuckle.

'I might have time for more than just a trip to the attic,' he said, and Kira's toes curled in her boots.

'Oh really?'

She looked back and his gaze was hot even out here in the snow.

'How can you possibly look at me like that when I'm dressed in a sleeping bag with sleeves?'

'I remember what's under it,' he said, waggling his eyebrows and Kira laughed, heat rising to her cheeks.

'Don't you have to work today?' she asked, as they dragged the tree up the front steps.

'I don't think either of us can do anything today until we're plowed out of here.' Bennett gestured to the still-covered driveway and the parking lot of the tree farm in the distance. It was all untouched whiteness and Kira wished it would last.

'Is it wrong that I kinda hope Logan's truck is outta gas?'

Bennett had propped the tree up beside the door and pulled her close instead. He smelled like pine and the metallic scent of cold air on warm skin.

'It's not wrong. I mean, it was my Christmas wish that got us snowed in in the first place.'

She glanced up at him and he was smiling, his eyes bright this morning.

'Right. I forgot you were responsible for this whole winter storm.'

'What can I say? I've been very good this year.'

Kira laughed, leaning into him. Had it really only been a week ago that she'd pictured doing this at the tree-lighting festival? And now it felt so easy, so natural. Already something she felt entitled to.

She pulled away. 'Wow. And so modest, too.'

He shrugged the playful smirk on his lips. 'How about some breakfast before we search the attic?'

'Sure.' Kira followed him into the house, appreciating what little warmth it held after being out in the cold. The power had been restored sometime in the night, so at least they had that. They shucked off their outerwear, hanging it over chairs and hooks to dry as Bennett talked about hopefully finding a tree stand up in the attic and needing to get some decorative fairy lights, too. And Kira tried desperately not to get too attached to the cozy domesticity of it all.

But it was too late of course.

Her gnawing loneliness was already eating this up. This time with Bennett, his aimless chatter, his warm body, his sweet smile. She wanted it. And the spoiled, rich girl inside her stamped her foot, fists clenched at her sides. She *wanted* it. She wanted him.

And the worst part was she could see perfectly how she could get him. It wouldn't take much to convince him. She could picture it.

Even with his assurances that he had no plans to stay, Kira knew a few well-placed comments, a few promises, a few more farm disasters and the scales would easily tip in her favor. Bennett would stay. He would fill the lonely bits in her heart. He would do all the shit around here she didn't want to do, or didn't know how to do.

And maybe for a while they'd be happy.

Except, underneath, she'd know she'd have trapped him here, she'd have manipulated him. And when had she ever been one for cozy domesticity, anyway? What happened when she got tired of it? Of him?

Although, as she watched him move around her kitchen pouring coffee and scrambling eggs, she couldn't picture getting tired of this. But it *would* happen one day, surely. And then she'd be forced to break this man's heart. This good man. All because she couldn't stand to be alone for a little while. All because she'd taken and taken and taken from him. Like she always did.

She tried to smile when he slid the plate of eggs and toast in front of her, but her face felt cold and immovable.

'You okay?' he asked and she met his eye across the table. His face was still a little red from shoveling and the cold, the hair along his forehead was damp with sweat. His gray eyes were warm this morning, more like her favorite soft wool blanket than a stormy sky. The way he looked at her made her physically hurt, a deep ache already forming in the hole he would leave when he went home.

Kira swallowed hard.

No more of this. Bennett is a holiday fling and nothing more. Something you've done plenty of times in your life. Now let it go.

She smiled her beauty-pageant smile, her mother's society-party smile. She faked it until her cheeks hurt.

'Yep. Just fine.'

Chapter Twenty-One

'How is it possible that it's even colder up here?' Kira blew on her hands and rubbed them together for warmth.

'Well, it's closed off from the rest of the house and there's no heat source up here so…'

She glared at him.

Right. She wasn't actually looking for an answer. Something had happened in between hauling that Christmas tree into the house and now, and he wasn't sure what it was, except that Kira's prickly spines were back out in full force. But maybe he did understand. After last night he was feeling torn open in ways he hadn't felt in years. If Kira was feeling half that vulnerable, she was obviously just protecting herself. Something he should probably consider doing himself. Instead, he just wanted to chop down trees for her and make her breakfast and coax that smile back onto her face. Because he was a sucker to his very core. A human doormat.

'There's a lot of boxes up here,' he said, changing the topic from heating issues to the task at hand. 'So we might find something useful.'

Kira ran her fingers over the top of a dusty box. 'He left so much behind.'

'According to Jeanie, there was a lot more but they had it cleared out before selling it.'

He scanned the attic. Stacks of cardboard boxes leaned precariously, slumped and crumpled with age, a few old lamps collecting dust in one corner, an ancient TV inhabiting the other. He could only stand up straight in the middle of the space, the slope of the roof on either side making it impossible not to hit his head along the edges of the room.

Kira peered at the handwriting scribbled on the sides of the boxes.

'Books, cassette tapes, clothes,' Kira read. 'Oh, this one says "holiday". That might be promising.' She opened the box and looked in. 'Hmm…' She pulled out a rather creepy, elfish-looking Santa doll.

'Yikes,' he said.

'The box is full of them.'

Bennett crossed the attic to look for himself. 'Wow.'

'An entire collection of terrifying Santas,' Kira said, rifling through the box. She pulled out another and held it up.

'I feel like it can see into my soul,' he said, as the doll stared at him.

Kira stifled a laugh.

'Why are old dolls so terrifying?' she asked as she put scary Santa back and closed the box.

'Because it's way too easy to picture their heads turning independently to look at you.'

'True.' Was that a trace of amusement he heard? He would run with that.

Bennett moved the Santa box so they could get to the one beneath it, also marked 'holiday'. 'I'm almost scared to look. Might be filled with deranged elves or something.'

'Baby,' Kira said, but the teasing tone was back in her voice as she nudged him out of the way. 'Jackpot.'

The box was filled with carefully wrapped ornaments.

Kira undid the yellowed newspaper around one and revealed a white ball with a delicate design in silver glitter snaking around it. She breathed a little sigh of awe and Bennett's heart stumbled in his chest.

'They're beautiful,' she said.

She took out another and another, passing them to him as she unwrapped them until his arms were filled with shimmering white and silver and gold ornaments and the smile was back on Kira's face.

And he didn't care that they were in a freezing cold attic or that the dust was tickling his nose or that he was pretty sure he'd heard the rumble of snow plows on the road. He would have stood there forever cradling the fragile decorations, wishing Kira would trust him to hold more than that.

Even though he didn't really deserve to.

Even though he was leaving.

She smiled at the bounty in his arms, unaware of the direction of his thoughts. 'Well, I was half hoping we'd find a box marked "treasure" but this is pretty good too.'

'And I'm glad we didn't find any skeletons.'

'We didn't open all the boxes,' she said, taking the ornaments back one by one and placing them carefully in the box to bring downstairs.

'Don't even joke about that.'

She laughed and it sounded like hope.

'I didn't realize you were such a scaredy cat, Ben.'

Ben. Ben like she knew him. Ben like they were more than just two people passing by each other in the randomness of life.

'Scaredy cat? No, I just would rather not find body parts in musty old attics.'

'Where would you rather find body parts?'

'Ideally, still attached to the person they belong to.'

Another small laugh as she snooped around in a few more boxes. 'Well, I guess that's it for holiday stuff. I'll come back to treasure-hunt another day,' she said, grabbing the ornament box before he could do it for her. She turned and her hip bumped another box. It toppled to the ground, spilling its contents across the attic floor.

'Shit.' She put the ornaments down and crouched to pick up the mess.

Bennett stooped to help her. 'What are these?' He picked up one of the envelopes from the floor.

'Old letters?' Kira sat on the dusty floor, legs stretched in front of her. She blew her bangs out of her face with a breath and her eyes widened as she turned the paper in her hand over. 'More old letters!' She peeled open the envelope and pulled out a yellow piece of paper.

'*Dear Ellen, my heart aches without you,*' she read. 'Oh, my God, they're old love letters!' Her gaze met his, uninhibited excitement written across her face and Bennett knew he was seeing something most people didn't get to. Were people ever more vulnerable than when they were unapologetically excited about something? He didn't think so.

'Cool,' he said, and she looked at him with an exasperated expression like he wasn't fully understanding the awesomeness of the situation.

'It's very cool.' She waved the letter between them. 'It makes me sad that we won't have anything like this.'

'We?'

She shook her head, hastily stopping his question. 'I meant our generation. Like no one will find their grandmother's old letters anymore.'

'Unless people are printing out their DM's.'

Kira rolled her eyes, but her lips tipped up in amusement.

'Right, unless someone out there is printing out their DM's, in the future no one will just stumble upon a box of old letters. It makes me kinda sad.'

She went back to reading the letter and he opened the envelope he was holding and scanned the letter.

'Kira…'

'Woah…'

Their heads snapped up at the same time. A delicious blush had crept up Kira's cheeks.

'They're dirty letters,' she said, eyes wide.

Bennett doubled over with laughter, a hand across his stomach, letting the letter fall from his fingertips.

Kira kept reading. 'This is absolutely filthy,' she gasped.

Bennett wheezed, sure he was sucking in so much attic dust that he'd be sneezing until New Year's, but the moment was too absurd not to.

'At least they're not your grandmother's letters,' he said between laughs.

Kira swatted his shoulder. 'Don't you dare bring my grandmother into this.'

Ben wiped the tears from his eyes. 'You did, not me!'

She frowned, still reading. 'I mean … it's still very romantic. He wanted her so bad, he pined for her.' She picked up another letter. 'That's hot.'

Bennett grabbed another letter to avoid staring at Kira while she read.

'Dear Ellen, I think about you constantly, day and night you haunt my thoughts. Your sweet mouth, the perfect curve of your breasts. The memory of the taste of your pussy keeps me alive, keeps me fighting, day after day…'

'Wow, Ellen must have been one hell of a woman,' he muttered, although he could relate to poor Edwin's feelings.

'He must have been in Vietnam when he wrote these,' Kira said, pointing out the dates on the letters.

'I wonder if she ever wrote the poor guy back.'

'They got married, so she must have at some point. Maybe they got lost?' She rifled through the letters looking for any response to Edwin's ardor. 'She must have responded. How could she not?'

Kira was on her knees now, examining the other boxes for more letters. 'She couldn't have just left him hanging. All his thoughts and feelings just flapping in the breeze. I mean, he loved her. Look at how he loved her. And he must have been so lonely … out there thinking of her…' Her voice cracked.

'Kira…'

She kept looking, opening box after box. 'They must be here somewhere.'

'Kira…'

'I'm sure they're here.'

'Peaches.'

Her gaze snapped to his. 'What?'

'I found one.'

Her eyes lit up. 'You did?'

She crawled back to the letters still scattered on the floor and he handed her the one letter he could see with Edwin's name and platoon number on it.

'*Dear Eddie,*' she read, spreading the letter out on her lap.

'Your letters never fail to make me blush. I had to start reading them in private, because my sisters are always trying to read over my shoulder. But I don't regret anything we did before you left and I'm happy the memories are keeping you warm while you're gone. Please come back to me.' Kira's voice cracked on that line and she sniffed a little but kept going. *'You're the only boy for me. I miss you. All my love, Ellen.'*

She looked up at him, tears glistening in her eyes.

'I didn't know you were such a romantic, Peaches,' he teased, his voice soft.

She huffed. 'I hide it well.'

'I think it's safe to assume Eddie didn't kill Ellen.'

'Definitely not.'

He crawled closer, leaning over the pile of love letters from Edwin to his beautiful wife. Kira lifted her face to him and he brushed his lips across her cheek. She sighed and his mouth found hers. Warm and soft and welcoming. A side of her no one else saw.

He pulled away and leaned his forehead against hers, and when her gaze met his, the force of his desire hit him hard in the gut. Not just desire for her body, although that was back, too, but God, how he wished he could be the one for her.

'Let's go back downstairs. You're freezing,' he said, her practical needs the only thing he could care for right now. She let him pull her up after they carefully returned the letters to their box.

He carried the Christmas ornaments downstairs and led

Kira back to the living room. He stoked the fire. He silently undressed first himself and then her, tossing their dusty clothes aside. He wrapped her in blankets and the warmth of his skin.

He kissed the fresh tears from her cheeks.

'Ben?'

'Yeah?' he whispered as he dragged his lips across her throat. She trembled in his arms.

'I'm glad you're here.' And he could hear the loneliness in her voice and he wanted to banish it forever.

Dangerous thoughts for a man who had to leave in two weeks.

'Me, too.'

She reached between them and guided him to her and he eased into her wet heat again, even though she must be sore and so was he but they were running out of time and there was nowhere in the world he'd rather be.

He pushed deeper and she gasped, her fingers in his hair, her ankles digging into his back.

'Yes,' she whispered. And *please*, and *don't stop*, and *Ben*, and *yes, yes, yes*. And he felt her tighten around him, the quickness of her pleasure surprising them both but she clung to him as it crested.

And then he found his, too, buried deep, his face pressed against the pulse rapidly beating against her throat. And for that brief moment she was his, and everything made sense.

Unfortunately, Logan never ran out of gas.

The rumble of his plow tore through the moment and Bennett vowed to never forgive the man for as long as he lived.

The snowstorm was officially over.

Chapter Twenty-Two

'Thanks, Santa.' Kira shook the old man's mittened hand and he actually 'ho-ho-ho'd' at her. She wasn't entirely sure if he thought he was really Santa or not, but she wasn't about to ask. He'd just spent the entire day in the cabin greeting dozens of sticky children, plenty of whom had screamed at the sight of him. The man had endured a lot in the name of Christmas joy. He could think whatever he wanted about himself, he'd just brought her a ton of business.

'My pleasure, Ms. North.' His eyes twinkled. Maybe he really was…

Kira shook her head. Owning this winter wonderland was making her nuts.

'Drive safe!' she called as Santa headed to his car.

The sun had set over an hour ago and the lights she'd strung up across the trees, twinkled merrily above her. Even a week later, the snow from the storm had stuck around, creating an ambience she couldn't have paid for. And she had to admit, looking around at the lights and the trees and the happy families piling into cars blaring Christmas carols from the speakers, she almost didn't hate Christmas. And she was sure as hell proud of what she'd built.

'Hey, Peaches.' The sound of Bennett's voice pulled her attention to the window of the cabin where his face peered out at her. 'Did Santa mean to leave this giant box of candy canes behind?'

'Oh, yeah. He said we could keep them. Something about having his own special supply.'

Bennett chuckled, the sound warm and familiar. 'That guy was bizarre.'

'Very.'

He gave her another smile and then popped back inside where he was probably cleaning up. It was one week until Christmas, and Bennett had sort of moved in and had kind of been helping her run the place since the snowstorm and it was all a terribly bad idea and yet…

He came out of the little cabin, down the steps and put an arm around her. 'Ready to head home?'

Home.

Together.

She was in so deep.

'Yep.'

They walked from the tree farm parking lot up the drive to her house, and it was all such an epically bad idea but she couldn't seem to walk away from it. After the storm,

Bennett had gone back to Jeanie's apartment, and they'd pretended that they were actually parting ways, that the end of the storm heralded the end of them. There really was no point in extending this fling until New Year's Day. She'd tried to tell herself it was for the best, that there was no need to drag this out. Better to say goodbye now.

But it was *Christmas*.

No one wanted to be alone for Christmas.

And Chloe was across the world. And her parents made her crazy. And what was she supposed to do, ignore the sexy man she liked just because he was leaving soon? Why start missing him before she had to?

So she might have invited him back in a moment of weakness, and he'd accepted, and he'd brought some extra clothes and his dogs and his laptop, and now for a week, he'd worked from her kitchen table and helped her when she needed it, and they'd slept on that mattress he'd dragged in front of the fire, and it was all so *good* that Kira couldn't give it up.

Not yet.

Describe yourself in two words. Selfish and stupid. That was her. But people could only change so much at one time, right? She didn't want to sprain something.

They walked into the house to find Elizabeth laid out on the bed by the fire and the two smaller dogs perched on the couch, snoring loudly.

'Off the bed.' Bennett snapped his fingers and the big dog looked at him with doleful eyes.

Kira laughed as he gave a sigh of frustration.

'Off the bed,' he growled, and the dog slowly unwound herself and sauntered over to the dog bed they'd put in the corner.

The other corner was filled with Kira's Christmas tree decorated with the attic ornaments and more lights than really seemed necessary, but Bennett had insisted. He'd also strung white lights across the mantle and suddenly Kira was living inside one of the holiday movies she'd once loved to mock.

But surprisingly, she didn't hate it.

The whole thing was very different from her mother's professionally decorated trees that she had in nearly every room of their house, each with a different theme, making the house feel like a Christmas museum. Whereas, this little tree, with its hand-me-down ornaments felt … cozy. Homey. It was an entirely new type of Christmas, one she was making with Bennett. One she'd never forget.

She sighed, tossing herself onto the couch, exhausted from removing her boots and outerwear.

'Winter is so hard,' she groaned, snuggling into the dogs' warm bodies.

'Why did you pick a farm so far north?' Bennett asked as he hung up his coat in the hall.

'Trying to get as far from home as possible,' she said through the blanket door. 'Also winter seemed pretty theoretical at the time.'

Bennett appeared back in the room a minute later. 'Why not California?'

'Too expensive. Too earthquakey.'

'Right.'

Right. Maybe in some other timeline, some other dimension or whatever, Kira and Ben would have met in California. Maybe their lives would have fit together better. Maybe she wouldn't have had to let him go.

But she didn't live in whatever timeline that was.

She was here.

In the winter.

He sat down on the other side of the dogs, laptop on his lap. 'Got a few things to finish up.'

'Sure. Of course.' He'd been fitting in his work in between loading trees onto cars and filling in for Iris when she'd come down with the flu. Guilt had been Kira's constant companion. He was doing too much for her.

Kira grabbed one of Edwin's old letters from the stack she'd gathered on the coffee table. She'd been going through them looking for clues about where he'd hidden his treasure, but so far had found nothing but smut. She'd also spent a few evenings sorting through the boxes in the attic. But besides a few boxes of old books, she hadn't found anything valuable. *Yet*. She was still holding out hope for a Christmas miracle.

Her phone vibrated in her pocket and she pulled it out.

'It's Chloe. FaceTiming. Do you mind?' she asked Bennett.

'Go for it.'

'Hey, Chlo.' She smiled at her sister's face.

'Kiki!'

Bennett gave a little snort at the nickname and Kira nudged him with her foot.

'God, you're hard to get a hold of lately.'

'I'm a very important business owner.'

She said it with a self-deprecating laugh, but Chloe beamed. 'I know. I'm so proud of you.'

Heat flooded Kira's face as her sister went on. 'I was worried about you at first. There were a few times you really looked a mess, I mean, like really bad…'

'Okay, Chlo. I get it. Thank you.' She didn't need Ben to hear exactly how much of a hot mess she had been, not that he hadn't seen plenty of it himself.

Her sister tipped her head to the side, studying Kira, her dark eyes seeing everything. 'You look different.'

Kira shrugged. 'Same old me.'

'No…' Chloe shook her head, her glossy hair flowing like dark waves over her shoulders. 'No, you're like glowing or something.' Then her eyes lit up in a way that made Kira wish she'd left the room to take this call, and risked freezing to death.

'You're getting laid!' her sister exclaimed triumphantly, and Kira wanted to dissolve into the cushions. Bennett chuckled softly at the other end of the couch.

'That's not it.'

'That's definitely it. You are aglow with orgasms!'

'Maybe I gave them to myself.'

Bennett shifted in his seat, a blush working its way up his neck. Kira bit down on a smile.

'Oh, my God, is he there right now?!' Chloe looked like she would climb through the screen if she could.

'Uh … nope.'

'Liar!'

'I'm not a liar. It's nothing, okay. I met a guy in town and we hooked up and that's it. Really.' She wished that was a lie. She wished Bennett was more than a hookup. But there was no point in telling Chloe about it. About him. Just one more thing for her sister to worry about.

Chloe narrowed her eyes, still not quite believing her. 'Well, he must have been pretty damn good. Your skin looks amazing.'

Bennett stood and gestured toward the kitchen, excusing himself from having to hear more of this painful conversation.

'I'm staying hydrated.'

Chloe nodded. 'Good.'

'So how are things with you?'

A small frown crossed Chloe's face.

'What's the matter?'

'Just a little homesick, I guess.'

'Homesick? What do you miss more, Dad's disapproving silence or Mom's disapproving lectures?'

Chloe huffed. 'I miss you, you idiot.'

Kira's heart ached.

'I miss you, too.'

'So, you're not going home for Christmas?' Chloe asked.

'No, although I did receive Mama's engraved invite for the Christmas Eve party.'

'Oh, lord, I hope you RSVP'd promptly. You know how she hates a late response.'

Kira laughed. 'I sent that thing right back with my "I regretfully decline" faster than you could say there's not a chance in hell I'd go back for that pretentious party.'

'We'll have to go back eventually.'

Kira frowned. It had taken a lot out of her to leave. She didn't want to think about going back. Not now. Not when she was just getting her footing.

'I suppose. But not today. I doubt Mama was torn up about it.'

'Your southern is coming out,' Chloe teased, her own accent thickening the longer she spoke. Kira could feel it happening, her words slowing down, thick and syrupy like the sweet tea Elaine used to make in the summer.

'Hush your mouth!' Kira gasped.

And Chloe giggled at the phrase. 'Well, I declare, sister. You look madder than a wet hen!'

Kira's laughter joined Chloe's. 'Remember how Memaw always used to say that about Mama when we'd get our good shoes dirty?'

'Oh, I remember.'

'I remember you always covered for me. Telling Mama tall tales about boys that splashed mud on us even though we had stomped in the puddles on the way home.'

Chloe shrugged. 'It wasn't like we didn't have plenty of shoes. Surely, we could ruin a pair or two.'

Their laughter died down. Maybe there were a few things Kira did miss about home, but it was all wrapped up in her sister. She was sure that wherever Chloe was would feel like home to her. But her sister was married to a Dane who designed those ubiquitous plastic toy building blocks for a living. And she wasn't coming home anytime soon.

'Kira, is that a Christmas tree?' Chloe's eyes grew in surprise.

'Oh … yeah… Had to play the part of a Christmas-lover if I'm going to sell Christmas trees.'

Chloe was studying her again like she could tell that a sexy man had cut down that tree for her and helped her decorate it, and that they made love by the glow of its lights every night and that Kira felt like she was building a home with someone else who would leave her.

Instead, she just smiled. 'I'm really happy you're happy there, Kiki.'

'Thanks, Chlo.'

'Let me let you go.'

Kira smiled at the phrase. Another one from their childhood. 'Okay, love you.'

'Love you.'

Kira snuggled into the closest dog, trying to swallow the emotions that always bubbled up after talking to her sister. Her childhood had been cold and strict, in some ways, and incredibly permissive in others. Her parents, mostly her mother, had incredibly high standards for her and Chloe: the way they looked, the way they talked, the way they behaved. Appearances were everything. Which was why Kira had spent so much time and energy doing everything in her power to fight against those restraints. And when she fell, when she screwed up, made a spectacle, her father's money had always been there to bail her out.

It was a toxic way to grow up.

She didn't need a therapist to tell her that.

'Is it safe to come back in?' Bennett peered in through the blanket door. 'Or are you still discussing my sexual prowess?'

Kira chucked a pillow at him and he laughed.

'What?' he said, rejoining her on the couch. 'I can't help it, if I make you glow.'

'Oh, shut up.'

He grinned.

She grinned back.

Stupid and selfish to her very core.

She gave the dogs between them a gentle shove and they hopped down to find Elizabeth and their doggie bed.

Kira moved and straddled Bennett's lap, his work put away for the day.

He raised his eyebrows.

'I have a glow to maintain,' she said.

He laughed a little, but the amusement didn't reach his eyes. 'Good thing your local hookup is here.'

'That's what this is, right?' She hated the look of hurt on his face. This would be so much easier if she was the only one getting hurt here. 'We agreed.' She leaned forward, kissing his neck. His hands grabbed her ass and tugged her closer. He was already hard against her.

'I know,' he groaned a little as she sucked on his neck,

letting her tongue run against the roughness of his stubble. 'Sometimes … it feels like … more than that.'

'It *isn't* more than that. It can't be.' She ran her hands through his hair, giving a little tug. 'Now let's see that sexual prowess you were just bragging about.'

He hesitated for a breath like he might argue further but instead he slapped her ass and growled at her to strip, which she happily did, as quickly as her layers would allow. This was good, this was better. Just sex. A holiday fling. Something they would sweep away after Christmas along with the fallen pine needles littering her floor.

'Come here,' he demanded. He was still sitting on the couch and he'd shed his own layers so he was sprawled naked on the cushions. 'I think I need some of that glow.' His smirk was wicked, and Kira loved it when he was like this, when he shed his niceness and let his true desires show through.

'Get on your knees for me, Peaches.'

A tiny part of her bucked at the command, but the rest of her reveled in it. She liked when he took charge here, during sex. It felt good to give in. To give to him instead of take.

But she also liked to torture him a little bit, so she stood in front of him a breath longer, letting him look his fill. And she did the same.

It would take decades or a head injury for her to forget the way he looked in the honey-gold light of the fire, spread out on her couch, long limbs, broad chest. His cock hard and heavy, his dark hair already mussed from her fingers, his storm-gray gaze locked on hers.

Merry Christmas to her.

'Kira.' Her name was a warning.

She grinned and dropped to her knees.

Bennett groaned and the sound had her pressing her thighs together, needing the pressure, already feeling like she would burst if he didn't touch her.

He wrapped his hands in her hair and tipped her head back so her gaze locked with his. She licked her lips and his eyes darkened.

He tugged on her hair and her lips parted on a whimper. He ran his thumb reverently across them.

'Perfect,' he rasped.

She sucked his thumb into her mouth, sinking her teeth into the soft pad of his thumb, needing a physical release for the emotions his words and his gaze sent tumbling through her. She didn't want to feel *feelings* right now. She just wanted to feel good.

With a twirl of her tongue she released his finger. She wrapped her hand around his erection and relished his sharp intake of breath when she gave his cock a few rough strokes. He still held her gaze and there was too much in that look, too much for her to handle, so she leaned forward and took him in her mouth with one, slick slide.

His groan joined the crackling of the fire as the only noise in the room.

His hand was still fisted in her hair and little sparks of pleasure and pain radiated from her scalp when he tugged on it, guiding her head, his hips thrusting mindlessly, his cock sliding between her lips.

And then Bennett, Mr. Fix-It, the too nice, too wholesome man she'd initially rejected, let the filthiest words flow from his perfect mouth.

'Fuck, Kira. You take my cock so good. You're so beautiful on your knees for me.' Another tug on her hair and she whimpered around him. He groaned. 'Such a good girl. Swallow me. Take it all.'

The words washed over her, the heat of them searing her, the ache between her legs growing. She took him and she gave him all of her in this moment, because it was the only way she could. The only way that made sense.

Another tug of her hair and she was off her knees and Bennett was pulling her to him and she was straddling him again. He kissed her swollen lips, praising her and whispering things he shouldn't say, things he shouldn't think.

Things about how perfect she was. How beautiful. How right she was for him.

Things about the future.

Things about staying.

She guided his erection into her, taking all of him in a fast, hard tilt of her hips and his forehead dropped to hers. His words stopped. His storm-cloud eyes met hers and he knew, he knew not to say those things anymore.

She rocked her hips, seeking pleasure, seeking release, seeking a distraction. It didn't take long to find it. It built with every thrust, every rock of her hips, Bennett's fingers digging into her hips, the flesh on her ass. And when she was so close, he thrust up into her, hard, and Kira broke, sobbing in his arms, thinking things she shouldn't think either.

Things about how perfect he was. How beautiful. How right he was for her.

Things about the future.

But because she was trying to be a better person, she didn't say them out loud.

Chapter Twenty-Three

Five days before Christmas, and Jeanie was at his door. Well, Jeanie was at Kira's door. Where he'd basically been living for a week, against all his better judgment, but Kira had asked him to come back after the snowstorm and he wasn't going to say no to that offer. He thought she would pull away. She sure as hell tried to and he was willing to accept that outcome, but when she called, he came running.

He wasn't in the mood for assessing what that meant about him or them or anything, really. He'd woken up with a naked Kira in his arms and that was all he really felt like thinking about today. Except for right now when he needed to talk to his sister.

'He lives!' Jeanie teased when he opened the door.

'Ha. Ha.'

'Hi, babies!' Jeanie ignored him to greet the herd of dogs who'd followed him to the door barking their welcome.

'Hello, hello, hello,' she crooned as she petted and scratched each dog in greeting. Eventually, she remembered he was standing there.

'I've been texting and you haven't responded. I haven't seen you in days!' She peered over her shoulder as she admonished him, clearly trying to get a glimpse of Kira, nosy thing that she was.

'The signal is spotty here. Sorry.' His sister didn't need to know that little problem had been fixed weeks ago. Or that he'd been avoiding her.

Jeanie eyed him suspiciously. 'And…'

'And what?'

'And what the hell are you doing here, Bennett?' she stage-whispered. 'You come to town to visit me, and then you just shack up with Kira? What's going on?' And then her eyes lit up in a very dangerous way. 'Wait, is it serious? Are you moving back east?!'

Bennett shushed her while he grabbed his coat from the nearby hook. He nudged his sister back out the door and onto the porch. It felt wrong to invite someone into a house that wasn't his, no matter what pretending he'd been doing lately.

Plus, Kira was just in the shower. He didn't need her coming downstairs to this conversation.

'It's not serious,' he told Jeanie once they were safely back outside.

She looked at him like he was the dumbest man in the world, which might not be that far off.

'You moved in with her, bro.'

'I mean … not really.'

'Bennett!'

'Okay, I mean, yes, I'm staying here for the rest of my vacation, but that's it.'

'Why?'

'Why what?'

Jeanie let out a little groan-growl of frustration. 'Why isn't it serious? Why can't you stay?'

'I have a life in California. A job and an apartment and friends. I can't just…'

'Do you even like it there?'

'I like it fine.'

'But don't you miss us? You could see me and Mom and Dad so much more if you lived on this coast, and now if you and Kira have a thing going, it makes even more sense! And you have told me on multiple occasions that your job can be done remotely, so…'

Bennett swallowed hard. Why did this all sound so reasonable coming out of his sister's mouth? Probably because she knew nothing about Nicole or just how bad his people-pleasing tendencies went and how he was trying to finally break them.

'It's not like that. That's not what she wants.'

She raised a dark eyebrow. 'And what do *you* want?'

He sighed. 'Well, right now I want this conversation to be over, and I'd love to know what you're doing here.'

His sister stared at him for another moment like she might continue the interrogation, but it was freezing out this morning and her breath hung in a cloud between them. Time was limited.

She gave up with a sigh. 'Fine. I just wanted to finalize Christmas plans with you.'

The door opened behind him.

'Oh … sorry… I didn't know you were out here.' Kira was dressed for the day, her fur-lined hood framing her beautifully flushed face. He wanted to kiss it, but he didn't need to give Jeanie any more ammo to use in her argument for him staying here forever.

'Don't apologize! It's your house.' Jeanie smiled and Bennett sensed danger. 'Actually, it's good that you're here. I was just trying to finalize Christmas plans with Bennett.'

'Oh, well…' Kira began, uncertainly.

Jeanie plowed forward. 'Logan and I will be spending it with his grandparents, and I assumed Ben would be coming.'

He nodded. 'Yep, sounds good. Thanks for confirming.' He tried to escort his lovely sister from the premises but she didn't budge.

'And now that you and Ben are such good … friends,' Jeanie's smile grew. 'You should come, too.'

'I couldn't possibly impose like that.' Kira held up her hands like she could fend off his sister with her body, but Ben just shook his head. There was no stopping Jeanie now.

'It's not an imposition at all! It's very informal. Plenty of other friends will be dropping in all day.'

Jeanie took Kira's hands in hers. 'Please come. It will be fun. And you can't stay up here all by yourself.'

Emotions flickered across Kira's face, but Bennett knew Jeanie had delivered the fatal blow. Kira didn't want to be alone. It was at least half the reason she'd let him stay. There were times he worried it was the only reason.

'Um…' Her gaze flicked to his, uncertain, like she didn't know if he would want her there, when in reality, the only reason he didn't want her there was because he wanted her there too much. 'I guess, I could stop by…'

'Wonderful!' Jeanie beamed. 'I will let Nana know to expect you.' She turned to go and Bennett nearly let out a sigh of relief. Nearly.

'Oh, and Kira,' she zeroed in on Kira again, her dark eyes dancing in the morning light, 'I'm so glad you've been keeping my brother company while he's in town.'

'I … uh … we're just…' Kira gestured between them, her hand flapping uselessly before she dropped it in defeat. 'Bennett has been … helping…' Her words trailed off as Jeanie's smile grew.

'I bet he has.'

'Jeanie,' he groaned.

'I'm going, I'm going!' She scurried down the stairs with a wave before Bennett could throw her into the nearest snowbank. This was why he didn't make a habit of filling Jeanie in on his dating life.

For one, she was horribly embarrassing. For two, he could tell she was already getting too attached to the woman he was already too attached to. Perfect. There was absolutely no way this wouldn't make his life more complicated.

Merry freaking Christmas.

He should have stayed home.

And then things got just a little bit worse.

'Hey, um Jeanie,' Kira called and his sister stopped in her tracks. 'Iris invited me to a wreath-making class tomorrow night. Any chance you'd like to come?'

Jeanie's face lit up like a Christmas tree.

'Absolutely!'

Kira smiled in return, and though Bennett was happy she was making friends here, he really was, did that have to include his sister?

Jeanie waved as she climbed into Logan's truck. It concerned him that she drove that monstrosity.

'See you tomorrow, Kira! Bye, Bennett!'

All he could do was stand there and wave goodbye, even as the tide of Dream Harbor threatened to pull him under.

Kira pulled up in front of the tiny florist shop on Main Street at half-past seven the next night. She'd left Bennett cozied up on her couch with the dogs and it had felt strange breaking the seal on the little world they'd created over the past week, but it felt important. If she was going to live here, it was about time she started to actually live here and not exclusively on her own property. Other than the evening Iris had dragged her out skating, she hadn't left the farm for anything fun.

She was in the process of taking a deep breath because, for whatever reason, she was nervous – probably something to do with the fact that she'd never had to try and make friends before – when Jeanie tapped on her window and scared the ever-loving shit out of her.

'Jesus,' she gasped, grabbing her chest. She gave Jeanie a weak smile and a wave.

Jeanie waved back, all smiles, but there was something so genuine about her that Kira found herself smiling too.

'Hi, Jeanie,' she said, climbing out of her car into the cold night air.

'You came!'

'Of course. I invited you.'

Jeanie shrugged. 'And it was such a nice invite, but I was planning to come anyway. You, though, you're a bit of a wild card, so I'm glad you showed up.' She smiled and took Kira's arm, steering her toward the shop.

'Iris is leading the class, you know that, of course. And Hazel's coming, and I told the book club about it so hopefully some of them will come too, oh, do you read romance?'

'I … uh…' Did Edwin's smutty letters count?

Jeanie waved away her hesitation. 'You should join anyway. It's fun and totally helped me when I moved to town.'

'Why did you move here?'

'We used to visit when we were kids. Bennett didn't tell you?'

'No, he didn't mention that.'

'Oh. Well, yeah, our aunt lives here, and I moved last year to run the café. But we always loved visiting her. I thought maybe the memories of being back here might convince Ben to stick around but…' She trailed off with a shrug and pushed open the door to the shop, leaving the thought of Ben sticking around in Dream Harbor lingering in the air.

'There they are!' Iris beamed from behind a long rectangular table that was covered in pine boughs and ribbons.

'Hi, Iris,' Kira said, taking in the room. It was small, with a counter at the back for the register. A refrigerator in the corner was filled with roses and the room was lined with red and white poinsettias. The middle of the room had two long trestle tables for the class. Most of the chairs were already filled with people, some she recognized, some were new faces.

'Come take a seat. We'll get started soon.' Iris gestured to a couple of empty chairs, but Jeanie was too busy saying hello to everyone to sit right away.

'Kira, you remember Hazel,' she said.

'Of course. I never forget the people that saved my ass. Hi, Hazel.'

Hazel smiled. 'That was a fun day. For us, anyway. I hope you've found some more reliable help.'

'Well, my brother's been spending an awful lot of time up at the farm since that snowstorm,' Jeanie put in suggestively.

'Oh?' Hazel asked, her eyes lighting up. 'Has Bennett been … helpful?'

God, this town loved gossip.

'He's … we're just…' Kira really needed to find a better way to say they were just having lots of amazing sex before Bennett had to return to his real life, but she hadn't come up with anything yet, so she just stammered her way through it. 'He's really … great.'

Hazel smiled. 'He seems really great.'

Jeanie and Hazel stared at her, waiting for her to go on, to explain what the hell was going on between her and Ben, but she had nothing more to say about that. How do you tell someone that their brother is a gentleman on the streets and a beast between the sheets? She was pretty confident there was no polite way to do it.

Finally, they relented and went back to introductions.

'Anyway, this is my mom, Maureen,' Hazel gestured to the woman next to her who was deep in conversation with another woman about the environmental sustainability of vegan meat substitutes.

'Mom, this is Kira.' Hazel tapped her mother on the shoulder. 'The new Christmas-tree farm owner.'

Maureen tore herself away from the discussion of tofurky to say hello.

'Nice to meet you, Kira.' As she turned to her, Kira was subjected to the full glory of the Christmas sweater Maureen was wearing.

'Are those your dogs?' she asked.

Maureen glanced down like she had forgotten what she was wearing. 'Oh, yes, those are my babies, Frieda and Diego.' She beamed.

'They are so cute!'

Hazel rolled her eyes and Maureen nudged her. 'Don't get jealous, Haze. You're cute, too.'

'You're insane,' Hazel said.

'You made me the shirt!' her mother protested, and Kira couldn't help laughing. But it was okay, because Hazel was laughing now, too.

'It was supposed to be a joke. I didn't think you'd actually wear a sweater with your dogs' faces on it.'

'Why wouldn't I?' Maureen seemed truly perplexed by this and Hazel wrapped an arm around her and gave her a squeeze.

'I don't know, Mom. Never mind.'

'So you're the new Christmas-tree farm owner?' Maureen's conversation partner chimed in, leaning forward. 'So nice to finally meet you! I'm Isabel. Jeanie, did you invite her to join the book club yet?'

'Of course I did,' Jeanie said with a laugh, finally sliding into a seat. Kira took the one next to her, in between Jeanie and Hazel.

'Oh, good! You have to join! Oh, and my kids had a blast at the tree farm last weekend. You're doing a great job up there.'

Kira's face heated with pride. People thought she was doing a good job. And it wasn't because of who her father was. Or her family's money or connections. It was because of what she'd done.

'Thank you.'

The bell over the door tinkled as the newest arrivals

entered.

'George! Andy! Come in,' Iris greeted them, and Kira gave a little wave to George, who'd dropped off a delivery of cookies at farm.

'Hey, Kira,' he said, unwrapping his scarf. 'Wasn't expecting to see you here.'

She shrugged. 'I'm trying a new thing where I leave my house and actually do things and see people.'

He grinned. 'That sounds good.'

'It's working out so far.' And it was. She was feeling better already.

'Okay, everyone, let's get started.'

Kira picked up the pine bough in front of her and followed along to Iris's instructions. Wine bottles were opened and ribbons were passed around and by the end of the evening Kira found herself laughing and chatting and promising to come to book club and for the first time since she moved to Dream Harbor she actually felt like she belonged here.

Maybe she hadn't screwed everything up by moving here.

Maybe one of her reckless decisions had worked out just right.

Chapter Twenty-Four

A small woman with gray hair opened the door at Logan's house. She had on the ugliest Christmas sweater Kira had ever seen, and that was saying a lot after she'd seen the sweater with Maureen's dogs on it.

'You must be Bennett!' she cooed, scooping Bennett into a tight hug before pulling back to study him. 'You are the spitting image of your sister.'

Bennett shifted next to her. 'We get that a lot,' he said, running a hand through his hair. Kira stood awkwardly beside him, ready to have this day over with. She'd stayed home with the dogs and bad movies yesterday on Christmas Eve, while Bennett visited his aunt Dot, but she'd already told Jeanie she would come to Christmas Day, so she was here even though she felt like she was intruding on Bennett's family Christmas. But the thought of being alone on Christmas Day was too sad, even for her. She'd never liked Christmas, but she'd also never had to suffer through it alone. Chloe had always been there.

So now here she was, her fake smile plastered on her face and the pie she'd picked up at the bakery in her arms, wishing she was drunk in front of her own fireplace instead.

'And here's Kira.' The woman, Logan's grandmother, obviously, turned her attention to Kira. 'Jeanie mentioned you two had been shacking up together.'

Heat flooded to Kira's cheeks. Could anyone do anything in this town without everyone knowing about it?

'We … uh…'

Logan's grandma patted her arm. 'Good for you, sweetie.' She winked, and Kira didn't know if she wanted to laugh or disappear.

'Nana, stop making them uncomfortable.' Logan appeared by his grandmother's side, looking every bit the big, grumpy lumberjack. He'd looked the same picking out a Christmas tree, plowing her driveway, and discussing agricultural engineers with her, so she supposed it was fitting that he looked like that on Christmas Day as well.

'I think it's nice! Two consenting adults finding pleasure with each other, it's lovely. Don't be such a prude, dear.' She looked up at her grandson with a beatific smile and Kira watched as Logan's cheeks blushed red above his beard. His nana chuckled. 'Come in, come in!' She took the pie from Kira's arms and hustled into the house.

Logan sighed. 'Merry Christmas. I'll take your coats.'

'Thanks.' They handed Logan their outerwear as Jeanie came over to greet them.

'Merry Christmas!' She wrapped Kira in her arms. 'I'm so glad you came!'

'Of course,' Kira answered from inside Jeanie's embrace. The woman was a good hugger. She had to give her that. 'Thanks for inviting me.'

'Hey, we crafted together. We're officially friends. Besides, I'm sure Ben wanted to spend Christmas with you,' she said, pulling away and turning her attention to her brother. 'Right, Ben?'

His perfect mouth was tipped down in a frown and Kira wondered if he regretted bringing her. He'd been quiet all morning. Maybe she should have stayed home, stayed out of this part of his life. It was one thing to make friends with his sister on her own time, but a sex-only Christmas fling certainly didn't involve an extended family get-together.

But again, she'd only been thinking of herself, of her own loneliness and now she'd put Ben in an awkward position.

Damn it, why hadn't she considered this before they left?

'Right. Of course.' He gave his sister a hug. 'Merry Christmas.'

'Okay, well come in. Nana Estelle's put out plenty of snacks, and Hazel, Noah, and Annie are already here.' Jeanie took Kira by the hand and dragged her further into the house, leaving her no graceful exit strategy. Maybe she could feign a headache after a little while?

'Hey, everyone, Kira and Bennett are here.'

Kira and Bennett, like they were a couple.

'Merry Christmas!' Hazel called from her spot on the couch. Noah sat at her feet and gave Kira and Ben a cheerful wave.

'Hi, guys,' Annie said, lifting her glass of wine in greeting. 'Merry, merry.'

Wine. That seemed like a very good idea right now.

'Hi, Merry Christmas,' she managed, before zeroing in on where the drinks were laid out on the drink cart.

'Hey, Annie, Hazel. Hi, Noah.' Bennett moved away from her side as he said hello to his sister's friends at his sister's fiancé's house. God, what the hell was she even doing here, crashing someone else's holiday?

'So how did your season go?' Annie asked. She was curled up in a chair by the fireplace. The room was cozy and warm without the need for blanket doors. It was nice.

'It went pretty well. We got a bit of a late start so hopefully it will go better next year.'

'Next year? So, you plan to stick around?'

'Uh … yeah.'

Annie smiled. 'Great, because I sold a ton of cookies.'

Kira laughed. 'Very lucrative for both of us.'

'Come sit.' Annie scooted over, making space for Kira and it was nice to be wedged in next to her. It was nice to be around people. God, why the hell had she been living like Quasimodo in his bell tower for the last four months?

'Thanks.'

She was not cut out to be a hermit. And for the first time it was occurring to her that she didn't actually need to do everything *alone* in order to be a self-sufficient, independent person. She could have friends. She could find people she liked here in this weird town.

Huh. What a novel idea.

Jeanie and Logan had rejoined the group after stashing their coats somewhere, and Estelle bustled in and out with more trays and platters of snacks.

'You could sit for a while, Nana,' Hazel suggested, but the older woman looked at her like she had eight heads.

Logan laughed. 'You know she doesn't sit.'

'Where's Grandpa Henry at?' Annie asked, looking around as though the man in question was hiding behind the enormous Christmas tree in the corner. Somehow, it had the kind of lurid giant lights and silver tinsel that Kira hadn't seen in real life ever. Didn't that stuff go extinct in the seventies? Were those lights even safe?

'He's attempting a deep-fried turkey again,' Logan said with a wince.

'I hope you have a fire extinguisher this year,' Annie said, dryly, taking another sip of wine.

Estelle waved away her concern. 'Oh, he'll be fine. His eyebrows grew back eventually.'

Jeanie looked up at Logan in concern.

'I'll go check on him.' Logan strode from the room and Annie giggled next to Kira on the loveseat.

'It's always interesting here on Christmas,' she whispered to her.

'So, you don't spend Christmas with your family?'

'Nah. We do Christmas Eve together. There's like a million of us and now most of my siblings have kids so they like to be at their own houses for Christmas morning. Santa and all that.' Annie rolled her eyes and Kira smiled.

'Anyway, Estelle and Henry have done this Christmas Day open house for years.'

Kira thought about her mother's parties, all the guests they barely knew, political connections and business associates. It was a far cry from this worn but cozy living room filled with friends and family.

'Who needs another drink?' Noah asked, standing up and heading to the drink cart.

Kira raised her hand. 'I'll take one.'

Noah grinned. 'Red or white?'

'Red.'

'You got it.'

'Me, too!' Annie lifted her empty glass. Kira smiled. Maybe this wasn't such a bad idea after all.

She caught Bennett's eye on the other side of the room, where he stood having an awkward-looking brother-in-law to brother-in-law chat with Logan, who'd apparently decided his grandfather was safe for the moment. Bennett's lips tipped into a private smile at her and something warm and unfamiliar settled in Kira's gut. Something comfortable, something content.

Was this what it would be like to be with him for real? To have someone to share a secret glance with across the room at a party? She'd spent so much time running from what her mother wanted for her: a stable man, someone who was 'husband material,' someone who wouldn't embarrass her, that she hadn't taken the time to consider how *nice* that could be.

Not that it mattered. What a shit time for that little epiphany.

'Ladies…'

She took the proffered drink from Noah.

'Cheers,' Annie said, clinking her glass to Kira's. 'To a successful new year.'

'Cheers,' Kira said, dragging her gaze from the man she couldn't have. 'To a *profitable* new year.'

Annie grinned. 'I like you.' And just like that, a little piece of her heart slotted back into place. Maybe she was likable. Maybe she could find people other than her own sister who would treat her kindly. Maybe she didn't need to be lonely.

'I like you, too.'

Annie tensed next to her. 'Oh, hell, no.' Her gaze had turned to the hallway where a man had just arrived with a small blonde woman next to him.

'What is it?'

'He brought a date to Christmas?' Annie's hiss was not nearly as quiet as she intended, and the man turned and locked eyes with her. Kira's head swiveled between the two of them.

'Who is he?'

'He's a bastard, that's who he is.'

He definitely heard her and responded with a smirk and a slight dip of his head like he was acknowledging that he was in fact a bastard. Kira could feel the rage emanating off of Annie.

'An ex?' Kira guessed.

'Not exactly.' Annie was still staring daggers at the man, but he'd turned to greet Logan and Jeanie. The woman beside him laughed nervously and Annie nearly snarled. There were clearly forces at play there that Kira didn't understand, but she definitely wanted to.

'Want me to slit his tires?' she offered.

Annie burst out laughing, leaning against Kira's arm. 'No, but I like you even more now.'

Kira smiled, laughter bubbling out of her, too. With or without Bennett, she could still make a life here. In fact, she definitely would make a life here. It was what she had wanted from the start.

'So, Hazel,' she said, turning her attention to Jeanie's other friend. 'When's the best time to start planting a cucumber garden?'

Chapter Twenty-Five

Kira was warm and soft and a little bit drunk with her head in his lap. She seemed to be humming some combination of 'Jingle Bells' and 'Deck the Halls' as he ran his fingers through her hair. The ends crackled with static, the silky strands clinging to his sweater. He didn't relish the idea of going into the cold, dark night to get home.

Kira smiled up at him and his heart lurched with the knowledge that his time with her was ticking away, along with the last few days of the year. He'd almost forgotten about that over the course of the day as they'd all talked and ate and drank. The house had been full of friends and family coming and going, of way too much food and way too many sweets. It had been a good distraction.

'So, when do you head back home?' Annie asked him now that the house had nearly emptied out again. It was just him and Kira and Jeanie and her closest friends sprawled out on the floor and draped over chairs, full and sleepy. He wondered how many of them would just crash here tonight. He was pretty sure Noah was already snoring from his position laid out in front of the fire.

'New Year's Day.'

Kira wasn't looking at him anymore; her smile had slipped.

'It's too bad,' Annie said, her chin propped on her arms on the coffee table. Bennett could barely see her past the empty wine glasses. 'You fit in so well here.'

'Yeah, Benny. You fit in so well here,' Jeanie repeated, from her perch on Logan's lap in the chair by the fire.

He winced. 'I told you, *Jean Marie,*' he emphasized her full name as payback for calling him Benny and she stuck her tongue out at him, 'I can't just uproot my life and move here.'

'I did it,' Noah piped in, apparently awake again. 'I highly recommend it.'

Hazel grinned at him from her end of the couch. Kira was now stretched out between them, her cozy-socked feet laid in Hazel's lap. She was the one who fit in so well here and he was happy for her. He'd much rather think of her here amongst friends than by herself in that cold house.

'It's definitely worked out nicely,' Hazel said and Annie groaned.

'Gross.'

Hazel laughed. 'Isn't it time for Secret Santa?'

'Yes!' Jeanie shot up from her seat. 'I almost forgot!'

Bennett breathed out a sigh of relief at the topic change.

He really didn't need all of Jeanie's friends joining the quest to get him to stay in town. Frankly, the woman whose head was in his lap was reason enough.

'I didn't bring a gift,' Kira hissed at him. 'I didn't know!'

'Don't worry about it. Jeanie handed the names out weeks ago.' His sister was excited to bring their old family tradition to her friends, but Kira hadn't exactly been in the mix at that point.

She still had a little worried frown on her face as she sat up. Bennett patted her knee and leaned in to whisper in her ear. 'You can help me guess.'

She gave him a relieved smile as Jeanie passed out the gifts.

'Annie, you go first,' she said, laying a sparkly red gift bag in her lap.

Annie waggled her eyebrows and pulled the tissue paper from the bag with a flourish. She peered inside and frowned.

'I know who it's from,' she said.

'Show us what it is first!' Jeanie said, and Bennett bit down on a laugh. His sister was always a stickler for the Secret Santa rules. She'd had a fit the year he switched the name he pulled with his cousin, Jesse.

'It is a roadside-safety emergency kit,' she said, pulling the package from the bag. 'It includes: flashlight, window breaker, and a first-aid kit,' she read from the description on the side of the box.

'Very practical,' Jeanie said, even as Annie scowled at the gift. 'And who do you think gave it to you?'

'Well, since he's given me one every year for the past five, it was obviously Logan.'

'And if you actually kept them in your car instead of throwing them in that bottomless pit of a hall closet, I would stop getting them for you,' Logan said, arms crossed over his flanneled chest.

Kira giggled next to him, and Bennett savored the sound.

'Okay, that means, Logan, you open next.' Jeanie laid a small perfectly wrapped box on his lap and Bennett immediately knew the giver. But he kept his mouth shut so Jeanie wouldn't murder him.

Logan unwrapped the box. He opened it and the frown on his face immediately melted.

'Is this…' He stopped, cleared his throat. 'Jeanie, is this…?' He looked up with tears in his eyes and Bennett couldn't imagine what his sister had put in that little box to make that man cry.

'Look on the inside.' She was kneeling next to him now as Logan pulled out the two rings that were in the box.

'What is it?' Hazel asked quietly as Logan turned the rings between his fingers.

He cleared his throat again. 'Wedding bands. Jeanie had them engraved with our initials.'

Jeanie wiped the tears that had traced down her cheeks with the back of her hand. 'Do you like them?'

He just nodded, clearly still unable to speak.

'I know we haven't even picked a date yet, but I wanted to get you something special and you surprised me with the engagement ring, so I thought I would surprise you, and—'

'They're perfect,' Logan said gruffly, cutting her off and tugging her into his lap before she could ramble on further.

'Oh, good.' Jeanie squeaked as Logan buried his face in her neck like he had forgotten they were in a room filled with their friends.

'Okay, that's enough you two. Jeanie, you have to open next!' Annie said, interrupting their cuddling, saving Bennett the pain of seeing his sister make out with her fiancé. He knew he liked Annie for a reason. 'Here.' She tossed the gift to Jeanie.

Jeanie tore off the wrapping paper and pulled out a giant fluffy scarf.

'Ooh,' Kira cooed. 'Looks cozy.'

'Annie, is this from you?' Jeanie asked, but Annie shook her head.

'Must be Hazel, then.'

Hazel smiled. 'I hope you like it.'

'I love it,' Jeanie said, already wrapping it around her neck. 'Okay, Haze, you open next.'

Hazel tore into her gift and Bennett held his breath. He didn't know much about Jeanie's friends, but his sister had mentioned that Hazel loved plants.

She grinned as she pulled out the little planter that looked like a person on a swing. 'How cute!'

'Jeanie said you were running out of space, but that one you can hang in the window.' He shrugged. 'Thought you might like it.'

'I love it,' Hazel beamed. 'Thank you.'

'Good job,' Kira whispered, and he wanted to lean into her words and the softness of her body next to him, but it was his turn to open.

The package was wrapped in random birthday wrapping paper. He raised an eyebrow but the group was giving nothing away. He opened it and found a Hawaiian shirt inside.

'Uh … wow…' He unfolded the shirt and that's when he saw that between the garish flowers were pictures of his dogs' faces. He burst out laughing.

'Does everyone wear their pets on their clothes around here?' Kira asked.

'Only the cool kids,' Noah said with a grin, giving himself away.

'Well, thanks, Noah.'

'Oh, man you got me!'

Bennett laughed again. 'It's a cool shirt, thanks, man.'

Noah beamed. 'You're welcome. Okay, where's my gift?'

Jeanie handed Noah a gift bag covered in pictures of fish. 'Cool bag,' he said, holding it up before digging around inside.

He pulled out four bars of soap and laid them out on the carpet in front of him.

'Wood Barrel Bourbon, Pine Tar, Alpine Sage, Bay Rum.' He read off the scents one by one. 'Wow, I'm going to be smelling very masculine. Who would have gotten me such a thoughtful gift?' He looked around the room as though there wasn't only one person left.

Annie threw a pillow at his head. 'It was me. Gotta keep that fish stink away.'

Noah laughed and threw the pillow back. 'Thanks, Annie. Very thoughtful.'

She winked at him.

'That was a great first Secret Santa,' Jeanie said with a smile. 'And maybe next year we can add even more friends.' She looked pointedly in Kira's direction, but didn't push it.

'Very fun, Jeanie. Thanks for planning it,' Hazel said. 'But we should probably get going.'

'But I'm so comfy!' Noah protested as Hazel got up and walked over to him. He'd already laid back down in front of the fire after opening his gift. She took his hands and tugged him up.

'It's comfier in bed. Come on.'

Annie stood too, yawning. 'I guess I'll go too.'

'Who's driving?' Jeanie asked.

'Already called an Uber,' Annie assured her with a hug.

'I stopped drinking hours ago,' Bennett said, pulling Kira up from the couch. She looked sleepy and grumpy and he wanted to carry her out to the car, but he'd never hear the end of that, so instead he led her to the door by her hand.

Coats and scarves and hats were donned as they wished each other Merry Christmas for the thousandth time that day, and they stumbled out onto the porch, the freezing night air shocking them into an unwelcome alertness.

'Bye, Bennett, Bye, Kira!' Hazel called as they made their way to the hired car.

'Goodnight!' Annie waved over her shoulder and Kira waved back.

'Night!'

Bennett's rental car was freezing cold when they got in and he really wished he'd thought to warm it up first. Kira sat with her shoulders hunched so high, her head had nearly disappeared inside her coat.

'Should be warmer in a minute,' he muttered, cranking the dials too high.

'Okay.' Her voice was quiet, small.

'Did you have a good time?' he asked as they pulled out of the driveway. The farmhouse twinkled with cozy lights behind them as they drove away. It filled Bennett with the melancholy that came with the ending of things: holidays, seasons, relationships.

Kira was looking out the window and he could see her face reflected in it.

'I think it was my favorite Christmas ever.'

'Then why do you sound so sad?'

She wiped a hand across her face, sniffling in a way that made Bennett want to tear the world down. She laughed a little, shaking her head.

'You know, I'm trying really hard to be a good person

here. I'm trying really hard not to ask you to stay, Bennett. I really am. But you are not making it easy. The fucking universe is not making it easy.'

'Kira—'

'No, nope. Don't say anything. We had an agreement. You promised. I promised. So that's it, okay? I'm not going to be selfish. I'm not going to ask you to give up your life for me.'

'What if I want to?'

Her head whipped to face him as he drove. 'You don't want to.'

'You're going to tell me what I want now?' Sadness was turning into frustration, into anger.

'You can't want to stay here! Maybe you think you do, but you don't. You just want to … you just want to help me, or whatever. I'm like a baby deer on the side of the road and you want to pull over and rescue me, but you can't, Bennett! You can't. I have to learn to be a deer all on my own now. And you can't fall back on old habits.'

'Kira, you aren't making sense.'

She growled in frustration and he pulled over. He couldn't have this conversation not facing her. When he turned to her, she had tears streaming down her cheeks. *Damn it.*

'I don't think you're a baby deer.'

She sniffled.

'I think you're a strong, smart, gorgeous woman.'

She shook her head. 'Please … please don't say things like that.'

'Kira, what are you afraid of?' What was he afraid of? Why had he agreed to this arrangement in the first place? He *did* fit in well here. He liked it here. He liked the people. He could be close to his family.

He could be close to Kira. Just because things had failed with Nicole didn't mean it would happen again. And so what if it did? Was he just never going to try again?

'This isn't real,' she said. 'People don't fall in love in a month. It doesn't make sense.'

'Feels pretty damn real to me.' *Fall in love*. He'd fallen in love with her. The realization hit him hard in the chest.

She wiped her eyes. 'No, it isn't. I was so lonely, Bennett. So fucking lonely. And then you showed up and it was nice to have company. That's it. That's all it was.'

Nice to have company. She was trying to convince him that he'd been just a warm body to her, but it was a lie. He could see it in her eyes. She was lying about all of it, but she was pushing him away anyway.

'And now you need to go back home to your real life and I need to live mine.'

Back home. Ha. How could any place that wasn't with her feel like home now?

'That's what you want?'

She nodded, her arms folded across her chest. She held his gaze a breath longer before sitting back in her seat.

'I think it'd be better if we end this now,' she said, addressing the windshield instead of him. 'You should probably go back to your sister's apartment.' She wouldn't look at him. Her mind was made up.

And Bennett wasn't about to beg.

Even though he wanted to.

Even though he wanted to throw himself at her feet and beg for her to see reason, to let him in, to let him stay.

Instead, he put the car back into drive and pulled out onto the deserted road. It was after eleven on Christmas night. Everyone was home with their families.

He fiddled with the dials; the car was suddenly stifling.

They rode the rest of the way in silence until Kira's house loomed ahead of them in the darkness. Bennett pulled the car up the driveway and killed the engine. But before Kira could jump out of the car, he grabbed her wrist.

She turned to him.

'Things might not make sense to you,' he said, his voice low and rough. 'But they make perfect sense to me. I *did* fall in love with you in a month.' She sucked in a little whimper like his words cut her, but he kept going. 'You are everything I want, and it has nothing to do with your broken house or your … your…' he shook his head with frustration. 'Whatever it is you think about yourself, that you're selfish or not worthy or … I don't know. I really don't know, Kira because I think you're fucking perfect.'

Tears rolled down her cheeks and her pulse fluttered in her wrist.

'If you want me to go, I'll go.' He tugged gently and she went to him, falling into him, her lips warm and wet and he kissed her hard and rough and fast, the taste of her tears on his tongue when he pulled away. 'I'll go. But know this. You are not a bad habit. You are something entirely new. Say the word and I will back here in a fucking heartbeat.'

He let go of her then. He couldn't look at her anymore, at her wide eyes, wet with tears, her swollen lips that he no longer got to kiss. She wanted him to go, he would go. He wouldn't stay here another second. He couldn't.

The dogs were less than pleased to be roused from sleep and ushered out the door, but there was no other choice. He stuffed the few things he'd brought over into his bag and followed them out. Kira stood on the porch, silent and stoic.

She didn't tell him to stay.

She didn't say anything as he threw his things into the car. And neither did he.

He'd said it all, and none of it had mattered.

There was nothing left to do but go. The only sound as he pulled out of the driveway was the whining of the dogs in the back seat, the last moments of Christmas music on the radio, and his own ragged breathing as he slowly fell apart.

The lies we tell ourselves are often stronger than the truth. They worm their way into our hearts and our minds until they are all we see, all we believe. And Kira had been telling herself a lot lately.

The main one being that she was not in love with Bennett Ellis.

But as she sat under her Christmas tree on Christmas

night, or maybe it was technically the next day at this point, unwrapping the small present Bennett had apparently left there for her, that lie was quickly unraveling.

She took another swig from the wine bottle she was drinking from and tore off the shiny red paper.

'Socks,' she said out loud even though she was completely and utterly alone. Again. 'He got me socks.' She wanted to be mad about it, mocking this silly gift but she couldn't bring herself to do it.

'He got me fuzzy socks with little peaches all over them,' she whispered, the tears starting up fresh. 'What a bastard.' She pulled a blanket off the couch and curled up under the tree. Pine needles stuck to her cheek but she couldn't seem to care. She'd fucked everything up, what were a few pine needles in her hair at this point?

She snuggled the socks closer to her chest and the sharp edge of a notecard pressed into her hand. Bennett's handwriting was scrawled inside.

Something to keep your toes warm until you get that boiler.

Merry Christmas

~B.

'Son of a bitch,' she cursed between sobs. She pulled the blanket over her head and worked on her next lie: tomorrow she would feel good about her decision. She would feel good that she had chosen not to keep Bennett here just because she was lonely. She'd made a good decision for once. She hadn't been rash or thoughtless.

She'd done the right thing.

That was what she'd tell herself in the morning.

But right now, she was sure she'd made a terrible mistake.

Chapter Twenty-Six

Kira had slept with her face practically on top of her phone so when it started ringing the next morning she nearly jumped out of her skin.

'No, no, noooo…' she groaned, fumbling for the phone with her eyes still closed. She knocked over the empty wine bottle and it went careening across the floor.

Ugh, God, every one of last night's bad decisions came tumbling back into her. Her conversation with Bennett, her conviction that it was better for him to leave. Finishing off the bottle of wine. She opened her eyes, blinking at the tree branches above her. Sleeping under the damn tree.

Her phone was still cheerfully ringing, and she managed to grab it.

'Chloe,' she croaked. 'Six hours ahead!'

Her sister winced. 'Oops! Sorry! I can't seem to remember that.'

'It's okay.'

'Kiki, where the hell are you?'

'Under the Christmas tree.'

'Uh… Are you okay?'

'No.'

'Do you need me to come home?'

Yes. 'No.'

'What's going on? You're freaking me out.'

'How long did it take you to fall in love with Erik?'

'Kiki, what does that have to do with anything?'

She sighed. Everything hurt. Her back from sleeping on the floor. Her face from sleeping on pine needles. Her pride. Her heart.

'I just need to know.'

'One day.'

Kira sat up, knocking low-hanging branches and rattling the ornaments. 'One day?! That's impossible.'

Her sister shrugged. She looked perfectly put together this morning. Mama would be proud. Kira attempted to flatten her bangs by raking her fingers through them. She was sure they were standing on end.

'It was possible for us.'

'Shit.'

'Kira, what the hell is going on? Why do you look like you slept in a dumpster?'

'Not a dumpster. I told you. Under the tree.'

Chloe stared at her, waiting for an explanation, but Kira didn't really have one. She had ping-ponged from one bad decision to the next so many times that now she wasn't sure which decisions were the wrong ones.

She didn't know if she was in love with Bennett.

She didn't know if she should have asked him to stay.

But she was pretty sure about one thing.

'Hey, Chlo?'

'Yeah?'

'Do you want to invest in my business? I'm thinking of opening a garden center to turn things into a more year-round operation but there's a lot I still need to do and one season of Christmas tree sales can only do so much—'

'Yes!' Chloe cut off her rambling explanation, her eyes bright with excitement. 'Of course I do! Whatever you need, Kiki. That's what I've been trying to tell you all along!'

'I'm going to pay you back. It would just be a loan.'

'Of course, of course! This is so exciting!'

'I'm going to send you a business plan.'

'Wonderful.'

'I'm going to do this for real.'

'Of course you are.' Chloe held her gaze through the screen, confident in her in ways Kira had never been of herself. She was going to do this. Maybe it wasn't exactly what she'd imagined when she'd been doom-scrolling after Chloe left, but none of that was real anyway. How off the grid were those people when they were livestreaming everything they did? She would set up her little homestead her own way. And she would support herself. But that didn't mean she had to do everything alone. Her sister wanted to help her, and Kira was finally ready to accept that help.

'I wish you were here.' She tried to swallow the tears

gathering in her throat, but it had been a rough twelve hours. Too many epiphanies crammed into too short a time period.

'Me, too.' Chloe wiped the tears in her eyes. 'But that's why I called. Well, sort of. We were both busy yesterday, but I thought we could watch a movie together today. Just the two of us.'

Kira raked a hand across her face. 'I love that idea. But I need a shower. Call you back in an hour?'

'Perfect.'

'Love you, Chlo.'

'Love you, too. Now go freshen up! I can smell your breath from here.'

Kira stuck out her tongue before ending the call. She still felt like shit about the way she handled the whole Bennett thing, but at least everything else was looking up.

Or it would be, once she changed out of yesterday's clothes and ran a brush through her hair.

'Are you sure you have to leave early?' Jeanie was nursing a cup of coffee at Logan's kitchen table. The remnants of last night's party were still littering the countertops even though it was late afternoon. No one else was home and it was just the two of them at the table.

'Yeah, it's time for me to get back.'

A llama? Alpaca? Wandered by the window. 'Uh … your uh, animal is escaping.'

Jeanie glanced at the window. 'Oh, that's Harry Styles. He won't go far.'

The creature came closer to the house, pressed its face up to the window and started munching on the screen. Jeanie remained nonplussed by the whole situation.

'But Dream Harbor has a whole New Year's Eve celebration,' she said, ignoring the farm animal destroying the house. 'There's fireworks!'

Bennett made eye contact with Harry Styles, and he could have sworn the beast winked at him. He shook his head. He clearly needed to sleep, but first he needed to get the hell out of Dream Harbor. 'I bet it's great, but really, I just want to get back home.'

She cocked her head, studying him over her steaming cup. She tapped her engagement ring against the ceramic. Tap, tap, tap. What must it be like to have so much faith in someone, in your relationship, to declare to the entire world that you intend to be together forever?

'And this rushing back home has nothing to do with a certain Christmas-tree-farm owner?'

'Nope.'

Her dark brows rose. 'Because the two of you looked awfully cozy last night.'

They had looked cozy. And felt cozy. So much so that Bennett actually thought that Kira might be cool with him staying in town for a while. So cozy that he actually considered uprooting his life again for another woman, because this one was worth it. This one was everything he wanted, and he knew it wasn't coming from some misplaced desire for her approval. He just wanted to be with her. All very cozy until the drive home when Kira blew the whole thing apart.

'We had an agreement. It was just a holiday fling. No one wants to be alone for the holidays.'

'Hmm. And what about the rest of the year?'

'Jeanie…'

'I just want you to be happy! And it was nice having you close by. I liked it.'

He gave her a begrudging smile. 'I liked it, too.'

'Well, my apartment is here whenever you need it.'

'You're going to have to rent it out eventually.'

She shrugged. 'I guess. But I'm happy to keep it open for you.'

He hated how tempting that offer was. He didn't need Kira's permission to stay in town. He could move here, stay above the café, and eventually get a place of his own. Jeanie would be thrilled. His parents would love it.

But then he'd be stuck here, a few miles from the most recent woman to reject him, in a tiny town that knew everyone's business. Not great for quietly licking his wounds.

No, he had to get out of here.

He never should have followed Nicole to California, and he sure as hell couldn't stay here if Kira didn't want him to.

'You should rent it out.' He stood from the table and put his empty mug in the sink. Jeanie stood, too, coming to give him a hug.

'Well, I am going to miss you,' she said, giving him one

more squeeze before pulling away. 'Maybe I'll come visit you sometime soon.'

'That would be great.' It would certainly be easier than him coming here ever again.

'Text me when you get in.'

'Will do.'

Jeanie walked him to his rental car where the dogs were already loaded into their crates for flying. He hated thinking of them stowed away in the cargo hold, but there weren't a lot of other options unless he wanted to claim these three miscreants were emotional support animals. Although, at the moment, he could use the support.

'Love you, Benny.'

'Love you too, Jean Marie.'

He kissed the top of his sister's head, got in his car and drove out of Dream Harbor before anything could convince him to stay.

The Pumpkin Spice Café was relatively empty two days after Christmas but Jeanie was behind the counter. Kira had never been to the apartment above it, so she didn't know if there was some way to knock on Bennett's door without coming through the main café area. She didn't have much of a choice but to talk to Jeanie. Especially since she hadn't texted him. The element of surprise seemed important.

She sure as hell was surprised she was here, but she'd woken up this morning and God, she'd missed him. So much, already, and it scared the shit out of her, but she had to tell him. In person. She had to tell him in person that she missed him, and he was perfect, too, and maybe … maybe they could figure something out. That maybe they shouldn't toss this whole thing out just because he was going home soon.

It had all made perfect sense in the hazy light of the winter morning when she'd woken up cold and lonely, but now standing in this welcoming café she was starting to question herself.

'Hi, Kira!' Jeanie looked surprised to see her, which she supposed made sense. She hadn't really made it a habit to come into town all that often during her hermit phase. Something she planned to remedy in the new year.

'Hi!' She glanced around at the space as she walked to the counter. It was adorable in here, with good lighting and colorful art on the walls. She could feel the will to make her own coffee every morning weakening. She could come here. She could chat with Jeanie and Annie and Hazel.

It would be nice.

'What can I get you?' Jeanie asked, her dark eyes never leaving Kira's face.

'Uh … actually, I was wondering if your brother was here?'

Surprise again crossed Jeanie's features. 'Oh, I'm sorry, Kira. He left yesterday.'

'Yesterday?' *Yesterday?!* Panic shot through her. *No, no, nooo*. 'I… Uh … sorry, I just thought he was staying until the new year.'

Jeanie was still studying her, not unkindly, like she was looking for the answers that Bennett clearly hadn't given her.

'He decided to leave early. I guess he needed to get back.'

Kira forced herself to smile. To nod. 'Right. Of course. That makes sense.'

Did it?! Did it make sense that he was just gone, just like that?!

'Do you have his number?' Jeanie asked. 'You could give him a call.'

'I…' Kira was slowly backing away. She needed to get out of here so she could fall apart in private. 'Yeah, I do. I'll text him. Thanks.'

She waved, turned, and nearly ran out of the café.

'You should tell him how you feel!' Jeanie called after her, only making Kira walk faster.

How could she tell him how she felt now that he'd left? *Bennett, I've decided you should stay,* was a pretty absurd text to send to the man who'd already boarded a plane and hightailed it out of here.

She turned out of the café and strode down Main Street not at all sure of where she was headed. She'd parked directly in front of the café, but she just needed to walk. The air was cold and sharp this morning, but for once she didn't mind it. It made her thoughts clearer.

He'd left just like she'd told him to. Why the hell was she surprised? This was Bennett, the most considerate man on earth. Of course, he'd done exactly what she told him to do.

And besides, he shouldn't have to wait around for her to get her shit together. As much as she hated it, as much as it felt like she couldn't breathe, like someone had carved another chunk out of her heart, she was proud of him.

Proud of him for leaving.

Proud of him for doing what was best for him. And that made her proud of herself. She actually cared about someone other than herself and the person that shared one hundred per cent of her DNA. Surely, that was growth. Unfortunately, no one really advertises that growth hurts like a son of a bitch.

Just say the word and I'll be there in a heartbeat.

She didn't know if he meant it, but she wasn't ready to say the word just yet. She *did* need to figure her shit out first.

And then … maybe then she'd take Jeanie's advice.

Chapter Twenty-Seven

Bennett had never been a big fan of New Year's Eve, but this year it sucked extra hard. He was back in his cramped San Francisco apartment, eating Chinese food out of the carton, surrounded by his dogs, which at any other time was actually his preferred way to spend an evening, but not now. Not anymore. Not when he wanted Kira next to him more than he wanted his left arm. More than he wanted air. More than he wanted…

A knock at the door interrupted his overdramatic thoughts. He needed to get a grip.

'Coming!' He emerged from the dog pile, pushing animals off his lap and making his way to the door. He pulled it open and his New Year's got a million times worse.

'Ben! You're alive!'

'Shit.'

Nicole frowned, her red-painted lips turned down in a little pout. 'What kind of greeting is that?'

Bennett sighed. He didn't have the energy to play nice. 'What do you want, Nic?'

'Can I come in?'

He squeezed the bridge of his nose. 'Sure.'

Why the hell not? Why not just dive headfirst back into his old life? Kira didn't want him but maybe Nicole still did. At least, as much as she ever did.

Nicole wiggled by him. She was wearing a tiny black dress covered in sequins and heels tall enough to turn her five-foot-three into at least five-six. Objectively, she looked hot. Unfortunately, it was doing absolutely nothing for him. Which seemed extra unfair. He couldn't have Kira *and* she had ruined other women for him, too? That was just cruel.

Elizabeth and Odie lifted their heads in interest, saw who it was, and decided she wasn't worth the effort. Pudgy didn't bother to wake up. Nicole ignored them in return. She'd never been a big fan of his little pack. And apparently, his dogs were smarter than he was. After enough rejections, they'd learned their lesson. Nicole just wasn't that into them.

'Well, first of all,' she said, glancing around at the coffee table strewn with takeout cartons, and his partially unpacked suitcase by the bedroom door. 'I was worried about you. You haven't been answering my texts.' She ran a hand down his arm and gave him that little smile that used to make him feel important, needed. Now it just made him feel annoyed. Annoyed at her. Annoyed at himself for not responding to it. Annoyed at Kira for breaking his brain.

'I was away.'

'Oh? That's good! A little vacation is always nice.'

A little vacation. A devasting heartbreak. Very nice. Highly recommend it.

'Well, you've confirmed I'm alive. So I guess you can go.'

Again, the little pout. He used to kiss it away.

'God, Bennett. Do you treat all your friends this way?'

'Is that what we are? Friends?'

Her pout turned into a sexy smile. 'With benefits.'

He huffed a laugh. 'They don't feel like benefits anymore, Nic. It feels like you are using me when you need me and ditching me when you're tired of me.'

Her eyes widened as he spoke, and he wondered if it was hard to open them that wide with the extra weight of her fake lashes.

'Is that really how you feel?'

Christ. He did not want to be having this conversation right now. 'It doesn't matter.'

'It does matter!' She put a hand on her hip, cocking it out to the side indignantly.

'Now you care about my feelings?'

'I've always cared about your feelings.'

He stared at her, disbelieving. He should kick her out. Or take her to bed. He wasn't sure which.

'Do you want a drink?' he asked, and her smile grew.

'Sure.'

His entire apartment was essentially one room, so he could still feel Nicole's eyes on him as he grabbed two beers from the refrigerator. He popped it open and handed it to her.

They drank in silence, Nicole watching him from her perch on the edge of his dining room table.

'Why did you move out here?' she asked, and he wanted to lie. But maybe the start of a new year was the perfect time to exorcize all this baggage from his past.

'You asked me to.'

She nodded, and took another sip. 'That was the only reason?'

'Yes. It was stupid. I'm aware of that now.' It was still so embarrassing to admit, even now all these years later. At the time, he'd claimed he had a job out here, too. That he'd always wanted to move to the West Coast. But he'd really just wanted to follow the pretty girl that he'd fallen in love with. If he was honest with himself, he'd known even at the time that she didn't feel the same. But she'd *asked*. She'd said she needed him, that she didn't want to be alone. And he'd fallen for it completely.

'I was glad you came with me.'

He huffed. 'You had a funny way of showing it. Ditching me after a few months didn't feel like you were glad.'

'We were so young! I didn't know what I wanted.'

'Clearly.'

'I'm sorry if I hurt you, Bennett, but I just had to get out of that town. I was scared and you were there for me.'

He shrugged like it didn't matter, like this one

experience hadn't shaped the way he'd thought about relationships ever since.

'And in my defense,' she said, twirling a piece of hair around her finger. 'You said you had other reasons for coming out here. You'd always wanted to live on the West Coast, remember?'

'I lied!' He laughed, the sound harsh and rough. 'I wanted to be with you.'

Nicole blinked like she hadn't considered that she was his entire reason for relocating his life.

'But you're right,' he said, shaking his head. 'We were young. But we're less young now and yet here you are.'

She pushed off the table and stalked closer, her hips swaying with every step. 'And you let me in.'

And he'd let her in.

Christ.

He always let her in. How much could he blame her when he'd never once told her how he felt? He'd never turned her away or said he didn't want to see her anymore. Every time she'd shown up on his doorstep or sent a late-night text, he'd been right there when she needed him. How could she possibly know he was unhappy with the arrangement?

He had never once tried to end this thing between them.

She stood in front of him now close enough that he could smell the perfume she always wore, the floral scent wrapping around him. It was tempting in its familiarity.

'I'm glad you're back,' she said, her eyes flicking up to his. She pressed a hand to his chest, the warmth seeping through to his skin. 'We always ring in the New Year together.'

'Why is that, Nic?' he asked and he really wanted to know. Why? Why did she keep coming back, even though she clearly didn't want to keep him around long term?

'Tradition?' She leaned closer, wrapping her arms around his neck, her body pressed against his. 'And I can always count on you, Ben,' she purred. 'You're always here for me.'

Ah, yes. Bennett, the human security blanket.

'Yeah, I don't think I can do that anymore.'

Her eyes widened in surprise as he unwound her arms from his neck. 'What do you mean?'

'I mean, I can't wait around here for you to need me.'

'I never meant for you to wait around, Ben. I thought we had an … arrangement. Like I said, friends with benefits and all that.'

'Friends implies that we're there for each other, not that you disappear for nine months of the year and then circle back when you're lonely or dumped or it's fucking New Year's.'

'Bennett…'

'No, no, I'm sorry, Nic. I can't do it anymore.' He stepped back, needing physical space between them, afraid he would accidentally fall back into bad habits. Because *this* was the bad habit. Not helping people, not caring for them, nor wanting to be there for Kira. The bad habit was staying in a relationship that made him miserable. The bad habit was not telling this woman exactly how he felt.

She was right. They had been so young when this all started.

But they weren't anymore.

He didn't regret the start of this thing. He'd been naive and in love and he'd followed a girl across the country and for a few months it had been amazing and exciting. And he was happy to have had that experience.

But he regretted that he hadn't let the end be the end.

He'd held onto this rotten thing for too long.

'You should go,' he said.

She was studying him with a little furrow between her brows. 'You met someone?'

Yes. And she was perfect even though she didn't believe it. And she was smart and funny and so fucking beautiful it hurt. And she loved dogs and reindeer and probably every other animal under the sun. And she was stubborn. And brave.

Braver than him because she was trying to change.

But Nicole didn't need to know any of that.

'It doesn't matter. I just…' he sighed and ran his fingers through his hair. 'I just don't want to be your standby anymore. I'm sorry.'

'What if I want more?'

'You don't.'

Her hands were on her hips again. 'Maybe I do. Maybe I don't want to lose you. I can try harder to be … what you want.'

She looked at him with big eyes and he knew she was scared. He believed her, that she would try for him, that she didn't want to lose him, but in this, he needed to be selfish.

'We had our chance, so many chances. I think it's best for both of us to finally move on.'

Tears filled her eyes and he opened his arms to her. She fell into them, pressing her face against his chest.

'I am sorry,' she sniffled. 'I thought you were okay with this. I thought you liked seeing me.'

'Of course I did. I still do.' He rubbed a hand down her sequined back. 'But I just ... I need to move on.'

They stayed like that for a long time, and he felt like he was holding his past in his arms. They'd spent so much of their lives connected to each other. Memories flooded him: spending nights in her way-too-small dorm-room bed, driving cross country in her crappy old hatchback, hoping they would make it, sleeping on an air mattress in their first studio apartment. After she left the first time, it had only been a few months before she returned, crying, needing a friend, comfort, and eventually they fell back into bed together.

And round and round they went.

Until now.

He kissed the top of her head and she pulled away. Miraculously, her makeup had stayed put.

'I was going to invite you to Sunny's party tonight, but I'm guessing that's a no?'

He gave her a small smile. 'That's a no.'

She nodded, brushing her hair back behind her ears again. 'So, what are the rules? Can I still talk to you?'

'Eventually. I just need some time.'

'Okay.' Her voice was a choked whisper, and his heart broke a little more.

At the door, she reached up and planted a kiss on his cheek.

'Happy New Year, Nic.'

'Happy New Year, Bennett.'

He closed the door behind her, and even though his heart still hurt, he felt lighter. Maybe the exorcism worked. Maybe this really would be a *new* year.

Chapter Twenty-Eight

The lights were still up at the end of January, because this was her place and she made the rules. Which she rather enjoyed. Besides, the twinkly lights made it easier to come home to her dark house.

'See you next week?' Iris asked as she shifted the car into park in Kira's driveway.

'Wouldn't miss it.'

Iris smiled. 'Great! I'll wait until you get in. It's so dark out here.'

'Thanks, but don't worry, Benny is here to protect me.'

Iris laughed as Kira wrestled her yoga mat from the tiny back seat before closing the door and giving her friend one more wave goodbye. She'd been taking Iris's Tuesday evening yoga class for three weeks now and she'd done Warrior 3 tonight without toppling over onto her head, so she was feeling very zen.

Or at least she did feel zen before she opened the door

and was nearly bowled over by her over-enthusiastic roommate.

'Hi! Hi, baby! I'm home!' She rubbed Benny, her big, not at all scary, pit bull rescue dog between his ears. His tongue lolled out of his mouth in pleasure.

'Did you miss me? You big baby.' She patted his giant head and attempted to wedge herself further into her house. 'You gotta let me in, bud.' She pushed him aside and he only gave an inch but it was enough to close the front door. He stuck to her like glue as she unraveled her scarf and hung up her coat. The radiator hissed happily in the hallway, filling the house with warmth. That new boiler was working like gangbusters.

She'd even taken down her blanket doorways and with Iris and Jeanie's help had hauled her mattress back upstairs. The little snowglobe-world in her house that she and Bennett had existed in for two weeks was officially gone.

And yes, she realized it was pathological to adopt a dog with the name of the person she was trying to live without, but at the time it had seemed like fate.

At least one Ben belonged with her.

'Come on, let's get you some dinner.' That got the big galoot detached from her side and running toward the kitchen, his claws scrabbling along the hardwood floors. Kira laughed, following along behind him.

It had been a strange month since Bennett left; hard but good. Now that she'd officially decided to emerge from her self-imposed isolation, life in Dream Harbor didn't seem quite so bad. In fact, she might have overdone her reentering society a bit. In the past month, she'd signed up for yoga, joined the book club, attended three different cooking classes at Annie's bakery, and picked up a few shifts at Mac's pub to bring in a little extra cash. Not to mention the meetings she'd had with Logan's agricultural engineer, and with Logan himself, for tips on how to run a farm and all the time she'd spent writing up a business plan for Chloe.

She was even starting to dream up ideas for that old barn. If she fixed it up, she could host events here.

Kira had been busy. And it had been … wonderful. And exhausting.

Benny whined at her feet as she heated some leftover soup for dinner.

'You already ate,' she reminded him, but he looked up at her like he was near death from starvation. She sighed but couldn't help her smile as she slipped him a little piece of chicken from the pot. This big guy had been the main thing keeping her from begging human Bennett to come back. At least for a while.

Because even though she'd filled her days and made friends and got her heat working and built a business plan and finally, finally convinced herself she could do this, she *could* exist in the world on her own, she still just really missed him.

She didn't want to exist in the world on her own.

Which was why she'd sent the letter.

She poured her soup into a bowl and moved to the table trying and failing to not think about the contents of the letter. It filled her with anxiety every time she thought about it.

Had he gotten it yet? She'd sent it a few days ago. How long did it take mail to get from here to there? What if it got lost? Mail got lost all the time, didn't it?

And worse, if he had gotten it, what did he think about it?

Maybe she'd been inspired by Edwin's prolific letter-writing. She was still sorting through them all on the off-chance he'd put a treasure map in one of them, but a letter had seemed like a good idea at the time. She wanted something less instant. Something that would let Bennett formulate his answer before he sent it. Something that wouldn't be like staring at the thinking dots on a text message. Those dots would have broken her for sure.

But now the waiting was just as bad.

Just say the word…

Had he meant it?

Maybe he'd gotten back out into the real world, away from their snowed-in fantasy land, and realized it had been just the circumstances. Just the magic of the season. Or the loneliness.

But even if that was true, she was still glad she'd sent it. He'd said so many beautiful things to her during that last fight, and she'd given him nothing but icy silence. He deserved to at least know how she'd felt about him. How much she'd loved their Christmas together.

And anyway, it was too late now. The letter was out in the world, in her sloppy handwriting, and there was no taking it back. She could still remember every word she'd written since she'd rewritten the damn thing so many times.

Dear Bennett,

Even after reading so many of Edwin's letters, I don't know how to start this one (sorry but it's not going to be dirty). I guess I just wanted to say a few things I didn't manage to say before you left, even though I probably should have.

I thought I was doing the right thing, the selfless thing, by ending things between us. I thought I should insist that you go home, but once again I wasn't thinking about you. About what you wanted. I shouldn't have doubted you. If you wanted to stay, I should have let you.

I am still a work in progress.

But I wanted you to know that to me, you are perfect, too. Which surprises me, honestly. You are everything I didn't know I wanted. But I fell in love with you because you are good and kind. A nearly unbearably handsome caretaker. Selfless and sweet. And by far the best sex I've ever had. I've used that little pink vibrator thinking about you so many times since you've been gone that I burned out the battery (okay, so, a little bit dirty).

I realized, maybe too late, that being independent doesn't have to mean being alone.

I miss you.

So, I guess, I'm saying the word…

All my love,

Kira

P.S. I loved the socks.

She ate her soup, listening to her latest podcast, *Horticulture and You*, with Benny snoozing, his big head covering her feet, and she tried not to think about Bennett reading those words. She was putting her bowl in the sink when Benny started growling.

'What is it, buddy?' The dog was staring at the back windows. 'Probably just a skunk or something,' she assured him, peering out into the dark but Benny wouldn't stop. His growls turned to barks.

'Okay, you're freaking me out.'

She followed the dog into the living room, grabbing her phone on the way, ready to call the cops, or Logan or someone, to come and scare away whatever was outside, scaring her big baby of a dog.

She looked out the front windows. The lights by the Christmas-tree cabin were on. So were the lights she had strung over the first few rows of trees. But it was the three dogs running through the farm that stopped her heart in her chest.

'Holy shit, Benny.'

He whined next to her, nudging his head against her leg.

'It's okay. They're … friends.' She was already moving toward the door, fumbling with her boots, pulling on her coat. She couldn't work the zipper; her hands were shaking too much.

He was here.

He'd come back.

For her.

She opened the door and walked onto the porch with trembling legs.

'Bennett?' Her voice was nearly a whisper. She felt crazy calling out his name. But his dogs were here, he had to be here somewhere.

Benny was still cowering next to her. 'Come on, bud. It's okay. Let's go investigate.'

They walked down the driveway toward the tree farm entrance. Elizabeth barreled out of the trees, heading straight for them. Benny growled low in his throat. The dogs circled each other, sniffing and growling.

'It's all right, Benny. Don't be scared.' A few more circles and the dogs seemed to come to some sort of truce, growling turned into happy yipping and the two ran off together.

She kept walking and somewhere along the way Pudgy found her and waddled along beside her. It only took her a minute to realize the tree next to the cabin was decorated.

'What is this?' she asked the little dog at her feet, but Pudgy just wheezed in response. The tree was covered in envelopes, tied on with red bows. One toward the middle had writing on the outside.

Open first.

Kira plucked it off the tree, her breath stuck in her throat and tears burned behind her eyes.

She tore open the envelope and pulled out the letter inside. Unlike the old ones she'd been reading lately, this one was crisp and white and written in Bennett's precise handwriting.

Peaches,

I got your letter.

She barely got through the first sentence before the tears clouded her vision. She swiped them hastily away.

I'm not much of a letter writer myself, but you said it made you sad that our grandkids would never find our old letters. I thought this would be enough to get them started.

I'm really glad you said the word.

I missed you, too.

Love,

Ben

She looked up, expecting to see him but he still wasn't showing himself so she grabbed another letter.

Peaches,

I think you are the most beautiful in the morning when your hair is a mess and you're all soft and warm from sleep. I could look at you like that forever.

Love,

Ben

And another.

Peaches,

You are incredibly stubborn, but I like that, too. You're fierce and determined. That's what will make you a great partner.

Love,

Ben

Her hands were shaking so hard now, she could barely hold the paper. She sniffled and wiped more tears.

'Where are you?' she asked out loud but he didn't appear.

Peaches,

I wrote all these letters on the flight here. I hope you meant it. I hope you want me here.

Love,

Ben

'Of course I do! Where the hell are you?' she yelled louder now but all that did was get the dogs to crowd around her. 'Damn you, Bennett Ellis.'

She opened another one.

Peaches,

This past Christmas was my favorite, too. I hope we have a lot more together. I was thinking a lifetime of them might be enough.

Love,

Ben

'Bennett,' her voice broke.

'Hey, Peaches.'

She turned and there he was, just like the first day, walking between the trees. Just like the first day but completely different. Because she loved him now. And he loved her.

'You came back.'

'I did.'

'And you'll stay?'

'I was planning on it.' That perfect smile broke through. 'If you want me to.'

She ran toward him and threw herself into his waiting arms. 'Yes. Stay. Please.'

He buried his face in her neck, his warm breath on her skin. 'Christ, I missed you.'

'I missed you, too. I should have never told you to leave. I'm so sorry.'

'You did what you had to do to be ready for this. I don't think you should regret that.'

'And you're ready for this?' she asked, still wrapped around him.

He grinned. 'Ready to love you? Fuck, yes.'

'Bennett, language! There are little doggie ears around.'

He glanced down at the dogs gathered at their feet.

'I see we have a new member of the pack.'

Kira laughed. 'This is … oh … uh … this is Benny.'

Bennett's eyes widened in delight. 'Kira, did you name your dog after me?'

'No! Of course not.'

He held her gaze, waiting, and she tried to keep a straight face but failed miserably. 'He came with the name … but I did sort of pick him because of it.'

The dog Benny whimpered. 'And because he's such a good boy,' she crooned, scratching the dog's head.

Bennett chuckled. 'Wow, I didn't realize you missed me that much.'

'Oh, shut up.' She smacked him playfully on the arm. He grabbed her hand and pulled her close again. She went willingly, so happy to be wrapped up in his warmth again. 'It's freaking freezing out here. Let's go inside.'

He kept his arm around her as they made their way back to the house, the dogs racing ahead of them.

'Did you bring any bags? Where is your car?' Kira looked around as they approached the house. 'How the hell did you even get here?'

'I … uh…' He looked delightfully sheepish. 'Jeanie dropped me off. I only brought the dogs and a carry-on bag which I think I left in Jeanie's car.' He gave her a chagrined smile. 'I was kind of in a hurry to get here.'

Her heart felt so full it ached in her chest.

'Don't worry, I have a bathrobe you can borrow for now.'

He followed her into the house, laughing, a tangle of dogs in the hallway between them and suddenly her house wasn't cold and lonely. It was full and loud and warm. And perfect.

'Hey, it's a reasonable temperature in here,' Ben said as he hung up his coat next to hers.

'Got that new boiler.'

'Oh, yeah?'

'Yeah, I have an investor in the business now, so I was able to make a few purchases around here.'

'An investor, huh? Good for you.'

Her face warmed with pride. It *was* good for her. And she was proud of herself for doing it. For leaving home and starting over. For asking for help.

For letting Bennett in.

'It's my sister, but it's all very official.'

'I'm sure it is.'

They were standing at the entrance to the living room now. The couch had a very respectable amount of pillows and only two throw blankets, the rest having been relegated to the bedroom and of course, the mattress was gone.

'How'd you get it back upstairs?'

'I had help.'

'I'm glad.'

'You want to come upstairs and see it?' she asked, waggling her eyebrows in a way Bennett obviously found super sexy because he outright laughed at her.

'Of course I do.' He pulled her close again, his arms around her waist and her face tilted up to his. 'But I don't have to stay here.'

'What? Why not?'

'I mean, I'm definitely back. I just don't want you to think I have to stay here. In your house. We can take it slow.'

'Take it slow? Bennett, are you kidding? You just flew

across the country to put letters for our grandchildren to find in fifty years in my trees and now you're saying we can take it slow?'

'I didn't specifically say they had to be our grandchildren *together*.'

'Yeah, okay.' She rolled her eyes and he pressed a kiss to her forehead. 'Look, I don't care if this is a terrible idea or it's too soon or too fast or doesn't make sense. I've learned something this month.'

'Oh?' He was looking down at her, and she realized she'd almost forgotten how long and dark his eyelashes were. It was still annoying, but now she loved him so she'd just have to deal with it.

'Yes. I learned that I don't want to be without you. Simple as that.'

'Simple as that, huh?'

'Yep.'

The smile that crossed his face was slow and sweet. 'Okay, good. I want to be with you, simple as that, too.'

'Perfect. Then it's settled.'

A little wrinkle of worry creased his forehead. 'I recently learned that I've misinterpreted people's intentions in the past, so if you could spell it out for me, Peaches, that would be great.'

She ran her fingers through his hair, messing it up just enough so he looked like hers again. 'You're moving, Bennett. Here to Dream Harbor, to live here with me and our far too many dogs and possibly a future reindeer or two. And we will live happily ever after. Is that clear enough?'

'Crystal. Thank you.' His smile grew into something mischievous, and she didn't have time to react before he hoisted her over his shoulder, caveman style, and headed for the stairs. She squealed and squirmed in his arms, but he held tight and gave her a swift smack on her ass.

'Bennett!'

He laughed. 'Now, let's go see this mattress.'

'Is it weird that I kinda miss the living-room blanket fort?' he asked hours later in the early light of the morning. They'd been awake all night, kissing and talking. Making plans. Getting reacquainted. He couldn't keep his hands off her. He had to keep convincing himself she was real. Any time they dozed off, he found himself waking up with a handful of her ass and a raging erection. It hadn't been a restful night but damn it had been a good one.

'No, I miss it, too, sometimes.'

Kira's head rested on his chest, and he ran his fingers through her hair. Her naked legs were tangled up with his.

'Maybe that can be our Christmas tradition,' she said. 'Sleeping in front of the fire.'

'That would be nice,' he murmured, letting his fingers trail from her hair, down her back. He could hardly believe he was here, back in this house, back with Kira in his arms. It was like a dream. Just a few days ago, he'd been home trying his best to live his life without her and now he didn't have to.

He must be the luckiest son of a bitch in the world.

'My sister is coming for a visit in the spring,' she said. This was how it had been all night, little pieces of their life spilled out for each other, filling each other in on all that they'd missed.

'Sounds good. Can't wait to meet her.'

'I've still been reading through Edwin's letters.'

'Oh?'

'Yeah, still kinda hoping he left some clues about this treasure.'

'Any luck?'

She shook her head, her hair brushing across his bare chest. 'Not yet. But I finally found those Tiffany lamps. They were hidden behind an old dresser in the attic.'

He smiled to himself, happy that she hadn't given up on finding something. He'd been skeptical all along that old Edwin had left something behind, but Kira dared to hope for good things, and he loved that about her.

She shifted in his arms so she could look up at him. 'Hi,' she smiled like she was just as surprised and thrilled that he was here as he was.

'Hey.'

'It's crazy that you're here.'

'I know.'

She grinned and he missed her, even though she was right here, he missed her. He needed her closer. He rolled them so he was above her, dipping his head to kiss her. She was sleepy and soft.

He should let her rest.

'Bennett,' she murmured.

'Yeah?'

'I love you.'

His breath caught, still shocked to hear it, still amazed it could be true.

'I love you, too, Peaches.'

She smiled and wrapped her arms around his neck, tugging him down into the cradle of her thighs. He braced himself on his forearms so that he didn't crush her, but she wrapped her legs around his back, holding him tight.

He nuzzled against her neck, breathing in her scent—shampoo and woodsmoke and pine and Kira—that made him dizzy with wanting her. She gasped as he rocked against her.

'Do you want to sleep?' he whispered against her cheek.

She shook her head. 'Not yet. I don't want to miss any time with you.'

He smiled. 'We'll have to sleep at some point.'

'Not yet,' she whispered, and he kissed her, stealing the words. He kissed her lips and her jaw; he kissed down her neck, dragging his mouth along her delicate skin. She arched her back as he kissed across her collarbone and down to her breasts. He licked and sucked and kissed until she was gasping for breath, her hips rocking against his, seeking relief even after all the times they'd done this tonight. It wasn't enough. It wouldn't ever be enough.

He slid down her body, burying his face between her thighs.

Christ, how he'd missed this.

Her taste, her scent, the feel of her against his tongue. The tug of her fingers in his hair, her gasps and whimpers. He held tight to her thighs, holding her in place for him, not willing to let go for a second.

He'd been an idiot to leave the first time.

Now he planned to hold tight to this woman forever.

'Ben!' Her thighs tensed around him, her hips rolling against his tongue. She tensed and then broke, trembling in his hands. He lapped up her pleasure, wringing out every last drop until her body went soft and pliable in his hands again.

He crawled back up her body and found her with a sated smile.

He grinned. 'Do you want to sleep now?' he asked and her eyes fluttered open.

'Not yet.' Her smile was downright wicked as she tugged him down again. Her legs were wrapped around him again and she was so slick he slid in in a single thrust.

'Kira,' her name was nothing more than a groan. He leaned his forehead against hers, steadying himself against the pleasure that was already rioting through him.

She kissed him, running her fingernails down his back, just enough to send prickling pleasure down his spine. He grunted and she smiled against his lips.

'I love you,' she whispered as he thrust into her again and again. She whispered against his mouth and his ear and into the crook of his neck as she held onto him, as he pushed into her, again and again, until he broke against her, falling apart in her arms.

'I love you, too,' he gasped, pressing his lips against her sweaty temple. They stayed like that for a long time, pressed together, unwilling to let go. Until finally, they slept.

After all, they had a lifetime to spend together. They could spare a few hours for sleep.

Epilogue

FIVE MONTHS LATER

'It's warmer out here than I thought it would be,' Kira said, wiping her brow and sitting back in the dirt next to him. 'It's nice. I feel like I'm finally defrosting after that winter.'

He chuckled. 'And just think of all the pickles you can line up in jars or whatever, if all these grow.'

She smiled at him, and she looked absurd in her gardening hat with dirt streaked across her cheek, but he'd never seen anyone so beautiful. It was how he always felt about her. First thing in the morning, covered in dirt, sweaty from that insane hot yoga she did; in any and all ways, he found this woman to be gorgeous.

'Thanks for making this…' She gestured toward the garden he'd dug out behind the house earlier in the spring where they were currently planting cucumbers. The radishes were already sprouting, and he was hoping to get some small tomato plants to add soon.

Kira had a stockpile of glass jars just ready to be filled. Over the course of the winter, she'd shown him some of her homesteading inspiration and he had to admit it was all very appealing.

'Happy to do it.' He leaned over and planted a kiss on her nose. Not to be outdone, Benny the dog, licked the side of her face.

'Ugh,' Kira groaned and pushed the dog away but there was laughter in her voice. She loved that dog. All of his dogs, too. Hell, she loved dogs she'd never even met but that was just one of the many things he loved about her.

'I'm going to go get us some lemonade,' she said, standing and brushing the dirt from her shorts. Benny slobbered along behind her. The other three dogs were in various states of sunning themselves in the yard. Odie was rolling on his back and wiggling his butt, ensuring that his white fur would no longer be white by the time they went inside. Elizabeth sat, ears perked, on alert even as she relaxed in the sun, and Pudgy, the old girl, was asleep by her side, snoring loudly.

And they were all happy here in their new home. They loved the space to run and roam around outside, so much better than his cramped apartment. And even though it had seemed completely insane when Bennett had boarded the plane to come here, he was happy here, too.

How could he not have come back?

He'd read the letter from Kira five times in rapid succession and had booked his flight within a half hour.

It was like Kira said. It was simple. He wanted to be with her. So here he was.

And of course, it was nice to be closer to family and all that. Not to mention, Kira had set up the smallest bedroom as the perfect little home office for him to work remotely and kept him busy with so many home projects that his Mr. Fix-It tendencies were not only well taken care of, they were also appreciated.

Santa really came through on that Christmas wish. The old guy went above and beyond. Christmas snow and the woman of his dreams, it was going to be hard to top.

Bennett smiled to himself, thinking about it, as he dug in the cool, damp earth. Getting his fingers dirty was his new favorite thing about living on the farm. That and waking up next to Kira every day.

He hit something. Something hard. Maybe a rock? He dug around it, moving dirt until the metal lid of a small box was visible.

'What in the world?'

Hearing the confusion in his voice, Elizabeth wandered over to investigate. She stuck her nose in the hole and huffed a loud breath, then turned back to Bennett, awaiting further instruction.

'Maybe let me handle it.' He nudged the dog to the side and dug around the box until he could lift it from the soil. It looked like the type of box you might keep money in at a bake sale. Or maybe an old Christmas-tree farm.

'Hey, Peaches!' he called. 'You might want to see this.'

He brushed the dirt off, but there were no markings on the box.

'Be right out!' Kira yelled from the kitchen window, but he couldn't wait.

He opened the box.

'Holy shit.'

He pulled out the letter sitting on top and immediately recognized the handwriting.

To whoever finds this box,

You're lucky, I didn't want my greedy cousin to get his hands on this, so I guess it's yours now. I can only hope you have someone worth giving it to. Good people are hard to find, so if you have one be sure not to let them go. Don't screw it up.

~Edwin

'I don't plan to, Ed,' Bennett whispered and Elizabeth cocked her head. He pushed aside the pearl necklace and two delicate bracelets before finding the diamond earrings at the bottom of the box.

He was holding them in his palm, the gems winking in the sunlight, when Kira stepped back out into the yard. She was barefoot, her legs long and tan in her cut-off denim shorts. The dogs rushed to greet her as she made her way through the grass, a tray of lemonade in her hands, and a contented smile on her face.

And Bennett knew Edwin was right. It was hard to find good people.

And he sure as hell wasn't going to let this one go.

'What is it?' she asked, as she got closer.

'Treasure,' he said, holding up the box. Kira's eyes widened. It wasn't hard to go from kneeling in the dirt to kneeling at her feet. It wasn't hard to say what he did next.

'Let's cash them in, Peaches.'

She somehow managed to put the tray down before tackling him, tipping him backward into the grass.

'Cash them in?' she asked, grinning down at him, the sky impossibly blue behind her, his heart impossibly loud beneath her.

'Yeah, let's see how much we can get for them.'

Her smile grew, her eyes glinting with fresh ideas. 'We can fix up the barn.'

'Just like you wanted.'

'Just like I wanted.' She laughed and the sound mingled with the birdsong above them and the breeze in the rows of pine trees around them. 'We can host parties. Weddings! Oh my gosh, it will be gorgeous. Can you picture it?'

It was his turn to smile. He'd help her fix up every inch of this place until it matched the dream she had when she moved here. He wasn't going anywhere.

'This is amazing,' she said, sitting up and starting to sift through the box. 'I can't believe there was actually treasure here. This stuff looks old. Old and valuable. We can do so much with this.'

'I think Edwin would be happy about your plans.' Ben tugged her closer again, brushing his lips across her cheek. 'As long as we do it together.'

'I'm all in, if you are,' she said. 'Unless you're getting tired of my crazy ideas.'

'Never.'

'Never?'

'I'm in it forever, Peaches. Crazy ideas and all.'

She grinned up at him. 'Okay. Me, too. It's a deal.'

'Deal.' And he kissed her to seal it.

Acknowledgments

As always, a huge thank you to the One More Chapter team and everyone at HarperCollins who makes these books possible. I am seriously living the dream because of all of you. Charlotte, Jennie, Emma, Chloe, Arsalan, Christina, and Jo, thank you for all that you do to make my stories into books and then to get those books into the hands of readers. I literally could not do this without you.

I, like many of you, love a good Christmas rom-com, but those super saccharine, super chaste ones always leave me wanting more. Hopefully, this story scratches that cozy Christmas itch but with a little more than one close-mouthed kiss right before the credits roll!

My favorite animated Christmas movie is *Garfield's Christmas* and so the 'finding old love letters' scene was a nod to that as well as Bennett's dog being named Odie, of course. So, a shout out to Garfield!

I have to give a special thank you to Jamie for being a mom friend, when those are so hard to come by, and for bus-stop brainstorming sessions, and for sharing the crazy notion that Scrabble can be sexy. You were right, and I hope I did that scene justice!

To my sister, Liz, we never did open that Christmas tree

farm, but writing about it was a pretty close second. And now you have two dogs named after you! A true honor.

To my husband for always doing anything involving technology in this house and for explaining to me what wifi is and how it's different from a cell signal even though I still don't understand it. You are the best and I look forward to asking you for computer help and frustrating you about my forgotten passwords until the day we die.

To my mom for always asking how the writing is going and my dad for telling me you're proud of me. To my kids just for being you. I love you all to pieces.

And to you, readers, we're three books in now and I cannot thank you enough for being here with me and the whole Dream Harbor crew! Thanks, as always, for reading!

The author and One More Chapter would like to thank everyone who contributed to the publication of this story...

Analytics
James Brackin
Abigail Fryer
Maria Osa

Audio
Fionnuala Barrett
Ciara Briggs

Contracts
Sasha Duszynska Lewis

Design
Lucy Bennett
Fiona Greenway
Liane Payne
Dean Russell

Digital Sales
Lydia Grainge
Hannah Lismore
Emily Scorer

Editorial
Arsalan Isa
Charlotte Ledger
Jennie Rothwell
Caroline Scott-Bowden
Emily Thomas

Harper360
Emily Gerbner
Jean Marie Kelly
emma sullivan
Sophia Wilhelm

International Sales
Peter Borcsok
Ruth Burrow

Marketing & Publicity
Chloe Cummings
Emma Petfield
Christina Storey
Joanna Surman

Operations
Melissa Okusanya
Hannah Stamp

Production
Denis Manson
Simon Moore
Francesca Tuzzeo

Rights
Helena Font Brillas
Vasiliki Machaira
Hany Sheikh Mohamed
Zoe Shine

The HarperCollins Distribution Team

The HarperCollins Finance & Royalties Team

The HarperCollins Legal Team

The HarperCollins Technology Team

Trade Marketing
Ben Hurd

UK Sales
Laura Carpenter
Isabel Coburn
Jay Cochrane
Sabina Lewis
Holly Martin
Harriet Williams
Leah Woods

And every other essential link in the chain from delivery drivers to booksellers to librarians and beyond!

When a secret message turns up hidden in a book in the Cinnamon Bun Bookstore, **Hazel** can't understand it. As more secret codes appear between the pages, she decides to follow the trail of clues… she just need someone to help her out.

Gorgeous and outgoing fisherman, **Noah**, is always up for an adventure. So when Hazel asks Noah to help, she isn't looking for romance, but as the treasure hunt leads them around Dream Harbor, their undeniable chemistry might be just as hot as the fresh-out-of-the-oven cinnamon buns the bookstore sells…

The *Sunday Times* bestseller

When **Jeanie's** aunt gifts her the beloved Pumpkin Spice Café in the small town of Dream Harbor, Jeanie jumps at the chance for a fresh start away from her very dull desk job.

Logan is a local farmer who avoids Dream Harbor's gossip at all costs. But Jeanie's arrival disrupts Logan's routine and he wants nothing to do with the irritatingly upbeat new girl, except that he finds himself inexplicably drawn to her.

Will Jeanie's happy-go-lucky attitude win over the grumpy-but-gorgeous Logan, or has this city girl found the one person in town who won't fall for her charm, or her pumpkin spice lattes…

As a renowned chef, single-dad **Archer** never planned on moving to a small town, let alone running a pancake restaurant. But Dream Harbor needs a new chef, and Archer needs a community to help raise his daughter, Olive.

Iris has never managed to hold down a job for more than a few months. So when Mayor Kelly suggests Archer is looking for a nanny, and Iris might be available, she shudders at the thought.

As Archer and Iris get used to their new roles, is it possible that they might have more in common than they first thought…

Available to pre-order now!

ONE MORE CHAPTER

One More Chapter is an award-winning global division of HarperCollins.

Sign up to our newsletter to get our latest eBook deals and stay up to date with our weekly Book Club!
Subscribe here.

Meet the team at
www.onemorechapter.com

Follow us!

 @OneMoreChapter_

 @OneMoreChapter

 @onemorechapterhc

Do you write unputdownable fiction?
We love to hear from new voices.
Find out how to submit your novel at
www.onemorechapter.com/submissions